# The Witches of Witherwack

# River of Bones

A Karen Dee Murder Novel

by

Tony Brassell

ISBN: 9798366663663

Copyright © 2022 by A V J Brassell

All rights reserved. This book or any portion thereof may not be reproduced or used in any manner whatsoever without the express written permission of the author except for the use of brief quotations in a book review.

# Dedication

This book is dedicated to the loving, kind, and inspirational people of the City of Sunderland and all those who live in the beautiful Northeast of England.

I moved to Sunderland in the winter of 2020. My wife was born and bred there but had lived away from the area for most of her adult life. For her it was a return home, for me it was a new adventure. As a fan of Roman History, the location was perfect for me. Now I had easy access to some of the best-preserved roman remains in all of England in the form of Hadrian's Wall.

That structure was started exactly 1900 years ago and remains a fine example of the strength and ambition of the roman empire.

We should never forget all the people who made us who we are. Whether it was the Romans, the Vikings or simply our immediate family. We are all a product of what went before. Yet we all have the chance to change the future, to bring about a better world.

I encourage everyone to follow their dreams, help each other along the way and live a life that will inspire others to make the best of their lives too.

# Prologue

The Dutch sailor wondered how life could be so cruel. Not that long ago he had been sleeping rough on the streets of Amsterdam, cast aside from his ship for one night of drunken stupidity.

Without an address or savings, all he could do was beg for money, hoping that the passing strangers might take pity on him. That had kept him alive until a 'friend' had found him and offered him a job.

He had been fed and given a roof over his head. For a couple of months life was good. Then he was given the chance to use his skills to make a journey. The boat was luxurious by the standards of the small boats he had been in before. It was a Sunseeker, admittedly a few years old, but it had all the navigation gear he needed to get him to the UK.

He was told it had been fitted with extra fuel tanks, sufficient for the North Sea crossing.

Jan was allowed to live on the boat and even take her out for sea trials to make sure he knew how to handle her in all weathers. While he was breathing the sea air and enjoying the open waters, he had the best time of his life.

When the day came for the crossing, he set off for the port of Sunderland. He had been told a berth was waiting for him in the marina, as was a welcoming party. He would be given accommodation so he could enjoy the city before he brought the boat back to Holland.

The journey was uneventful, apart from spotting a Minke Whale with cub not far from his destination. Nature was wonderful.

He forced himself to smile at the memory.

Two men had been standing on the pontoon when he arrived in the Sunderland marina. They seemed friendly, and helped him secure the boat. From there he was taken to a cottage in one of the many streets around the city. A blind man was to be his landlord, until the boat was ready to make its return journey.

Jan had known in his heart that there was something dodgy on board the boat, but he had chosen not to look too closely. This was a dream job. He didn't want to lose it.

He had been in the city just over a week when things changed. One of the highlights of the trip had been a visit to see Sunderland play football in a pre-season friendly. He had got very drunk after the match, telling a lot of people where he was from, and how he had travelled to Sunderland.

There was a fight later that evening. He remembered little about it, apart from waking up in a police cell. He had given the police his address and told them where he was from. They had let him out on remand, pending further investigations.

He had been due to report back to the police station that day, but he was going to miss the appointment. In fact, as he lay there naked, tied to a cold metal table, he had the sinking feeling he wasn't going to make any appointments ever again.

Two men in white coats walked in. They were both wearing masks. One, he noticed, had bottle blonde hair. He tried to speak to them but for some reason he couldn't formulate the words. The drugs he had been given had done that to him.

One picked up a small electric saw, checking it in the glare of the white light that shone down on his body.

He felt his bladder release.

The blonde-haired man tutted, picking up a towel and wiping away the mess.

The man with the saw came closer and looked straight into his eyes.

"I'm sorry about this, but the boss is the boss. If only you hadn't given the police your address, we wouldn't all be here now. But as the boss says, waste not want not, and your only value to us now," he looked Jan up and down, "is you."

The blonde man walked behind Jan and covered Jan's face with a cloth. As Jan drifted away, the last sound he heard was the electric saw whirring into life.

That was three years ago.

# Chapter One

*Monday 16th May 2022*

Karen Dee drove her brand-new Audi Q2 into the car park, stopping in front of the main entrance to the Southwick North police station. She ran her hand over her short dark hair, then checked her makeup in the car rear view mirror. She smiled to check her teeth for lipstick stains and climbed out of the car.

"Oi. You can't park there!" The voice came from one of the windows above where she had parked.

She looked up at the policeman looking down at her. "The boss parks there, stick it round the back, pet."

With a half-smile she got back into her black Q2 and reversed out of the prime parking spot and drove around the back of the brick-built building.

Convinced she was no longer encroaching on anyone's territory, she got out, opened the boot, and took out a battered looking khaki shoulder bag. She checked that her precious laptop was safely inside and was pleased to note that the cheese and tomato sandwich she had made while she was preparing her breakfast, hadn't been squashed. Karen had no idea whether the station had a staff canteen, so had decided not to take a risk on starving on her first day.

Karen glanced at her reflection in the glass window of the car; she was happy with what she saw.

She then took a walk around her Q2. Karen had bought the vehicle with a loan based on the new rate of pay she had been given, following her promotion. It was a big step up from her old mini, and she loved it.

She was wearing a black jacket over a plain white blouse. Karen had opted to wear practical black trousers; the skirt would wait for the arrival of warmer weather. *It looks like I'm going to a funeral*, she thought to herself.

Since her husband had died, nearly five years ago now, black had become her favourite colour. She hoped the move from Newcastle to the Southwick North station would give her a new focus. Her husband's face seemed to appear alongside hers in the reflection in the car window. He was never far from her thoughts. *You've got this*, he seemed to say. That gave her strength.

She forced herself to smile as she walked to the station entrance.

Her heart was beating faster than normal as she reported into reception. She was experiencing a heady mixture of nerves and excitement.

At five foot ten inches tall she was rarely shorter than other women and saw eye to eye with most men. It meant she had little need for heels and was wearing a comfortable pair of smart black Skechers. They squeaked slightly on the stone floor as she walked to the reception desk.

"Detective Inspector Dee reporting for duty," she announced to the handsome desk sergeant.

"First day, pet?" He smiled at her, ignoring the rank difference. "Welcome to Southwick North. Just pop through the door over there, the offices are up the stairs, I'll buzz you in until you get your pass. You'll spot the signs."

"Thanks sergeant....," she read his name badge. "Moore."

"Tom Ma'am. Tom Moore."

"Thanks Tom, no doubt I'll see you again soon."

"Anything, you need, just let me know. I've been here since God was a boy so know my way round a bit."

They smiled at each other, Karen noting his wedding ring as she turned to walk towards the stairs to the offices on the floor above. *Out of bounds Karen*, she chided herself, with a smile, as she climbed the stairs. Not that she felt ready for anything like that yet. She had met and married the love of her life. No-one could take his place.

The magnolia walls were stark compared to her previous station in Newcastle. If it wasn't for the computers and modern telephone systems, she could see through the doors and windows as she walked along the corridor, she could have been forgiven for thinking that she had been transported back to the seventies.

Karen was looking for the office of her new Detective Chief Inspector, William 'Billy' Roberts. She spotted a group of plain clothed officers sitting in a briefing room, drinking and chatting before the start of their day's work. She decided to knock on the door.

The conversation stopped dead as she entered the large room.

Ignoring the awkward silence, her eyes were attracted to the windows. From where she stood, she had an excellent view of the River Wear and the new Spire Bridge.

"Can I help you Love?"

"Detective Inspector Dee reporting for duty. I'm looking for the DCI."

"New blood, brilliant. I'm no longer the newest on the team."

The young woman who spoke got up from her desk in the far corner of the room and walked over to shake Karen's hand. "I'm Jacqueline White, Jack to my friends, and we should call you?"

"Karen, Karen Dee, fresh in from Newcastle."

There was a collective groan from around the room.

"You'll win no friends mentioning that around here."

"Does it help if I am originally from Durham?"

"That's better," one of the men in the room replied.

"We're all waiting for Billy. We'll do all the introductions when he gets in. Billy's not the best timekeeper, especially on a Monday morning. But my names Mick, or Michael when me Mam is in the room."

"Thanks guys," Karen replied. "Where's my new home?"

"You're over there in front of the boss's office," Mick pointed to a tired looking empty desk. "Your ID is in the top drawer with the key to your locker. The locker room is down the end of the hall, as are the toilets. If you need anything else just ask anyone, we're all happy to help."

"Thanks Mick and thanks everyone."

Karen walked over to her desk and sat down, hanging her bag over the back of her chair. She opened the top drawer.

BANG! Several party poppers taped to the inside of the drawer went off at the same time. Karen nearly fell off her chair. The room erupted into laughter. At that precise moment DCI Billy Roberts burst through the door.

"What the hell is going on here?"

"Just having fun with the new blood, boss."

"You almost gave me a bloody heart attack, you idiots. Are you alright Dee?"

Karen brushed the debris from the party poppers off her jacket. "Fine boss," she muttered, trying unsuccessfully to hide her annoyance. "Their cards are marked."

"Good for you, this lot love to dish it out, and I am sure they'll be more than happy to get something back in return."

He glared around the room. The DCI looked like he had just got out of bed.

"Dee, with me." He opened the door to his office and Karen dutifully followed him in. The room was a mess. He pulled a pile of files off the single chair in front of his desk and added them to the two piles on top of a filing cabinet in the corner of the room.

Billy took his jacket off, draping the denim like a rag on the back of his chair.

Karen noted there were no photos on the desk or on the shelves behind where he sat. A small trophy, most likely for golf, sat on a shelf behind his desk. It consisted of a ball on top of three crossed golf clubs, fixed to a wooden base. Several certificates and a photo of Billy amongst a group of other police cadets adorned the wall above the shelf.

There was an odd smell in the room. The pizza box sticking out of the unemptied bin was no doubt the source of the stale odour.

Billy sat down, pointing to the empty chair for Dee to do the same.

"Welcome to Southwick North, Dee." He handed her an envelope with her ID, lanyard, and locker key. "I am guessing the guys told you this lot were in your desk. Standard welcome from the detectives I'm afraid. Some things never change."

"No worries, boss, I've handled worse."

"I've read your file but tell us a bit about yourself."

Karen paused for a moment, deciding on what to reveal.

"Well, I'm Karen Dee, 35, widowed, no kids, ex-army, born in Durham and moved to Newcastle when I joined the police. I've been in the force five years now. I saw this opportunity for promotion and here I am."

"Any hobbies?"

"Not really, I'm a cat lover, like a glass of wine and read a lot. Oh, and I like to keep fit and enjoy a good walk."

"There are plenty of pretty walks around here, so I am told." Billy smiled. "Walking is not my thing, unless I am hitting a little white ball around one of the local golf courses."

"Isn't golf defined as a good walk spoiled?"

"Yeah, something like that. It's a bit of a social thing with me rather than a vocation. I play off eighteen."

Karen had no idea what that meant but smiled anyway. She guessed it wasn't that brilliant.

"We've got some good people here Karen. I am hoping you will fit in and add some real strength to the team. I'll introduce you in a minute." He looked back to the piles of files. "I'll be passing some of these over to you. Don't worry, nothing exciting is happening right now. You'll soon get a feel for the place when you read through the cases."

He looked out through the window to the officers working in the open office area.

"I've put you outside my door for two reasons. If you have any questions, just stick your head around the door. As long as I'm not in a meeting or on the phone." He paused then lowered his voice a touch.

"Second, I want you to be my guardian. Try to keep the wolves from my door. I need time to think, and I hope you will give me that. I know it will take a while to get your feet under the table but after you do, you will be the first point of contact for the guys. They should only get to me if you can't handle their problems or questions."

Karen felt a little intimidated by the new role she had been allocated, yet a part of her was quite excited. She craved responsibility and this sounded the perfect opportunity to lead a team and direct how they operate. She imagined herself sitting behind Billy's desk one day. She put on a brave smile.

"Sounds fine to me, boss. I hope I can do justice to the role."

"I'm sure you will, but please don't be afraid to ask me anything. My door will always be open to you."

"Thanks, much appreciated."

"Right, let's go meet the team. I've allocated you a Detective Sergeant to be your partner in crime so to speak. They'll take you around the city for a day or two to give you some idea of your new patch. By the time you settle back down you'll find some case files on your desk to work through. Is that OK with you?"

Karen nodded her consent.

With that nod of agreement the DCI got up from his desk and walked out into the main office, Karen following along. He clapped his hands. Everyone stopped what they were doing and turned in his direction.

"Guys, despite your sad attempt at causing grief to our new colleague, I am pleased to say she has agreed to become our new Detective Inspector." The detectives cheered and clapped.

"Jack, I'm allocating you to work with Karen so shuffle your desks around, so you are sitting close to each other." He went on to introduce the rest of the team.

Mick, she had already met. It turned out he was the oldest in the team and another Detective Inspector. He was mainly desk bound now because of a back injury sustained while on duty. He was looking forward to his retirement.

John Phillips was a Detective Sergeant as was Matt Jones. They were supported by three Detective Constables. Jordan, Rachel, and Catherine. Catherine was a tech guru, spending most of her time on her computer, carrying out research for the team.

Once the formalities were over, Billy collected all the mugs from the office on a tray, and then walked Karen down the corridor to the canteen. Together, they brewed up for the team, making sure each had their own mugs. Karen took a standard issue police mug, making a mental note to bring one in from home the next day. She had a mug in mind which she thought would guarantee a laugh.

For the next half an hour the detectives traded stories while Billy retired to his office. Once they had enjoyed their tea and coffee together, Jack and Karen gathered their phones and their bags, then made their way down to the car park for a drive around Sunderland.

They took an unmarked police car, heading towards the centre of the city. Karen had visited Sunderland briefly a few years ago for a concert but this was all new territory to her. Led by Jack they toured some lesser-known areas. She found the maze of brick cottages confusing.

*This will take some getting used to*, she thought to herself. They went on to visit Seaburn, and Roker, with their beautiful beaches, ending up at the National Glass Centre where they parked so they could get some lunch.

Jack treated Karen to a hot chocolate and one of her favourite meals. Jacket potato covered in baked beans. Later they enjoyed a quick peruse around the latest exhibits and watched some guys blowing glass. Karen was impressed by the city; from what she had seen so far, she thought she would feel at home here.

"Where are you living?" Jack asked as they munched their way through lunch.

"I'm renting a place in Witherwack."

"That's a coincidence, I was born and brought up there. The people are super friendly."

"It's been fine so far. Betty's café by the post office has been a godsend while I was busy moving in."

"Is it still there? Me Mam used to take us to Betty's for our breakfast once a week when I was a bairn."

Karen smiled at the accent.

"She does a delicious bacon roll and pink slice."

Karen looked wistfully at the river. Remembering walks with her husband along the river in Durham. Jack noticed the mood change.

"Fancy a walk along the river?" Jack asked.

"I am sure it's all legitimate research. I need to know my way around," Karen replied with a smile.

Together they took a stroll up the Wear towards the Wearmouth Bridge. The sun had broken through the early morning mist, turning a damp dawn into a warm spring day. Karen took her jacket off, tying the arms around her waist. Bike riders tinkled their bells, as the fitness brigade rode their expensive machines, up and down the paths. Joggers were everywhere.

Two young lads rode past as they walked; one wolf whistled in their direction.

Jack laughed. "Guess they wouldn't be so keen if they saw our badges, little tinkers. They should be at school."

They stopped and looked over the railings. The tide was out, leaving a stretch of mud between them and the water. Gulls and waders picked through the thick goo, looking for food. Numerous traffic cones and a couple of shopping trolleys poked out of the mud, all covered in weed.

Jack pointed to one of the trolleys. "Can you see that? It looks as if someone has left their shopping in that trolley."

Karen peered in the direction Jack had indicated.

"That is weird, fancy popping over to see what's in the bag?"

Jack looked again. "Who me? I don't have my rubber boots in the car."

Karen thought for a moment. "Let's call it in and let uniform have a paddle. I'm curious."

Jack had her radio in her hand. "They won't thank you for this, they'll be sleeping off their lunch somewhere." She pressed the button and spoke into her radio. "DS White to base, there's a suspicious package in the mud on the north side of the river, between the glass centre, and the bridge. We need someone to investigate."

"DS White acknowledged, we'll send over a team. Stay in situ until they arrive."

"Ask them to bring boots, I fancy having a look," Karen whispered.

"The DI asks if they'd bring some boots, she fancies getting dirty on her first day."

There was a pause on the other end.

"Will do."

Within twenty minutes a group of uniformed officers approached where they were standing, carrying a mix of kit.

"Hi guys, Detective Inspector Dee, and Detective Sergeant White. Did you bring some waders?"

"Here, we brought a couple of sets in case you both want to get wet."

"I'm good." Jack was obviously not keen to climb into the stinking mire next to the river. Karen took the offered waders and kicked off her shoes.

"It's a bit sticky out there Inspector, are you sure you want to give it a go."

"Sure, my spidey senses are twitching. I'd like to have a look at that bag up close."

"OK, let's gear up," a rather well-built sergeant suggested, and they all got into waders ready to make their way out to the shopping trolley. Karen could tell by the mutterings amongst the men that they were questioning the necessity for the mission, but they grudgingly accepted their orders.

Ten minutes later they were making their way through the thick mud towards the shopping trolley. Memories of army training flooded back as Karen struggled in the mud. In those days, their uniforms would get covered in muck. She had no intention of getting her clothes dirty if she could help it.

When they arrived at the trolley, they found that the black sack was tied to the inside of the frame, which they all agreed was a little suspicious. The sergeant took out a knife and was about to cut the bag open, when one of his team interrupted. "Careful Sarge, it could be a bomb."

"Don't be daft. Who would leave a bomb out here in the river? I'm going in."

A bit more gingerly than he first intended, the sergeant cut the bag open. As he did, a human head fell out of the bag into the trolley. One of his men was violently sick.

Karen took out her phone, taking a few pictures of the scene. "I guess my spidey senses are still working well," she uttered to herself.

"Shall we bag the remains up Inspector?" The sergeant asked.

"Might as well, I don't think this is where he died so it's not worth trying to preserve the area as a crime scene. Keep the black sack intact, if you can, just in case."

One of the policemen took a body bag out of a backpack, laying the thick black plastic container out on the mud. Gingerly, they lifted the black sack into the body bag and placed the bearded head in the bag alongside it. Karen took a few pictures of the face before they zipped the bag up.

"Better bring the trolley up too just in case it holds some evidence worth collecting."

"OK boss. You heard the Inspector boys. Let's get this job done before the tide turns."

Karen left them to their task, wading carefully back to the

riverbank. She almost fell at one point, waving her arms around like windmills before regaining her balance. She climbed up to where Jack was watching.

"Nice save boss. I thought you were going to end up face down in the mud. What's the score?"

"We have a murder, Jack. And on my first day. The bag contains human remains, all cut up." She handed Jack her phone so she could check out the pictures while she took off her waders, hanging them over the railings to dry out.

"Well, that's not a pretty sight, thank goodness I've a strong stomach. The boss will be furious, he's all for a quiet life," Jack laughed.

"Not as mad as those poor lads, they've got to carry the body and the shopping trolley out of the river. Who do we talk to in forensics?"

"Oh, you're in for a treat there." Jack laughed again as they walked back to the car.

## Chapter Two

*Tuesday 17th May 2022*

The next day Jack took Karen to the Sunderland Royal Hospital to meet the local pathologist. Her name was Dr Laura Rae.

Karen was concerned the Doctor would be more than odd. She assumed you had to be mad to do such a horrendous job.

After they had made their way to the mortuary, Jack introduced Karen to Dr Rae.

"Pleasure to meet you," said Karen, offering her hand.

"Likewise." Dr Rae gave Karen a hint of a smile, ignoring the offer to shake hands.

She wore a regulation white lab coat and blue rubber gloves. Her long red hair was tied back, and she wore a pair of goggles which looked as if they were prescription, as they magnified her eyes in an almost comic way.

Every time Jack looked at her, a picture of minions flashed through her mind for some random reason. It made her smile.

On the table were the remains of the man they had retrieved from the river. Dr Rae had laid out the pieces of the body where they should all go but they could clearly see a lot of bits were missing.

Jack hung back as Karen walked over to the body, scanning the face and the bits of skin and bone, looking for any marks or wounds.

"Any thoughts on how he died Dr Rae?"

"Laura please. Would you like to discuss the results of my examination over a coffee? I have a peaceful sanctuary next door."

"That would be lovely," Jack replied, seemingly unable to take her eyes off the body.

Laura took her rubber gloves off and led the way into the side room which contained a complicated looking coffee machine. Dr Rae proved an excellent host and soon they were all sitting around a coffee table with steaming drinks of different kinds in front of them. Karen had her regulation cappuccino, while Jack had an espresso and Dr Rae had a flat white.

Laura handed Karen a file.

"You can take this away with you for your team to process, but in short, he was drugged before he was cut up, bagged up, then thrown off the bridge. There is a small puncture wound in his neck and his blood, what we could find, was flushed with gamma-hydroxybutyric acid, GHB. Some call it liquid ecstasy."

Dr Rae untied her hair which fell like a red waterfall over her shoulders. The effect was stunning. She then took off her goggles which instantly converted her from weird nerd to stunning beauty. Karen wondered for a moment if the Doctor was flirting with her.

"Do you have any idea when he died?" Jack asked.

"I think the bag had been in the water less than two days. The weight of the trolley pulled the body under the water but the air in the bag gave it some buoyancy, hence the reason the trolley travelled down the river a short distance." She paused to take a sip of her coffee. "Over the last few days there have been some heavy showers inland, so the river has been flowing quite strongly."

They all sipped their drinks, deep in thought.

"As you could see the hands were in the bag, so I've taken a set of fingerprints and included them with his DNA records. They're all in the file. I've also emailed out a set of his dental records for you. You shouldn't have much difficulty identifying him."

"Thank you, Laura," Karen replied, downing the last of her drink. "And thank you for the delicious coffee."

"Well, you can thank the NHS for that. I told them I couldn't do this job without a decent supply of coffee. It seems they value my skills more than the exorbitant cost of a professional barista machine."

She laughed a loud cackling laugh which seemed so out of place in a mortuary. Yet it was infectious and both Karen and Jack were soon laughing too, though they had no idea why.

Laura asked Karen what had brought her to Sunderland. The Doctor was amazed to discover she had only been in the city a few days before starting her new job.

"This is a fine start to your time in Sunderland."

"Isn't it just?" Karen replied. "The boss is quite upset with me, so I am told. I haven't had the chance to talk to him yet."

"I've never met him. I think he might have a phobia about dead bodies. You on the other hand don't seem bothered?" The question in her voice was obvious. "More coffee?"

"One's enough for me thanks. I'll be buzzing later. I'm ex-military, so I've seen my fair share of dead bodies, I'm afraid." As she spoke, she seemed distracted, as if recalling memories. Bad memories.

"Well, that's all behind you now," Jack suggested, trying to move the subject away from the topic of death. She had spotted that the conversation had the potential to upset Karen. "I guess we'd best take all this information back to the team, so we can start trying to solve this mystery."

Karen snapped out of her daydream. "You're right. Thanks, Laura. I look forward to meeting you again soon. Are you local to these parts?"

"I sure am. I live with my parents in Witherwack." Dr Rae smiled a smile which lit up the room.

"What a coincidence, so do I, and Jack was born in Witherwack."

"They'll call us the Witherwack girls if we're not careful," Jack laughed.

"Or worse," Laura suggested, tying her hair back up, laughing that cackling laugh of hers at the same time.

Karen and Jack got up. Both shook hands with the Doctor.

"Thanks for all your help, Laura, I'll be in touch as soon as we find out who our victim is."

"It's been a pleasure. I look forward to meeting you again soon," she added with a wink and a smile.

With that they left the mortuary.

Out in the car park, they both took a deep breath. "Interesting aroma in those places."

"It is that. It wouldn't be top of my perfume list that's for sure."

"She likes you," Jack added, as they climbed into the car. Karen smiled but chose not to reply.

Jack drove them back to Southwick North Station while Karen

thumbed through the file of information Laura had given them. She stared at the face of the dead man for some time, trying to imagine what he was like. Was he a good man or a bad man? *Only time will tell*, she thought to herself.

By the time they returned to the office the team had set up the incident board which had been dug out of a cupboard down by the toilets. Mick was still running a duster over it when they walked in the room.

Karen took the file to her desk and pulled out a picture of the dead man's head. She pinned the photograph to the centre of the board, near the top.

Billy came out of his office. "Well, this is a fine start to your time here Karen."

"Sorry boss, to be fair Jack spotted the bag in the trolley."

"Hmmm," Billy muttered unhappily. "What have we got?"

"The remains of this guy were found not far from the Glass Centre, in a black sack attached to a shopping trolley." Karen pointed to the photo. "All we know so far is that he was drugged before he was killed. There's every chance he was thrown off the Wearmouth Bridge into the river."

"Do we know when he went into the river?" Mick asked.

"Less than two days ago, Dr Rae reckons."

"So, you've met the delightful Dr Rae," Billy chipped in with a smile. "Bit of an odd ball that one."

"But excellent at her job," Karen replied quickly, defending her newfound friend. "I've got fingerprints, DNA and dental records in the file so hopefully we can identify this guy quickly. Any reports of missing persons?"

Catherine waved her hand in the air from behind her computer. Her petite spectacled face looked up at Karen. "Nothing on the system or on the local socials."

"Thanks Catherine, can I hand you the data on our victim to see if you can track him down."

"No problem. Please call me Cat, everyone else does."

"OK, it's Cat from now on."

Karen picked up the file and walked it over to Cat to work on.

"Well people, the board is a bit sparse. Let's aim at filling it up by this time tomorrow. Some mother is missing a son. Check all the CCTV and traffic footage in the area. With luck we can find out exactly when he was thrown off the bridge." Karen stared at the board and then noticed the team were all watching her.

Billy stepped in. "Chop chop, guys. You heard the DI. Let's try and sort this out pronto. It's odds on the top brass will be over this one like a rash, and the media will be wanting answers. No doubt someone saw us fishing this guy out of the Wear."

Everyone turned back to their desks as Billy went back into his room. The work had barely begun when Cat waved her hands in the air again.

"I've got a name."

Karen was sitting on the edge of her desk still looking at the photo on the board as if she had missed something.

"Well done, Cat, what have you got?"

"His name is Peter Bailey. Had a few minors many years ago so we had his fingerprints. He's been off the radar for almost thirty years."

The printer in the corner of the room started working as Cat printed off his criminal record.

"Not a hardened criminal then?"

"Doesn't sound like it, Ma'am," Mick replied.

Karen looked at Mick, startled by the way he addressed her. She hadn't thought of herself as their leader until now. She smiled at him. "Not heard his name before then?"

"Doesn't ring any bells I'm afraid. I'll have a word with a few of my contacts."

"Thanks Mick, let me know if you find anything."

Cat walked over and pinned Peter Bailey's record to the incident board. She also added a printed label with his name on it directly above his photo. She then walked back to her seat.

"We've an address here for Mr Bailey. It is thirty years out of date but let's start there. John, Jordan, do you want to take a drive over to Roker and check out this address. It's in Roker Avenue."

"Aye aye, Ma'am. We'll give it a knock."

John and Jordan left the room leaving Mick, Matt and Rachel to focus on the CCTV research with Cat. They were all watching video feeds of the area around the Wear Bridge.

Karen had a thought. "Where's the nearest supermarket to the Bridge?"

"That will be Tesco Ma'am," Mick offered.

"Can we check the CCTV around the supermarket as well please? Someone took a trolley to the Bridge that night."

"You'll find trollies everywhere Ma'am. The little tykes take them all over. Not sure what they do with them, but the trolley could have come from anywhere," Matt suggested.

"Well, my money is on it being commandeered by our killer or killers on the same night Mister Bailey was thrown over the Bridge."

"Killers Ma'am?" Rachel asked.

"Looking at the Bridge yesterday, I think someone on their own would be hard pushed to lift the remains of Peter here," she pointed to the photograph, "and a trolley over the railings and into the river."

There were a lot of nods around the room as people cracked on with their various jobs.

Karen sat back down opposite Jack.

"I've just been looking through the files Karen, we have a Prudence Bailey on our watch list. She was a person of interest in a drug distribution case we were looking into. Must be over a year ago now. Could be a coincidence?"

"I'm not a fan of coincidences. Do you have an address for her?" Karen asked.

"We do. She lives in Whitburn."

"Right, Jack, let's pop over and find out if she knows, or is related to, our victim."

They grabbed their jackets and hurried out of the room down to the car park.

# Chapter Three

Jack drove out from the station towards the seafront in Seaburn. Sun FM was on the radio playing a mix of local news and music. She headed towards the village of Whitburn, taking the coastal route, passing a string of restaurants, the new Seaburn Inn, the Stack and amusement arcades on the way. She turned into the leafy avenue known as Front Street and parked up not far from Whitburn Church.

The house they were looking for was set back from the road on top of a high bank. The views across towards Sunderland were beautiful.

"A house like this must cost a pretty penny," Karen mused as they walked up to the front door, taking in the lovely gardens and the views as they went.

The fields opposite were full of oil seed rape, offering a huge yellow carpet as a foreground to the wider view. The blue sky above the field reminded her of the Ukraine flag; that country was a regular, albeit tragic topic of conversation both on the radio and in the station.

"More than a normal salary could afford, that's for sure," Jack commented.

Karen knocked on the wooden door.

After a short wait a woman answered, just as Karen was about to knock again. She was dressed all in white with a shock of black hair. Given her age Karen guessed that her hair must be dyed. She was carrying a small dog under her arm and had a cigarette in her mouth.

"Yes?" she asked, after removing the cigarette from her mouth with her spare hand.

"Police. Mrs Bailey?" Karen showed her identification badge to the woman.

"What do you want?"

"We'd like to ask you a few questions about a man called Peter Bailey. May we come in?"

"Sure, come on through. What's that idiot done now?"

The woman stepped away from the door to allow the two officers in. After closing and bolting the door behind them, she showed them through to a huge lounge situated at the rear of the house. Karen and Jack were directed to sit on a large white sofa, while Mrs Bailey sat in a matching armchair opposite them. She put the dog down which happily ran off.

"When did you last see Peter, Mrs Bailey?"

"Ms please, I left the missus bit go a long time ago. I haven't seen Peter in over twenty years. If I walked past him in the street, I am not sure I'd even recognize him."

"I'll not beat about the bush Ms Bailey, Peter's dead."

Prudence stubbed her cigarette out in a marble ashtray, set on a glass coffee table. The table stood on a plush sheepskin rug which filled the space between them.

"Would you like a coffee?" she asked the two officers with barely a pause.

Karen and Jack looked at each other. "Yes please."

Karen replied for them with barely a moment's hesitation.

Ms Bailey reached out and touched a small pad that was sitting on the table. As if by magic a young girl appeared. Ms Bailey asked her to bring coffee for the three women. The girl nodded before quickly hurrying away.

"Forgive me asking Ms Bailey ......" Karen began to ask.

"Prudence please."

"Thank you, forgive me asking Prudence, but all this doesn't come cheap, what do you do to be able to afford all this luxury?"

"I am a dog breeder. I supply exclusive customers across the country with top end pedigree dogs. There has been a huge spike in the market and the value of my dogs has increased substantially since the pandemic began."

"What type of dogs?" Jack asked.

"The most expensive ones," Prudence replied with a smile. "I'll show you my kennels after we have had our drinks. Where is that girl?"

A door opened, and the young girl reappeared pushing a trolley loaded with coffee and biscuits. The three women sat in silence as the girl placed the cups in front of the women, adding a plate of high-end chocolate biscuits to the table. She poured the coffee, her hand shaking ever so slightly. A jug of milk was added to the table as well as a bowl of brown sugar cubes.

The girl turned and left the room. Not a word was said.

"I'll be mother. Milk ladies?"

"Yes please," they both said eagerly.

"Help yourself to a biscuit. I have these sent up especially from London."

The detectives both took a biscuit, carefully unwrapping the gold foil to get to the sweet treat inside.

"How much do pet dogs go for these days?" Jack asked as she nibbled on the delicious biscuit.

"The English Bulldog is the most expensive, but I'm not a fan. I breed Cavapoo mainly, which are a cross between a Cavalier King Charles Spaniel and a Poodle. I also have some Dachshunds and Cockapoos. I charge £3,500 for my dogs which is a little above the norm, but people know they are getting the best from me. Some of my dogs are national champions."

The girls tried to act impressed though neither were dog lovers.

"Do you have any problems selling your dogs?" Karen asked.

Prudence laughed. "My dear girl. I have a waiting list as long as your arm. I can't breed them fast enough. If you've finished your coffee, I'll take you to meet my babies."

Karen and Jack drained their cups, Jack stuffing the last of her biscuit in her mouth as Prudence got up from her chair. They followed her through a pristine utility room which led to a door to the back garden of the house. Outside they walked down a long path between manicured lawns and flower beds until they arrived at a door. The plain grey portal was almost hidden amongst the greenery. Prudence took a key from her pocket and opened the door.

The women were assailed by the sound of dogs which had been completely hidden from outside.

"I try to keep this place as secret as possible. The last thing I want to do is upset my neighbours."

The building was well lit with white walls. A central corridor led away from the entrance area which was home to a desk and a computer. A calendar hung above the desk with various dates ticked off and notes made against each day.

Prudence led them down the corridor. On both sides were a series of cages, each containing dogs. Many were full of puppies, dozens, and dozens of puppies. Karen had never seen so many dogs in her life. The noise was deafening as the dogs reacted to the visitors, no doubt hoping for food. The odour was not that pleasant either.

"I have a team of girls who come in twice a day to feed the dogs and keep the place clean. They are due here soon, so the dogs are quite hungry." Prudence had to raise her voice to be heard. "Have you seen enough?"

"Yes, thank you." Karen was keen to return to the fresh air.

Prudence led them out into the back garden. As she shut the door, peace was restored. All they could hear was the sound of birds singing and bees feasting on the many flowers which filled the space between the kennels and the house. All three took a deep breath.

As they walked back to the house, Prudence made them an offer. "Look I don't owe Peter anything but if he has no money or family, please let me know and I'll be happy to fund his funeral. I have a friend in the trade."

"That's kind, I'll bear that in mind," Karen responded.

They went back into the house, where Prudence led them straight to the front door. Jack was a bit disappointed she wasn't going to get a chance at another biscuit, but she noticed the table had been cleared already. The small dog, a Cavapoo, was asleep on the sofa where they had been sitting.

As they stepped outside, Karen stopped.

"If you do think of any reason that Peter might have been killed, Ms Bailey, please let us know. Jack, have you got a card, I haven't had mine printed yet?"

"Yes Ma'am. Here you go." Jack gave Prudence her card.

"Thank you. It has been so long I can't imagine I would think of anything, but I will be in touch if I do."

"Thanks for the coffee and biscuit," Karen said genuinely, as she turned away to walk back down to the car. "The biscuit was delicious," Jack added with a smile, then followed Karen down the path.

Prudence stood by the door and waved as the officers walked away. She closed the door and walked back to the couch sitting down next to the sleeping dog. She took out her gold Samsung flip phone and dialed a number. "Phil, we have a problem."

*****

As they travelled back to Southwick North, the two detectives were deep in thought. They were driving past the Sunderland AFC training ground when Karen asked a question.

"How many puppies do you reckon were in those kennels?"

"Well, that's the question I was wrestling with. I am guessing well over a hundred."

"One hundred and twenty-four, to be exact. Unless there were a few hidden away I couldn't see."

Jack glanced at Karen in amazement.

"It's a numbers thing. I must count."

"That's impressive. A valuable skill in this job."

"Not sure if it's a skill. I am quite OCD in a lot of ways. I've a good memory for faces too." Karen seemed almost guilty when she mentioned her 'attributes'.

"What was your thinking about the puppies?" Jack asked.

"One hundred and twenty-four puppies at say £3000 a time after vet's bills and the like gives her a damn good income. In fact, if the dogs were bred twice a year that would be worth a cool three quarters of a million pounds, annually."

"Yes but think of the food bills and the staff you'd need. There's a lot of expenditure before you earn that sort of money."

Karen pondered that for a while as they drove through Southwick. "You're right. But I still think there is enough profit to account for her lifestyle. Something still smells off though."

"What do you want to do?"

"I think we should keep an eye on her for a few days. Check who comes and goes and get a better picture of Prudence Bailey. I'll also ask Cat to do some digging, to see what we can find out about her."

They pulled into Southwick North station and climbed out of the car. Karen put her hands on the car roof. "I think we should check companies house and find out if she has any other business interests."

"I'll do that," Jack offered. "Let's see if the others have any news for us."

With that they headed back into the station. Tom Moore buzzed them in with a smile and the pair headed up to their office.

"That Tom is quite dishy," Karen whispered as they climbed the stairs.

"Quite the charmer. I'll tell you all about him when we are

having a coffee one of these days."

"Intriguing," Karen muttered as they entered the office. It was buzzing with conversation.

They went to their desks to dump their bags and jackets, then Karen walked back to the incident board. "Attention guys, what have we got so far?"

Detective Sergeant John Phillips was first to respond. "Jordan and I went over to check out that old address this morning in Roker Avenue. The place is a bit of a dump to be fair and is being used as an HMO. No-one had ever heard of a Peter Bailey. Jordan did have some luck when we checked with the neighbours."

"Yes Ma'am."

Jordan flicked open his notebook. "A neighbour remembered him from thirty years ago. Said he was a likeable chap: liked a pint at the Wheatsheaf in those days. The man said he just stopped coming to the pub. No-one knew what had happened to him. The guy's wife thought she might have seen him begging for money outside one of the bookies in town a few months ago."

"Thanks Jordan. So, he might have needed money. We visited his ex this morning and she has cash to spare. Maybe he went to her to look for money though she says she hasn't seen him in years?" Karen paused. "Any luck with the CCTV coverage in the area?"

It was Cat's turn to speak. She put up her hand from behind her computer screen as the printer started whirring. "We've found the moment the trolley was thrown into the river. We spotted two youths in hoodies pushing the trolley to the centre of the bridge three nights ago, then heaving the trolley with the bag inside, over the railings."

"I am guessing we have no viable ID on the youths."

"Nothing specific Ma'am, but one was wearing a pair of red trainers which show up on one of the cameras."

Karen mulled that over as Cat pinned a still from the CCTV camera to the incident board. It showed the moment the two youths threw the trolley into the river.

"Wouldn't someone notice that and report it in?"

"Trolleys are thrown in the river all the time Ma'am," Matt Jones commented. "It's not easy to spot if there was something in the trolley."

Karen thought for a moment. "Do we have access to a dive team? Maybe this isn't the first time a body has been disposed of in this way."

"Good call Ma'am. I'll call up the experts." Jack picked up the phone and was soon talking to the police marine unit based in Jarrow.

Karen looked at her watch. It was just after noon. "Anything else useful guys?"

"Dr Rae has been after you Ma'am. Can you call her back?" Rachel responded.

"Damn it. I forgot I was going to let her know when we had identified the victim. I'll give her a call."

"The Dive team can be on location at two o'clock Ma'am. Do you want to be there?"

"Yes. Tell them I'll meet them under the Bridge, Jack. Right guys let's find everything we can on Prudence Bailey. Cat, can we have her picture on the board as a person of interest. Can we also do some digging as to Peter Bailey's recent movements, soup kitchens, hostels, that sort of thing. John, Jordan, can you do some digging in those circles?"

"Aye, Ma'am, we're on it."

"Come on everyone, we can do this. Where's the DCI by the way?"

"He's been summoned to City Hall Ma'am. Meeting with the top brass apparently. The media have been asking questions."

"Fair enough, I'll catch up with him later. I'm gagging for a coffee, anyone else want one?" A forest of hands went up. "Drinks all round by the look of it, can you give us a hand Jack?"

"Right behind you."

Together they walked down the hall and filled up a couple of trays with coffee mugs. Karen had brought her own mug to the office. It was a retro Sunderland AFC mug celebrating their victory in the FA Cup final in 1973. She'd decided against the rude one which was derogatory against the Mags. She didn't think it was that appropriate for someone of her rank.

"So, what can you tell me about dishy Tom?" Karen asked as the kettle boiled.

"Well, he's a bit of a one with the ladies, likes to flirt. His wife had enough of all the talk so dumped him just a month or so ago. Rumour is he is devastated, which is why he still wears his wedding ring, but she won't have him back."

"Doesn't sound like my type. Still, he's a good looker," Karen laughed at her own words.

"Just you be careful Ma'am," Jack added as she started to pour out the hot water.

When they returned to the office everyone was impressed by

her mug although no-one was old enough to remember that special moment of Sunderland history. They all longed for the return to those heady days. She quickly realized Sunderland was a town desperate for football success. Football dominated the discussion as the detectives paused to enjoy their bait, as many called their sandwiches.

Cat continued to work, ignoring the football banter. A picture of Prudence Bailey was soon added to the board, with her name neatly printed underneath. It had come from a dog show Prudence had attended in Newcastle. By the smile and the rosettes, at least one of her dogs had been very successful.

Karen noted that part of a shoulder was evident in the picture, showing someone had been with her at the time.

"Cat, can I see the full picture please."

"Coming right up Ma'am." The printer whirred again, and Cat walked over with the full image.

"Do we know who this is?" Karen asked, pointing at the man alongside Prudence Bailey.

"I'll find out." Cat rushed back to her seat and started typing.

"Guys if I can have your attention?"

The team stopped chatting, focusing on Karen.

"I'm going to head down to the river to meet the dive team. Mick and Matt, can you head down to Whitburn and keep an eye on Prudence Bailey's house. I'd like to know who comes and goes. Look out for this man. Cat will get us an ID on him soon." Karen pinned the full photo to the incident board.

"Cat. Call me as soon as you have a name for our mystery man."

A hand appeared from behind the computer screen in the corner giving a thumbs up.

"Jack, you're with me. I'll drive this time. Let's see if I can find my way to the National Glass Centre."

Jack smiled as she gathered her things and followed Karen out of the room. "This should be interesting," she whispered to Mick as she walked out the door.

Half an hour later they arrived at the river. It had been an interesting drive as Jack predicted with a couple of wrong turns and last-minute lane changes, but she could tell Karen was a good driver. "The roads take some getting used to."

"I'll say. Any sign of the dive team?"

"There they are." Jack pointed towards the mouth of the river. A black rib was heading upstream towards them with a team of divers on board.

# Chapter Four

The six-man rib team had been briefed on what to look for and simply waved across to the two detectives as they approached. They anchored the rib slightly downstream from the Wearmouth Bridge. The tide was out again so they couldn't manoeuvre the rib close enough to the shore to be able to speak to Karen.

Jack took out her radio and was soon patched through to the dive team just as the first diver went over the side. Two divers took to the water, both attached to the rib by a rope which was played out by a colleague. Another diver stood by in case the team in the water got into difficulties.

The sixth member of the team kept in touch with the divers in the water as well as with Jack on the riverbank.

Karen walked down to the Glass Centre to buy two coffees and was walking back to where Jack was watching when one of the divers surfaced.

"Is something happening?" Karen asked as she handed Jack the coffee.

"It looks like they've found something. The visibility is terrible, so they have been feeling their way around down on the riverbed using their hands."

"Doesn't sound very pleasant. I wonder what they've found?"

The radio burst into life. "Dive team to Jack. We've found three trolleys, all contain packages. We've marked them. Do you want us to recover them now?"

Karen looked up and down the busy riverbank and made her decision. "Not yet. It will attract too much attention. Can we recover the trolleys tonight, after dark?"

Jack relayed the message which was received with a thumbs up from the rib.

"Ask them to meet us down by the Marina. We'll make the arrangements there."

Jack spoke again to the team on the rib, and they were soon motoring off towards the harbour. They left a small pink buoy floating where they had found the trolleys.

Karen and Jack drove around to the marina, parking opposite the Snow Goose Cafe. The team on the rib took off their dive suits and walked up to join Karen and Jack. After handshakes all round, they all sat down on the outside tables to enjoy tea and cake while planning the recovery operation.

The operation was set for 10.30 that evening. The team arranged for a larger vessel from Newcastle with a winch to join them. Jack and Karen would be picked up from the Marina at 10pm and accompany the divers down to the recovery point. Once all the details were finalized, Karen picked up the bill for the food and drink, then together with Jack they headed back to Southwick North station.

When she returned to her desk, she made her long overdue call to Dr Laura Rae to bring her up to date. On a whim she offered her the chance to join them that evening. Laura accepted without hesitation.

*****

Across in Whitburn, Mick and Matt had spent a rather boring day, watching the front of Prudence Bailey's house. Coffee cups and empty sandwich boxes lined the dashboard and conversation had all but run dry. It wasn't until three in the afternoon that they saw Prudence leave the house and head across the road towards Cornthwaite Park. Matt got out of the car and followed her at a distance, eventually walking past her as she took a seat on the other side of the bowls green.

He carried on walking until he exited the park opposite Latimer's Seafood shop. He then called Mick on his mobile to tell him where she was before doubling back to the car along the road.

Mick walked into the park some five minutes later, with a newspaper, and took a seat thirty yards from where Prudence was sitting. She was obviously waiting for someone. She was constantly looking around, trying to spot whoever she was about to meet. Mick didn't have to wait long.

A man approached from the south end of the park. Mick instantly recognised him from the photo in the office. The man was almost totally bald, dressed in a dark suit with a strong tan. He was around six feet tall and looked to be in his fifties. He oozed money by the cut of his clothes. His shiny shoes seemed out of place in the park.

Prudence stood up and gave him a hug when he arrived at her seat. They sat down close together and began a hushed, yet intense conversation which Mick was unable to hear.

After around ten minutes, the couple got up, kissed, then went their separate ways. The man went back the same way he had come. Matt, who was now back at the car, watched Prudence enter the house just before a team of girls arrived to feed and clean the dogs. Having established the link, the detectives returned to the office to report in.

With everyone back in the office Karen called for an update.

Cat was first to report in, her hand popping up from behind her computer screen. "Ma'am, the man is Phil Brookes, a funeral director. He lives across in Ashbrooke, near Backhouse Park."

"Thanks Cat, add his photo and name to the incident board."

"Prudence did say she could arrange Peter Bailey's funeral,

maybe she was just telling him what was happening in case we take her up on her offer?"

"That's plausible Jack, but why meet in the park like that and why did he walk to the meeting?"

"We didn't notice him come from a car, Ma'am. He must have parked further along the coast towards Seaburn."

"Thanks Mick. Anyone have anything else to add?"

No-one offered anything further, so she explained to the team that they had potentially found three more bodies in the river under the Wearmouth Bridge.

Just as she was finishing, the DCI returned to the office. Billy walked over to the incident board to get up to speed. He was looking slightly smarter than usual.

"How has your day been boss?"

"Meetings Mick, you know how I hate meetings."

"We'll be dragging the river tonight, boss, we think we may have found three more bodies down there."

"That will attract a lot of attention, Karen. Maybe we need a deflection."

"Deflection? What have you in mind?" Karen was curious.

"Let's put out a story that an unexploded World War two bomb has been discovered near the Wearmouth Bridge. We can say that we will be closing it for an hour from ten fifteen tonight as a precaution." Billy seemed pleased with himself at the idea.

"Sounds good to me boss, Jack and I with Dr Rae will be on the boat tonight. Can we leave you to create the deflection?"

"Well, I think I've done my bit, I've been facing questions from City Hall for most of the day. Now it looks like we may have a serial killer on the loose. Cat, can you send out a message to the media and Mick can you let uniform know that we want the bridge closed for an hour. They can put out some advance warning signs to let everyone know about the closure."

He looked around the room to check everyone was happy before heading into his office, closing the door behind him.

*****

The man in black was annoyed when his mobile phone rang. No-one disturbed him while he was playing his favourite sport. He was even more annoyed at the subject of the call. How had this happened? He demanded answers and needed to find out who was at fault. The blame had to stop with someone, and they would be punished for their mistakes. Punished severely.

Maybe it was time to visit the Sunderland operation. He had not been in the area for a few years, believing all was going well.

People were scared of him; he knew that, and he encouraged that. Yes, he would visit Sunderland and personally make sure this mess was cleared up, fast.

*****

That evening, Karen and Jack met Dr Rae at Sunderland Marina. The Dive boat was already there, as were the team they met earlier, plus an extra couple of boat hands and a skipper. An awning had been set up at the back of the boat to protect the deck from prying eyes. Three spotlights lit the deck and the surface of the water at the back of the boat. A winch with a hook sat at the rear of the vessel on the starboard side.

The night was quite chilly out on the water, with a ghostly sea fret rolling up from the coast. Both Karen and Jack accepted heavy coats from the team. Dr Rae had come better prepared and was well wrapped up against the elements in a thick red puffer jacket. She stood out from the rest of the team, who were all dressed in black.

The boat slowly made its way up the river. The mist seemed to follow them, powered by a gentle wind off the North Sea. The boats lights created strange patterns in the mist.

"It looks like the souls of the departed are joining us tonight," Jack noted quietly.

Karen looked at Jack and felt her skin prickle at the thought. Dr Rae simply smiled and watched the crew work.

The anchor went over the side at precisely 10.30pm. From where they were, Karen could see the flashing blue lights of the police roadblocks either side of the bridge.

A few lights lit up the darkness from the Echo Building flats overlooking the river. Karen was sure she could spot a few people on their balconies but that couldn't be helped. She hoped the mist would help hide what they were doing, and that the watchers would soon become bored and head back into the warmth of their homes.

Within minutes two divers entered the river and the winch was lowered into the water. Ten minutes later, at a signal from the riverbed, the winch started to pull up an object from the cold, inky waters.

A shopping trolley, with a black bag enclosed, appeared out of the river, and was quickly brought on board. The divers worked with military precision and soon three trolleys were sitting on the deck.

"A shout from the stern sent the winch back down again."

One of the dive team came over to Karen. "We've found another one Ma'am."

"Dear God. How many are down there?"

"It could be loads more, Ma'am. It's virtually impossible to cover the whole of the riverbed between here and the river mouth."

Dr Rae was virtually beaming with excitement.

"The Dr seems pleased," the dive team leader mentioned to Karen with a grim smile. Dr Rae was itching to open the bags.

Once all four trolleys were on board, the boat lifted anchor, and Jack gave the all clear over the radio so the bridge cordon could be lifted.

Back on the Marina an incident tent had been established on one of the pontoons, but Dr Rae couldn't wait that long. She pleaded to Karen to be allowed to open the bags.

"Just one Laura, to make sure we have found what we think they contain."

Laura Rae pulled out a pair of blue rubber gloves from one pocket of her jacket and a penknife from the other. She walked from trolley to trolley then decided on one that seemed less rusty than the others.

Carefully she studied the bag in the trolley before gently cutting the cable tie which attached it to the trolley frame. She then made an incision in the top of the bag about a foot long. She put the knife back in her pocket and took out a small torch.

"Hold this please." She gave the torch to Karen who took it gingerly. "Shine it in the bag when I pull it open."

Karen stepped closer to the trolley and shone the torch down on the bag. Dr Rae eased the bag open.

Their worst fears were realised. The remains of a foot and a hand were visible through the gap.

Karen stepped back as the smell of rotting flesh assailed her nostrils. It didn't seem to bother Dr Rae who took back the torch and delved a bit deeper into the bag.

"We have a head," she said proudly. As if she had found some hidden treasure.

"That means we have some sort of serial killer," Karen stated. "The boss will be furious."

Then to everyone's surprise she made a request.

"Can we have a minute's silence please, for these people. It is our job to find out who these people are and why they ended up this way. Let us think about the task ahead and the sadness that this will bring to their families."

With that, all activity on the boat stopped, as the dive team, crew, Dr Rae and the detectives all took a moment to reflect on what they had found.

When the minute was over, Karen clapped her hands.

"Right, let's take these trolleys to the Royal, so Dr Rae can make a start trying to identify these individuals and what happened to them."

"Yes Ma'am," came a collective response from the dive team.

When the boat was safely tied to the pontoon, Karen and Dr Rae climbed ashore, leaving Jack to work with the dive team to move the trollies on to dry land. Together they walked the short distance to where Dr Rae had parked her car.

"Fancy a lift home?"

"That would be kind," Karen smiled to her new friend.

"Well, we are almost neighbours."

Karen sent Jack a message to let her know she had a lift home.

Dr Rae walked over to a bright red mini, the original kind, with a union jack on the roof. She unlocked the door and got in, leaning across to open the door for Karen.

"This is cosy," Karen muttered, once she had squeezed herself into the car.

Dr Rae turned the key and the car coughed into life. With a slight wheelspin, Dr Rae drove up the hill away from the Marina towards Witherwack.

They travelled in virtual silence. Both lost in thought as to what they had found. When they arrived at Karen's house, which it turned out was just a street away from Dr Rae's home, Karen invited the Doctor in for a drink.

Dr Rae looked at her watch. "Best not, I have to be in work at seven to make sure the bodies have been catalogued properly. I have a big day ahead of me."

"No worries, maybe next time."

"I'd like that." Dr Rae touched Karen on the knee.

Karen climbed out of the car and headed up the short path to her front door. As she turned the key, she looked back just in time to see the red mini wheelspin away. *That was weird*, she thought to herself, as she walked into her new home, She was met by the hungry meows of her cat.

# Chapter Five

*Wednesday, 18th May 2022*

The following morning after a briefing with the team, Karen and Jack headed over to the Sunderland Royal Hospital to meet Dr Laura Rae. They arrived at 10am.

Laura had already been at work for over three hours. When they met her, she was literally bouncing with excitement. Forensic teams had already checked the trolleys but there was no usable material on those.

All four tables in the mortuary carried human remains which Dr Rae had laid out methodically. "This is so cool," Dr Rae offered.

"That wouldn't be my choice of words," Jack muttered as Karen walked over to the tables.

Karen studied the remains, one by one. They were in varying degrees of decomposition though the last of the bodies was in far better condition than the others. Laura followed her like a little schoolgirl waiting for permission to speak.

Eventually Karen stopped in front of the more identifiable remains. "OK Laura, what do we have here?"

Dr Rae clapped her hands in excitement.

"All the remains have been dismembered in the same way as the first body you found. The first three are too far gone to give us much. I can probably tell you if they are male or female, if you can give me some time. Apart from dental records, there is little else left to help identify them."

She walked up to the head of the fourth body. "As you can see this person is a far more recent addition to the river. Killed two or three weeks ago I reckon. You can still make out from the colour of his skin that he has a decent tan, despite the degradation of the remains. The weird thing is that his left hand is quite pale compared to his right." Dr Rae moved the hands together to show the difference.

Jack had hung back from the tables as she was more than a little uncomfortable with the morbid sight of all the bodily parts laid out before them.

The curiosity of the hands made her overcome her revulsion and she joined Laura and Karen at the table. "The nails are well manicured too," she noted.

Karen nodded. "Someone somewhere must have some idea who this guy is. Any idea how he died Laura?"

"Same MO. I found a puncture wound on his neck. I'd lay good money that I'll find GHB in his blood."

"Dear God. You know what this means Jack."

"We have a psycho serial killer on the loose here in Sunderland."

"There's that," Karen replied, "but this could be the tip of the iceberg. The divers reckoned that potentially there could be dozens of trolleys with bodies like these in the river."

"Why have we only found out about this now. Why haven't we received reports of missing people?"

Karen looked at Jack. "People go missing all the time Jack, all over the country. For all we know these people might not even be from the UK."

"Coffee?" Laura asked.

"Love one," the girls replied in unison.

The three women retired to the breakaway room where Dr Rae kept her Barista machine, and they were all soon enjoying cups of top-quality coffee.

Karen noticed the cups this time. They were all different, coming from different tea sets. Dr Rae saw that Karen was studying her cup.

"Car boots and charity shops."

"They're great," Karen replied.

Karen, shook her head, snapping back into the reality of their situation. "When will you be able to get back to us with your findings?"

"I hope by the weekend. Monday, at the latest."

"What about the recent guy?"

"I'll start with him. I should be able to let you have dental records, fingerprints, and DNA by the end of play today."

"Thanks Laura, much appreciated. While we are all here, do you fancy meeting up at the weekend. Say Saturday morning at Betty's Café."

"I'd love that, I don't get out much. Say 10.30am for brunch?" Dr Rae suggested.

Jack nodded enthusiastically. "It's a date. The first official meeting of the Witherwack girls." The women laughed, Dr Rae with that cackle that was guaranteed to turn heads.

Once they had left the mortuary, Karen and Jack returned to Southwick North. On the way Jack raised a question which had been playing on her mind.

"Any thoughts on why the bodies are being cut up like that?"

Karen thought for a moment. "I've had the same thought but for the life of me, I can't work it out. Usually, the head and hands are removed to stop us identifying the bodies but here, well it's as if they don't care."

"They are either very confident or stupid."

"I'll go with both. They are confident but never thought they would be discovered. If you hadn't spotted that the shopping trolley had a bag in it, we would be blissfully unaware that this was going on."

Jack turned the car into the police station and parked around the back. As she got out of the car, she waited for Karen to climb out then clicked the key fob to lock the vehicle. "There is a common denominator here. None of the dead have been reported missing, we'd have a pile of missing persons files if they had been."

Karen looked over the top of the car at her new friend. "You're right. That either means they are loners, like Peter Bailey perhaps, or more likely they are not from around here. This gets more curious all the time."

At that moment it started to rain so the women hurried into the station before they got wet.

They both nodded at Tom Moore, who was manning the front desk.

"Just in time Ladies, it's pouring down now."

They both smiled at the charming sergeant before heading up to their offices.

When they entered the office all the team were working. More information had already been added to the incident board ready to account for the four new bodies.

"We're going to need a bigger board," Mick muttered as Jack sat down. Karen, walked over to the board, looking at the new details.

"I think you're right. Especially when we start to put some meat on the bones. No pun intended." Jack was about to say something when the DCI walked in. "What have we got, Karen?"

"Four more bodies boss, all dismembered like Peter Bailey. So far, he is the only one we have identified but Laura, over at the Royal, is confident we'll have some details about at least one of the bodies by the weekend."

"Why just one?"

"The other three are much older and decomposed but one is quite recent. We could even make out some skin colour, which was a bit weird."

Matt was following the discussion intently. "Why was it weird Ma'am."

"Well one hand was quite tanned while the other was pale in comparison."

"Like this?" Billy held up his hands. His left hand was quite pale compared to his right. "Exactly but a lot more defined. How did you get your hands like that?" Karen asked, stunned to see the similar pattern.

"Your dead man is a golfer. I'm right-handed so I wear a glove on my left hand. I would guess if the colour difference is more substantial than mine, the man played golf a lot more than me."

"So, we are looking for a right-handed golfer from somewhere a lot warmer than here?" Jack summarised for the team.

"Seems like it," Karen replied. "Cat can we be ready to approach our European colleagues when Dr Rae sends us the fingerprints, dental records and DNA."

A thumbs up wave came from behind Cat's computer screen.

"Carry on guys. Karen, can you come with me?"

"Yes boss," Karen replied, and she followed Billy into his office closing the door behind her.

Once they had both sat down Billy placed his elbows on the desk, rested his chin on his hands and stared at Karen. Karen felt distinctly uncomfortable for a moment.

"You've been here five minutes and we have a bloody serial killer on our hands. What the hell Karen?"

"It's not my fault boss. Some of these poor people were killed and dismembered long before I arrived in Southwick North."

"I know Karen. I'm getting a lot of stick from upstairs. We need to find out what the hell is going on."

"I'm not convinced there aren't more bodies in the river boss. I'm reluctant to put the divers down again as we have enough to be getting on with. What do you think?"

"I think that is a good call. Let's work with what we've got. Keep the team at it. I'd like to think we'll have some idea of what is going on by this time next week."

"We'll do our best, boss. We just don't have much to go on."

"I've got faith in you. Don't let me down."

"You can count on us. The team are an excellent bunch, we'll find the answers."

"Off you go then, I've a conference call with City Hall in five minutes. I'll stall them for now but they're going to want answers soon. I'm hoping the media don't get too pushy. I know a few rumours are doing the rounds but tell the team to keep what's going on to themselves. Careless words cause me hassle."

Billy smiled at Karen, and she took the gesture as a signal to go.

Once back in her office she stood again in front of the incident board. She stared at the sparse details as if something was going to jump out at her.

"Guys!" She announced as she turned around. "There are a few questions here that we need to think about, and they all start with why. "Why did these people all have to die? Why were they dismembered in this way? And," Karen paused for a moment, staring out at the river, "why throw them into the River Wear?"

"Let's call it a day. I want you all in sharp tomorrow morning. If you get a chance, have a think about those questions. Maybe we can come up with some possible answers tomorrow."

"Cheers Ma'am. A few of us are heading over to Granny Annie's down on the seafront at Roker, if you fancy joining us?" Rachel offered. "It promises to be a beautiful evening."

"Thanks Rachel, perhaps another time. I want to focus on the case this evening and wouldn't be much company. I'll see you all in the morning. Just don't speak about the case if there's people around. The boss wants to keep it hush hush for now to keep the press off his back."

"Understood Ma'am," Rachel responded as she put on her jacket. With the scraping of chairs, the team all left their desks and headed down to the car park.

Jack was last to leave the office. Before she closed the door she turned to look back at Karen. "If you need some company, please give me a call."

"Thanks Jack, I'll be alright. Go and enjoy yourself but tell them to be careful. I don't want any mention of this to go beyond this office if possible. Not until we have more information anyway."

"I'll keep an eye on them. See you tomorrow. Don't stay here too late."

As the door closed behind Jack, Karen turned back to the incident board. "I'm missing something," she whispered to herself. With a shake of her head, she collected her jacket and computer case and headed downstairs to take the short drive home.

# Chapter Six

That evening she sat watching her favourite soaps, trying to rid her mind of the puzzle that she faced at work. She had a glass of Sauvignon Blanc on the table next to where she sat, and her beloved Ragdoll, Jinx, was stretched out against her legs.

As she gently stroked the cat with her right hand she thought once again of the bodies that they had found.

*Why were they disposed of like that and what had happened to the rest of them?* she thought to herself. She considered that the others were golfers too but wondered where did Peter Bailey fit in? He obviously was not a golfer.

At 9pm she switched over to her favourite crime series, Silent Witness. She was watching on catch up and had somehow managed to avoid reading about the latest story on social media. Karen was always amazed at how involved the forensic pathologists were in the cases. In her experience the people she had worked with were, if anything, underutilised. Maybe she would invite Dr Rae around to talk about the case at some point over a glass of wine.

*As long as she didn't get the wrong idea,* Karen thought to herself. She was still convinced Dr Rae had a soft spot for her.

Just as the title credits began to run, Karen's mobile rang. It was Jack. She pressed the pause button on her remote.

"Ma'am, sorry to bother you. I thought I would let you know that Cat has received details of our golfing victim from Dr Rae, she must be working overtime. Cat went back to the office to run the fingerprints and dental records. She found an immediate match from Spain."

Karen picked up her wine but thought better of it. "Spain? Who was it?"

"His name is, or was, Miguel Victor. He has a string of aliases and a list of minor convictions. All to do with drug handling.

He seemed to drop off the radar about ten years ago and became a keen amateur golfer, travelling all around Europe and the UK playing golf. The Spanish police were convinced he was still dealing in drugs but could never pin anything on him."

"That's good progress. I'll thank Cat for going above and beyond in the morning. Let's try and pin down his movements and find out where he was staying or playing the last time he was here. I'll ask the boss; he'll have some ideas. He's into his golf."

"Good idea. Are you OK?"

"I'm fine, why do you ask?"

"You sound a bit flat."

"Guess the case is getting to me. A decent night's sleep and I'll be fine in the morning. Thanks for asking."

"No worries, Karen, I'll see you tomorrow."

With that, Jack hung up, leaving Karen to ponder the news. She had smiled at the informality of the last part of their conversation. She already thought of Jack as a friend. As long as she was formal in the office, Karen was happy to be on first name terms.

She took a sip of wine and pressed the play button.

For the next hour she would let someone else solve the murders. Then it would be an early night.

\*\*\*\*\*

*Thursday, 19th May 2022*

The next morning Karen was in the office, bright and early. Jack was at her desk, as was Cat and Mick. The others streamed in one by one until they were all beavering away on the case. DCI Billy Roberts was last in, looking a little worse for wear.

Instead of heading straight into his office he stood and looked at the incident board. Cat had added an image of Miguel Victor to the board along with some details they had received from the Spanish police.

"Who is this guy, Karen?"

"He is the most recently killed victim we fished out of the river after Peter Bailey. He's a pretty good golfer apparently, played on the amateur tour but has past links to the drug world."

This seemed to pique Billy's interest more than usual.

"What do we know about his last visit to the UK?"

"That's what we are working on now. We are checking Newcastle airport, looking for flights in from Spain and trying to establish when he arrived. The trouble is, he uses a number of aliases so it could be hard work tracking him down."

"Well let me know when you find the date, then I'll check the golf fixtures. With luck we can place him at a tournament."

"Thanks boss."

Billy turned and went into his office, closing the door heavily behind him.

"He's a bit rough this morning," Jack whispered across to Karen.

"It will be one of two things, "Karen suggested, "either a good night or a bad night." They both laughed.

As usual it was Cat who came up with the first bit of useful information. Her hand went up from behind her computer screens. "I've got him, Ma'am."

Karen jumped up from her chair and walked across to Cat's desk.

"He arrived in the country on the 8th of April, Ma'am."

On Cat's screen were details of a Jet2 flight from Alicante with the name Floran Paulio, one of Miguel Victor's known aliases.

"Can we access the CCTV of the airport that day to try and spot him?"

"I'll have a look," Cat promised.

Karen went across and knocked on Billy's door.

"Come," shouted Billy from inside. He was nursing a glass of water which was fizzing away. A tub of Andrews Liver Salts was on his desk. "Good for a hangover."

Karen was unimpressed.

"8th of April, boss. Can you find out why he would want to be here then?"

"I'll check the golf fixtures and let you know."

"Thanks boss."

Karen backed out of Billy's office, shutting the door gently behind her. She had barely sat down when Cat again put her hand up. *How does she do it?* Karen thought to herself as she walked across the room to Cat's desk. A couple of the other detectives joined her.

On Cat's screen was a video feed from the baggage collection area at Newcastle Airport. A man with a flowery shirt could be seen collecting a set of golf clubs from the carousel along with a large shoulder bag.

"He was challenged by the customs officers, but nothing was found." Cat threw the comment in as they watched Miguel Victor leave the airport and climb into a taxi.

At that moment the DCI opened his office door.

"There was an amateur event at Ramside Hall on the 10$^{th}$ of April, Dee. He was probably signed up to play in that."

"Thanks boss, we'll check that out. Matt, Rachel, can you drive over to Ramside Hall and track our victim down. He may have stayed at the hotel as well as played in the competition."

"Will do Ma'am." Matt replied as the two officers grabbed their jackets and headed out. As they left Karen's phone rang. It was Dr Rae.

"Hi Karen. I have taken a long hard look at the other bodies but apart from dental records I haven't got much else to offer."

"Were they all men?" Karen asked.

"Yep. Are we still on for Saturday?"

"Of course. See you then." Dr Rae hung up the phone without replying.

Karen looked at her phone and shrugged. "Rude."

"Everything alright?" Jack asked.

"Just Dr Rae being a bit weird."

"I told yoooou."

"You did," Karen laughed, "Saturday will be interesting."

"I can't wait."

Jack went back to her computer while Karen stared at the incident board. For a while the room was quiet as the detectives clicked away at their keyboards. Most of the focus was on missing persons or CCTV footage.

Uniform had been given pictures of the youths that had been seen throwing the trolley off the Wearmouth Bridge. The team hoped someone would recognise the red trainers as they had precious little else to go on.

A telephone rang which caused a couple of the detectives to jump. It was Jordan who answered.

After a few words he concluded the call with. "Can you send the details over to Detective Constable Cat Groves please? ..... Thank you." He hung up.

"Ma'am. That was the SOCO team. They have a partial fingerprint from the first shopping trolley. It was on one of the wheels."

"How's that possible. It had been in the water for a few days," Karen was incredulous.

"Apparently it was tucked under the wheel support which protected it from the flow of the river," Jordan explained.

"Let's have a look at that video footage from the bridge again," Karen suggested.

Cat called it up on her computer screen and the detectives gathered round to watch the moment the trolley went in the water. As the two youths lifted it over the railings, the one with the red trainers grabbed the wheel to give it one final heave.

"That's it. You can see him hold the wheel as he throws it over. If we can find a match, we should be able to track 'red trainers' down."

"Except, we don't have a match," Cat reported.

"Damn it." Karen was frustrated. Try as they might they weren't getting the breaks she had hoped for. Patience wasn't one of her finest virtues.

"Dee!" The shout came from DCI Billy Roberts office.

Karen walked into his room and shut the door behind her.

"What's happening Karen. We've a mass murderer on the loose and we don't seem to be making any progress?"

"I don't think that's fair boss. We've found a partial print for the kid who threw the remains of Peter Bailey in the river. We'll soon know what happened to Miguel Victor and we have dental records for the other victims. I reckon we are due a break soon."

"Well let's hope so. I am getting phone calls on the hour, every hour asking what progress we are making. I'm sick of telling them I have nothing to report."

"We'll get a result, boss. Have faith."

About three in the afternoon, Matt and Rachel returned from Ramside Hall. Karen could tell they were excited by the way they burst into the office.

"What have you got, guys?"

"They serve the most amazing lunches at Ramside Hall," Matt enthused.

Karen looked at him. "Really!"

"Sorry Ma'am. Perhaps you should sit down for this."

"Just tell us what you found."

"Well, Miguel Victor did play in the competition in April. In fact, he won a prize. He registered as Floran Paulio for the tournament."

Rachel reached into her jacket pocket. "This is a picture of him collecting his prize." Karen looked at the smiling face of Miguel Victor holding a new golf bag.

"Anything else?"

"Well, this is the interesting part. We talked to the professional in the golf shop. Apparently, when he arrived, he bought himself a full set of golf clubs and all the kit. He told the professional that his had been lost by the airline."

"But we saw him collect his golf clubs at the airport," Mick reminded everyone. No-one spoke for a moment.

"Brilliant. Now we have a missing set of golf clubs. What the hell is the relevance of that?" Jack asked.

"Let's try and trace him to any other competitions. Hopefully it will give us something to go on. In fact, I'll ask the DCI to help. I am sure as this is golf related, he would be happy to make some calls."

As Karen walked into Billy's office the other's looked at Matt.

"Are you serious," Jack asked.

"What?"

"The lunch comments!"

"Well, it was a great lunch," Matt said guiltily as he returned to his desk.

## Chapter Seven

*Friday, 20th May 2022*

Friday dawned bright and clear. Karen was woken by the distant sound of sirens. The only other sound was the screech of gulls. She ate her breakfast while listening to Simon on Sun FM. The music drowning out her thoughts as she came to terms with her first full week in her new job.

When she reached the office, the team were already busy, working on the case. Billy had discovered two further tournaments where Floran Paulio had played. On each occasion he bought new golf clubs before the tournament started.

The incident board now included a picture of Miguel Victor and another with him collecting his golf clubs at the airport. The detectives wrestled with how these elements were all linked. The discussions went on for hours.

They were about to break for lunch when they received a call. Uniform had arrested two 'scrotes' who they'd found smashing up a piece of children's playground equipment in Roker Park. One wore a pair of red trainers.

Karen and Jack headed off to the Sunderland station where they were being held. For a Friday afternoon it was remarkably quiet, peaceful even, until they reached the holding cell where the two youths were being held. The pair screamed, shouted obscenities, and kicked the cell door, generally being a pain in the, you know what, to anyone who paid them any attention.

On a request from Karen, the one with the red shoes was dragged into a separate cell. Karen and Jack walked in to join him and a rather large sergeant who was standing guard.

"What's your name?"

"No comment," came the snidey reply. The arrogance of youth oozed out of him.

"Have you ever thrown a shopping trolley in the river?"

"No comment."

Karen thought the smile was begging for a slap.

"Sergeant did you take his fingerprints when you brought him in?"

"Yes Ma'am."

"Good." She turned to Jack. "I am willing to bet his prints will match the one's on the shopping trolley and then we will be able to charge him with murder."

"Wait, what?" The smile was gone.

"Well, you threw the body off the Wearmouth Bridge."

"What body? We threw a few trolleys off the bridge, that ain't a crime."

Karen ignored the fact that it actually was a crime.

"There was a bag in the trolley."

"The guy told us it was full of stones to weigh the trolley down."

"What guy?"

"The guy who called us to tell us where to collect the trolley. We thought he might be from a rival supermarket."

"Are you that stupid?"

"He left us £50 in the trolley for us to throw it off the bridge. We didn't ask any questions."

"How many have you thrown into the river?"

"I've not been counting."

"How many?" Karen's voice went up a notch and she gave him her best evil eye.

"About ten."

"Dear God." Jack was appalled.

"You know you're in deep trouble son."

The boy had suddenly lost all his bravado. Realisation dawned that he had been party to the disposal of ten bodies. It was not how he expected his day to work out. He simply nodded.

"Lock them both up in separate cells sergeant, until we can question them properly. Oh, and I want his phone so we can try and track the calls."

"Aye Ma'am, it will be my pleasure. Come on you."

By now the boy was shaking and close to crying as the sergeant led him away. As they left the building another officer handed Karen an evidence bag with a small phone in it. She would get Cat to look at it when they got back to Southwick North.

On the way back she got Jack to drive by the river. They walked down to the bank and stood for a while, looking out at the calm waters. At least five more bodies waited out there to be recovered.

"Jack, when we get back, see if Cat can get anything from the phone. It might give us the date each body was disposed of if nothing else. My guess the number will be untraceable, but Cat can try."

"What about the other five bodies?"

"I guess we'd better get the dive team back out there, but not before the weekend. Let's take stock and enjoy a couple of days rest. I think we all need a break. Next week we are going to solve these crimes, or I'll hand in my badge."

"That's a bit extreme, Karen. Tell me you don't mean it?"

"I do Jack. Everyone needs answers and it's up to me to get to the bottom of this, with your help. The guys need to be on the ball next week or as any football manager knows, I'll be out the door."

"It happens a lot in Sunderland."

"Does it?" Karen asked.

On the way back to the station, Jack listed all the Sunderland football managers that had led the club over the last few years. It was quite a list.

Back in the main office the incident board was filling up nicely. They were yet to connect all the dots, as Karen put it, but the team had a lot of dots to work with.

Officers tried to match dental records for the bodies yet to be identified, while tracking down the movements of Miguel Victor between golf tournaments. Efforts were also made to find anything on Peter Bailey which would provide a motive for his murder or offer a potential link to Victor or Prudence Bailey,

"Is it worth keeping Prudence Bailey on the board?" Mick asked as the officers assessed the progress of the investigation before the weekend.

"My gut tells me she's involved somehow." Karen studied Prudence's face on the board. "Let's leave her there for now or until we can rule her out of the investigation. Can we spare anyone to watch her house next week?"

"We're a bit short on numbers," Jack replied.

"I'll ask the boss if we can get some help next week. By the way, where is he?"

"I think he is playing in a golf competition this weekend Ma'am and took the day off to practice." Matt Jones looked guilty, as if he was sharing a well-kept secret.

Karen pulled a face, the one she used when Jinx made a mess on the floor. She was annoyed Billy hadn't told her he was taking a long weekend, especially with such an important investigation under way.

She glanced at her watch. It was 4pm.

"Well, as the boss is away, let's pack up for the day. The sun is shining, and I doubt we can make much more progress between now and the weekend. Get some rest and relaxation people, because I want this investigation put to bed next week."

A chorus of thank-yous accompanied the scrape of chairs as the team packed up their desks and headed home. Just Cat and Jack stayed behind. Cat was beavering away on her computer, seemingly oblivious to the fact everyone had left the office, while Jack waited to chat to her boss.

"Looking forward to brunch tomorrow?" She asked.

"Very much so. It should be interesting. Doing anything tonight, Jack?"

"I think I might head into town and grab myself a drink or two. Fancy joining me?"

"I think I'll pass, thanks Jack. I'm feeling my age a bit these days, Sunderland on a Friday night is probably more suited to youngsters, like you."

"For goodness sake, you're hardly old. Maybe you should let your hair down. You might enjoy it."

Karen looked wistful for a moment which Jack immediately spotted. She decided not to push Karen.

"Maybe next time. I'll see you in the morning at Betty's Ma'am."

"Don't get too mortal Jack and be careful."

"Don't worry about me. Pity the bloke who rubs me up the wrong way." Jack smiled at Karen as she pulled on her jacket and headed home.

Karen walked over to talk to Cat. The young detective constable had earphones in and was fully engrossed by her computer screens. Karen tapped her on her shoulder and Cat pulled out one of her earpieces.

"Sorry Ma'am, I was miles away."

"Everyone's gone home. Don't stay too late."

"I won't Ma'am. I'm trying to pin down some of these dental records. It's proving a bit difficult. There's no central database so I am sending what we have to the list of dentists in the area as well as a national list of dentists. If the victims are from outside the UK, we might never find them unless Dr Rae has some success extracting DNA from the remains."

"I'm seeing her in the morning, so I'll find out how she's getting on."

"Thanks Ma'am, have a great weekend."

"You too Cat. You've impressed me with your efforts this week. Keep up the good work."

Cat reddened noticeably. "Thank you, Ma'am."

Karen collected her things, took one last look at the incident board, and walked down to her car. She lovingly stroked the bonnet as she pressed the button to unlock the Audi Q2. As she left the car park she put on her favourite album, the soundtrack from Les Miserables.

As she drove home, 'One Day More' boomed out of the car's speakers. She sang all the way, until she parked on her driveway, the case forgotten for a few minutes.

That evening she sat with a notebook on her knee as a film played in the background on the TV. Jinx was curled up alongside her, a glass of white wine sat on the coffee table. She was trying to piece together what all the bits of evidence meant; specifically, how they linked together.

The pages stayed frustratingly empty for a while until she decided to doodle a type of mind map. She put Peter Bailey in the middle of the left-hand page and Miguel Victor in the middle of the right-hand page.

She then started to put key words around each name looking for common denominators. Murdered and drugs were the only two words which were consistent to both pages. Even the drug link was tenuous as they had no reason to think Peter was involved in drugs in any way.

Karen finally put the pad away as Jinx stretched out, looking for some attention. She stroked the cat as she took a sip of wine. *Why does wine have to be so nice*, she thought to herself as the delicious New Zealand Sauvignon Blanc slipped across her tongue.

The film came to an end, and she thought about watching something else but in the end opted for an early night. She was in bed reading a crime novel on her kindle by 10.30pm.

*Saturday, 21st May 2022*

The next morning, Karen was up early. After a shower and a light breakfast, she dressed in her favourite black track suit and went out for a run. She was no athlete, but she enjoyed the countryside and reckoned combining the fresh air with some exercise was good for her physically and mentally.

She ran through the countryside towards West Boldon and was soon on the outskirts of Boldon Golf Club. She paused for a rest and a drink, watching the early morning golfers teeing off. She wondered if Billy was a member here and resolved to ask him about his golf, to show interest if nothing else.

The players all treated their clubs with respect, cleaning them after some shots, the woods being covered to stop them getting scratched. She thought about the missing clubs and why Miguel Victor would buy new clubs before a game.

The germ of an idea started to formulate in her head, and she knew Billy would know the answer. Pleased with herself she turned and ran back home. She had brunch with the girls to look forward to.

## Chapter Eight

After a short walk, Karen arrived at Betty's Café, a few minutes before 10.30am. She had taken another shower but still wore the black tracksuit. It was comfortable.

Jack was already there, sitting in a window table which looked out at the road. As Karen was taking her seat, there was an almighty screech of tyres from outside. The red mini of Dr Rae had arrived in a cloud of tyre smoke, stopping inches short of the cars already parked in front of the row of shops.

"Why didn't she walk?" Karen was amazed someone as trim as Dr Rae would drive such a short distance.

They watched through the window as Laura got out of the mini and headed over to the Café. She had spotted them watching and waved enthusiastically at the two policewomen.

Her choice of clothes could not be more different to Karen's. She wore bright orange trousers, a yellow jacket over a green t-shirt and her red hair hung loose over her shoulders. The effect was stunning.

Even Jack in her white jeans and pink top felt dowdy as Laura burst through the door with a big smile and proceeded to hug and kiss both the women as if they had been apart for years.

Betty immediately stopped talking to her regulars and came over herself to serve the girls.

She stared at Jack.

"Now I might be wrong but aren't you that Jacqueline White who used to live around here?"

Jack smiled at the use of her proper name. "What an excellent memory Betty, lovely to see you after all these years."

"Lovely to see you too pet. What are you up to these days?"

"I'm with the police, this is my boss Karen who I think you've already met, and this is Dr Laura Rae, she works in......"

"I work in the hospital," Laura interrupted to stop Jack potentially mentioning the mortuary. "I've been here a few times too. I live with mum and dad just around the corner.

"Are your parents Pauline and John?"

"That's them."

"Lovely couple, they come in here now and again. Give them my best. Now what are you all having?"

"We're here for brunch, I think it will be full English breakfasts all round." Jack looked at the others to check she was right.

"I'll have the vegetarian breakfast if that's OK?"

"I didn't know you were a vegetarian Karen." Jack sounded surprised at the revelation.

"Since my husband died."

"Oh, I'm sorry pet." Betty said quietly, putting her hand on Karen's shoulder. "I'll get these orders started. Does everyone want tea?"

Karen chose decaffeinated, Jack had a normal with two sugars and Laura went for an earl grey.

"Coming right up." Betty returned to the counter and passed the order into the kitchen while one of her Saturday girls made the teas.

"I feel a bit of a frump compared to you two."

"Is black your favourite colour?" Laura asked.

Karen thought for a moment "I guess it has been since my husband died. I'm not in mourning or anything, it just feels the right thing to wear."

"Tell us about him, your husband." Laura put her hand on Karen's hand.

"Laura, Karen might not want to talk about him."

"No, it's alright. I've not had anyone to talk to about him for a while now. It seems I've finally found some friends who I can share things with. Where do you want me to start?"

"What was he like, was he tall and handsome, was he a generous lover?"

"Laura, for goodness sake."

Karen laughed as the tea arrived and was handed out in a flurry of cups and saucers. She picked up her cup, holding it with both hands as she stared out of the window for a few seconds, as if recalling her man and what he had been like.

"Gary wasn't tall, nor was he handsome in the conventional sense, though I thought he was gorgeous. He was a Captain in the army, a career soldier like me. Yes, he was a good lover, Laura."

"I knew he would be." Laura laughed her cackling laugh and smacked the table drawing the attention of everyone in the Café.

"When we were in the same place we were joined at the hip. My only regret is that we didn't get enough time together, mainly thanks to our careers keeping us apart for long periods of time."

"Never thought about having kids?" Jack asked.

"There wasn't enough time. We were always travelling; never settled long enough to build a nest."

"That's a shame. How did it happen, you know?"

Jack glared at Laura again, not believing she could ask such a question. Karen noticed the look.

"It's alright Jack. It's nice to be able to talk. He was on a training exercise in the arctic circle, some sort of joint mission with the SAS. The snowmobile he was travelling on ran into a crevasse. He was killed along with another man he was travelling with."

"That's terrible." Laura put her hand on Jack's again smiling at her in sympathy.

"The army were brilliant. They couldn't do enough to help me but in the end, I didn't feel like I could stay. I was given an honourable discharge and a pension, but I missed the camaraderie, so I joined the police."

"The army's loss is our gain." Jack spoke as the three plates of food arrived. Betty had excelled herself. The plates were piled high with sausages, bacon, eggs, hash browns, mushrooms, beans, tomatoes, and Karen's favourite, fried bread. Karen's plate had veggie sausages in place of the sausages and bacon.

For a while the conversation was forgotten as the three friends tucked into their meal.

Karen glanced around to see if they could be overheard but there was nobody close enough to eavesdrop.

"How's your side of the case going Laura? Any progress?"

"Are we going to talk shop?"

"I just thought I would ask." Karen sounded apologetic.

Laura laughed again. "Sorry, I was pulling your leg. It's going well, I think I managed to obtain some viable DNA from two of the bodies so far. I'll be sending the information through on Monday." Laura had lowered the tone of her voice to make sure no-one could hear her.

"What about your end? Any idea as to why these people ended up like they did?"

"Not really. I have an idea which came to me last night, which I need to pursue with the boss. He's a golfer so will be able to tell me if I am barking up the wrong tree or not."

"Interesting." Jack spoke while chewing on a sausage. "What are your vegetarian sausages like?"

"You can taste a bit if you like." Karen placed a piece of her sausage on Jack's plate which was quickly eaten.

"Different, a bit herby but quite tasty."

Karen smiled. "You didn't like it, did you?"

Jack laughed. "No, it's certainly not for me."

"Do you want to try a bit, Laura?"

"No thank you. My parents are vegetarian, I get enough of that at home,"

They all laughed.

As the friends began to clear their plates, Karen asked what they would be doing for the rest of the day.

"I'll be watching the match at the Stack in Seaburn," Jack said, wiping her face on a napkin.

"What match?"

"What match? The match! Sunderland are in the League One playoff final at Wembley this afternoon. If we win, we'll go up to the Championship. It's been a long time coming but we've an excellent chance today. I can't believe you haven't heard about it."

Karen shrugged as she finished her last piece of fried bread. "I need to join some local social media groups, I guess, or subscribe to the Echo."

"You can join me down at the Stack if you like?" Jack was almost certain she knew what the answer would be.

"Thanks Jack but I think I'll stay home this afternoon. The housework needs doing. I'll try and watch the game on the TV. No doubt it will be a hot topic on Monday morning."

Jack was disappointed but it was Laura who asked the question.

"Do you stay home because you miss your husband?"

Karen stared out of the window again. This time both her friends could see her eyes start to water. She put her face in her hands.

"I'm sorry." Laura offered her a tissue. "I didn't mean to upset you."

"Thanks Laura." Karen took a tissue and dabbed at her eyes. "I don't know why I still get so upset. It's been nearly five years now."

Laura and Jack each held one of Laura's hands. Karen felt a tingle, like a mild electric shock. It warmed her and stopped her tears instantly. Neither of her friends appeared to notice.

"We're here for you Karen, all you have to do is ask."

Karen looked at her friends. "Thanks Jack. Please don't stop asking me out. I'll surprise you one day. I guess I just don't feel ready to go out and enjoy myself yet. It doesn't feel right."

Laura squeezed Karen's hand. "Well, if it's any consolation, an afternoon in the Stack with hundreds of drunk football supporters wouldn't be high on my list of things to do on a Saturday afternoon."

They all laughed again drawing more attention to their corner of the Café. Betty came over. "Look at you three all holding hands and having fun. You sound like a coven of witches: we'll have to call you the Witches of Witherwack." They all laughed again at their new moniker.

"The Witches of Witherwack! I'll drink to that. How about another round of teas?" Karen ordered more teas from Betty as they all laughed again.

Laura had to leave first which gave Karen the chance to ask about Sergeant Tom Moore.

"Is there anything else you can tell me about Sergeant Tom?" She asked Jack.

"Well, he keeps himself to himself, but the goss' is that he has suffered from depression since his wife left him. He has been off work for short periods of time but when he is at work he puts on a brave face."

"Interesting, anything else?"

Jack smiled. "Nice to see you so interested."

"I'm just curious," Karen replied, trying to play the innocent.

Jack laughed. "I believe you, thousands wouldn't."

She tried and failed to get another cup of tea out of the teapot, so settled on filling her cup with the spare milk.

"He's a fair bit older than you. We had a party for his fiftieth last year."

"That doesn't matter. He looks much younger than that," Karen replied smiling.

"I know. He's very fit. A good runner too. I sponsored him in the Great North Run last year."

Karen thought for moment. Jack just smiled at her. "You're interested in him, aren't you?"

"He still wears his ring, Jack. I reckon he still hankers after his wife."

"You're right on that score, but she's moved on. One of the lads saw his ex with a guy at a restaurant a few weeks ago." Jack sipped at her milk.

"Maybe he needs to be shown that there is life after you lose the love of your life."

"You're a fine one to talk. Are you ready to move on?"

Karen looked sad for a moment. "You're right, talk is easy, but making that decision to move on, well that's the biggest step of all."

"Jack reached out and held Karen's hand. "Well maybe you and Tom could make that step together, one day."

"Maybe. Come on, let's do the rest of the day. Thanks Jack, I've really enjoyed our brunch."

"Me too."

Jack called Betty over and divided the bill after taking off the £10 that Laura had left on the table. After a final hug, they went their separate ways.

That afternoon Karen sat on her sofa, Jinx by her side and a glass of wine in her hand. She watched Sunderland beat Wycombe Wanderers in the playoff final and raised a glass to her new home.

She picked up the photo frame that sat on the sofa with her. It was a photo of her husband in his dress uniform, He smiled at her, and she smiled back.

"I miss you so much my lover," she whispered, kissing the glass protecting the photo. "Maybe it's time to go out again, what do you think?" Gary smiled back at her and a voice in her head said, *"I love you too."* It was his voice, the voice she missed so much. "Maybe not yet then," she said to the picture of her soul mate.

The brick smashed through her window, catching her on the side of the head. She fell off the settee, unconscious, dropping and smashing the precious photo.

# Chapter Nine

The blackness started to clear and awareness gradually dawned. She was moving, the sensation almost made her throw up. The nausea raged for a moment then began to fade. She tried to open her eyes, but the light was too bright.

Karen realised she was lying down so tried to sit up. She was shocked to feel that she was being held down. Someone touched her arm.

"Stay still pet. You've had a nasty bang to the head."

"Where am I?" Her voice was slurred and hoarse.

"You're in an ambulance pet. On our way to the Royal."

"My cat, where's my cat."

"Your cat is fine. One of your neighbours has taken it in. She called the ambulance when she heard your window break and saw what had happened."

Karen relaxed a little, then seemed to sleep as the next thing she knew she was being wheeled into the accident and emergency department.

A junior doctor was soon checking her over for injuries. All the time Karen became more aware of what was happening as the fog of the bang on the head started to clear.

After a series of tests, including having a torch shone in her eyes, Karen was fully awake when the doctor announced she had been very lucky. An inch to the left and she could have lost an eye.

She did have a nasty cut next to her eye and a few more minor cuts where glass from the window had peppered her skin. Her hand was also cut from where she had fallen on to the picture frame.

"We'll keep you here for a couple of hours just to check you are okay to go home. Can we call someone to come and get you?"

Karen thought for a moment. "Can you call my friend Detective Sergeant Jacqueline White?" Then she hesitated, recalling what Jack was doing that afternoon.

"No forget that. Just order me a taxi when I'm free to go, I'll find my own way home."

"Are you sure?"

Karen hesitated again, thinking about Laura Rae.

"Actually, I'm good friends with Dr Laura Rae who works here, maybe you could give her a call for me."

The doctor smiled. "Will do."

An hour later Laura was sitting by Karen's bed holding her hand. A set of Steri Strips held the cut next to her eye in place and a few plasters marked where she had been cut by flying glass.

"What the hell happened Karen?"

"Well one minute I was watching the football then a brick comes through the window and nearly kills me."

"Probably vandals, we get a few around home."

"Hmmm. I'm not sure. Maybe someone was sending me a message or trying to kill me. It just seems a bit too timely to be a random piece of vandalism."

Laura looked at her friend. "Have you told Jack?"

"No, I didn't want to spoil her fun. Sunderland won you know."

"I heard. The city will be buzzing for weeks to come. You'll have no bother catching your killers now. The team will be really fired up."

Karen managed a smile. "I hope so. We need to stop more people ending up in the river."

"You will Karen, but not now. Rest easy, then I'll get you home."

An hour later Karen was being helped into the small red mini. She had been given the all clear by the on call doctor. She also knew Accident and Emergency would need the bed. It was a Saturday night in Sunderland after all.

Laura drove slowly home, something which didn't go unappreciated by Karen. The last thing she needed was to be thrown around in such a small tin box.

When they reach Karen's house someone had already boarded up her front room window. Inside, the lounge was still a mess. Laura wouldn't hear of Karen doing anything to clean up. She did allow Karen to boil a kettle and make tea in the kitchen.

Laura took out Karen's vacuum and hoovered the lounge, picking up the glass and assorted debris. The larger bits needed a dustpan and brush.

The photo frame was given special reverence and carefully laid on a coffee table next to where she thought Karen sat. The brick was picked up using a cloth and placed next to the TV.

Eventually, satisfied with her work, Laura allowed Karen into her front room and sat her down on the sofa.

"We'll get a new frame for that picture tomorrow," Laura suggested as she drank her tea.

"Thanks Laura, you've been a star."

"No worries, what are friends for. We witches must stick together."

Laura managed a weak laugh at the reference to the name Betty had given them.

"I'll stay the night, just to keep an eye on you."

"You don't have to do that." There was surprise in Karen's voice at the offer.

"It's OK. I'm a doctor remember. They taught me to keep people alive before I learned how to work out why they died. You'll have your own personal doctor on hand just in case you feel unwell in the night."

"Where will you sleep?" Karen was almost nervous to ask.

"That sofa looks comfortable, I'll sleep there. Just yell if you need me."

"Thank you."

Karen was grateful and smiled at her friend as she drank her tea. She did feel awful and was a little worried about being alone.

Karen flicked the TV on, and they watched Casualty.

"That drip is turned off," Laura laughed. She pointed out the same mistake several times during the programme.

"You should get a job as an advisor to Casualty."

"I don't think they would put up with me. I prefer working with the dead."

"Why did you take that path Laura?"

"My brother was killed in a car accident, several years ago. The driver of the car that hit him died too. Everyone thought the driver was drunk and our family were blaming him for Brin's death. The pathologist discovered that the driver had suffered a heart attack and was probably dead when his car hit my brother."

Laura paused as if she was recalling memories of her brother.

"The thought that justice could be done in such a way fascinated me and I studied to become a forensic pathologist. I changed from helping the living to helping the dead. They don't have a voice; they can't tell me what's wrong. I do my best to tell their side of the story. I love my job."

"Do you fancy a glass of wine?"

"Thanks Karen, but as your doctor I suggest we keep to the tea for tonight."

Karen laughed. "Right you are doc."

"And I prescribe an early night, maybe take a paracetamol before bed."

"How about a hot chocolate. Am I allowed one of those?"

"I think that's a very good idea. I'll make a couple of cups. I think it will help us both sleep."

As Laura busied herself in the kitchen, Karen smiled to herself. She had found a couple of real friends here. She promised herself to call Jack in the morning, not too early, and let her know what had happened.

Laura came back with two steaming hot mugs of chocolate.

"Here you go."

"Thanks Laura, I think I'll take this to bed with me and maybe read for a minute or two. Will you be OK here?"

"I'll be fine thanks. I'll have the TV to keep me company. Just try and get some sleep." As Karen stood up, Laura leaned in and kissed her on the lips.

"Something to keep you warm tonight. Sleep well."

Laura took Karen's place on the sofa and settled in to scan the channels.

A shocked Karen, walked to the door and looked back at her friend. She could taste the lipstick or chapstick Laura was wearing. It tasted nice.

"Good night, Laura."

"Night," came the casual reply.

Karen walked up to bed, for a moment her headache forgotten. She took a couple of paracetamol tablets out of the bedside draw and washed them down with the cocoa. She reached for her kindle but as soon as her head hit the pillow, she fell asleep.

*****

*Sunday, 22nd May 2022*

The next morning, she awoke with a banging headache. The first thing she noticed was the kindle on her pillow, then movement in the bed next to her.

She rolled over to see Jinx making a pudding in the bedclothes.

A knock on the door brought back the memory that Laura had stayed the night.

"Wakey, wakey. You have a visitor."

Karen gingerly sat up, realising she was still wearing the clothes she came home in last night.

"Who is it?"

"It's me." The voice was Jacks.

"Come in."

The door opened and in walked Jack and Laura, the latter carrying a tray of breakfast consisting of toast and tea.

"What time is it?"

"It's just after 10, sleepy head," Laura answered.

Jack came over to help Karen sit up, pushing pillows behind her friend to give her some support.

"How did you hear what happened?"

"Laura called me this morning, so I came straight around. I picked up Jinx from your neighbour. I've also called a glazier to replace your window. He's doing me a favour and should be here in an hour."

"Thanks Jack," Karen replied as she munched on her toast. "And thank you for my breakfast, Laura."

The two friends sat on the end of Karen's bed and watched her devour her breakfast. She was very hungry.

"Are you not having anything?"

"We've already eaten thank you. We decided to let you sleep but thought by 10am you would have had enough. We thought Jinx should be the one to wake you up."

Karen reached out and stroked her cat which had curled up next to her.

"Thanks guys. You've been good friends."

"I'm sure you'd do the same for us."

"For sure." Karen kept on eating until every crumb had gone.

"What's the plan for today?"

"We thought after the window is replaced, we'd take you out for a little drive, maybe grab some lunch somewhere and then let you rest up for the evening before work tomorrow."

"What's the weather like?"

"It's a beautiful day. How about a run out to South Shields and a walk along the beach?" Jack suggested.

"Oooh, can we go on the rides and amusements?" Laura clapped excitedly.

"I might take it a bit easy and avoid the rides, but the sea air should do me good. Let's do that."

"I'll drive," Laura volunteered.

"No, we'll go in my car. It's a bit bigger and has a more comfortable ride for our invalid friend here."

Laura pouted but agreed to Jack's suggestion.

For a while the case was forgotten as the girls enjoyed a day out in South Shields. They bought fish and chips for lunch, took a paddle around the lake in a giant swan, ate candyfloss and enjoyed a long walk along the beach.

The sea air seemed to do Karen the world of good, and by the end of the afternoon she was back to her normal self.

They went back to her house to drop off Laura so she could drive the short distance home. The doctor wanted to have an early night as she planned to start early on the Monday morning.

Karen and Jack sat for a while in Karen's lounge, enjoying a cup of tea while watching the antiques roadshow on the TV.

As the programme finished, Karen turned to Jack.

"She kissed me last night."

Jack turned to her friend visibly startled.

"What? Laura?"

"Yep, full on the lips."

"Did she try anything else?"

"Nope. She was lovely. Just looked after me in the evening and kissed me before I went to bed."

"Well, that's weird. She knows you're not gay."

"I know. But she was nice. Her lips tasted great."

"Karen Dee, you're not on the turn, are you?"

"No! Of course not."

Jack gave Karen a stare. "Are you sure?"

"Jack, stop it. I'm sure. But It's nice that she cares."

"You should have rung me last night."

"What and spoil your celebrations."

"Well, I guess I was a bit worse for wear."

"Exactly. No. I did the right thing. You do realise that any other time I would have rung you first."

"I know. Look I'd better go. We have a lot to do tomorrow."

"Thanks Jack and thanks for all you did today."

"Oh, I have one more gift for you." Jack reached down behind the cushions on the sofa. She pulled out the picture of Gary in a new frame and handed it to Karen.

"I popped into Home Bargains this morning while you were asleep and bought you a new frame. It wasn't expensive so please change it if you'd rather have something better."

Karen looked at the picture and kissed the glass. "It's perfect Jack. Thank you so much."

Jack got up and headed for the door. "Don't forget to lock me out. See you in the morning Ma'am."

Karen laughed. "See you in the morning and thanks again for everything."

After Jack left, Karen locked the door, turned off the TV and headed up for bed. She looked at her face in the mirror, studying the damage the brick had caused. "You'll not get away with this, whoever you are?"

She cleaned her teeth and went to bed. Jinx joined her. This time she read a couple of chapters before turning the light out and going to sleep.

*Monday, 23rd May 2022*

The next morning Karen was in the office just before 8am. Cat was already there.

"Have you been here all weekend, Cat?"

"I came in yesterday, Ma'am, and have just beat you in. What happened to you?" Cat was concerned when she saw the damage to Karen's face.

"I'll explain when everyone is here. Has all your hard work paid off?"

"I think it has Ma'am. I've been trawling social media images of the town centre. I was looking for Peter Bailey but look what I found."

Karen walked around Cat's desk and watched video footage of a man carrying a set of golf clubs through the centre of the town. It was Miguel Victor.

# Chapter Ten

As soon as all the team were in, Karen called for the detective's attention. The DCI was yet to appear.

"Thanks to Cat, we have ourselves a breakthrough. She found CCTV images of Miguel Victor walking through Sunderland City centre carrying a set of golf clubs."

Everyone turned to Cat who received a spattering of applause from the team.

"We've studied the images closely and we are pretty sure those are the same golf clubs he brought to the UK."

"Could you see where he went with them?"

"Afraid not Mick. We followed him on various cameras from the train station, past the Peacock and then on towards the Empire Theatre. We lost him when he turned into Garden Place."

"Shall we get over there and see where he might have gone, Ma'am?"

"Definitely worth a look guys. Mick, you stay here with Cat and see if you can find any more footage of him, maybe leaving the area. The rest of you, let's meet up by the Dun Cow and check out the area."

Everyone started to move. As they did, Karen walked over to Mick. "Mick, when the boss arrives, tell him what's happening and offer him the chance to join us. If he can't, ask him to give me a call."

"Right you are Ma'am. Will do."

With that, Karen followed Jack out of the office, and they headed off towards Sunderland City centre. They parked up alongside the New City Hall and were just getting out of the car when Karen's mobile rang. It was the DCI.

"Thanks for calling, boss. Has Mick filled you in?"

"Yes Dee, I'll come over. How can I help?"

"Your golf clubs, boss, are they hollow?"

"Yep, the shafts are all hollow."

"What about the club heads?"

"Hmmm. I'm not sure about the irons but I'm sure the metal woods are hollow."

"Thanks boss. I have an idea that we need to check out. I'll tell you all about it when you get here."

The team gathered at the back of the Dun Cow and looked around. There were a couple of narrow lanes with bins at the end. Both were potential locations where Miguel Victor may have dumped the clubs or met someone.

A large grey building which looked like it had been abandoned stood out as another potential meeting point.

"Let's start over there. Can you find a way in John?"

"I think there may be a security office, let me have a look."

John went off to try and find a way in. While he was gone, the others looked around to see if there were any other ways into the large site.

Matt discovered a gap in the fence where the fencing material was loose and slipped into the site. "Here you go Ma'am. I reckon some nippers have been using this way in to access the building. You know this used to be the Gilbridge Police Station?"

"No, I didn't. Kind of ironic, right?"

Matt smiled. "It sure is. I think Mick used to work here."

The others followed Matt's lead and were all in the site by the time John came back with the duty site officer.

"Oh, I see you've breached our defences."

"Sorry, I think you need to check the fences, mate," John suggested with a smile.

"Do I need to call the police to let them know I have some trespassers."

All the officers raised their badges.

"I guess that answers that, then. I'll leave you to it, but be careful, the site is in quite a bad state. The building is being refurbished and in some places the floors have been removed. Just watch where you are walking. There are hard hats by the gate if you need them."

John clambered through the gap and followed the other detectives to a hole in the building's wall which seemed an obvious point of access.

The inside of the building was grey and bare. In places you could see where the developers had just started working. A few of the windows were broken and there was evidence in some rooms that the place had been a favourite haunt of local youths. Graffiti was plastered on some of the walls, and in one room a few mattresses were laid out on the floor. The smell was not very pleasant.

The detectives spread out to look through the lower floor for any sign that Miguel Victor had been there. While they were searching, the DCI arrived in the building wearing a suit and a hard hat.

The first person he saw was Rachel. "Where's Dee, Rach?"

"Up ahead boss, I'll give her a shout."

Rachel went off to find Karen and brought her back to meet Billy.

"Where are we to, Dee?"

"Just doing a quick search of the building. I have a hunch this might be where Miguel Victor dropped off the golf clubs."

"I'll help. The security guard is a bit annoyed with you."

"He'll get over it. If we report all this to his boss, he'll be lucky to keep his job. Look at all this mess, kids must be in here every night."

Billy wrinkled his nose at the smell.

"You're right, let's get this done."

The team had no joy on the ground floor so went up a level to the first floor. In places there were gaps in the concrete floors, which meant everyone was being extra careful when they looked in each room.

They had been in the building nearly an hour when Jack shouted out. "Over here boss!"

The team gravitated towards her location which was in an old toilet block at the far end of the building. The floor was solid which allowed several of the detectives to enter.

In the third of a block of six cubicles were the remains of a set of golf clubs. All the grips had been pulled off the clubs and the heads of the woods had holes in their bases, seemingly drilled out using a large diameter drill bit.

"What the hell happened here?"

"If my hunch is right boss, these clubs were used to smuggle drugs into the country. We need to get these tested to see if I'm right."

"I'll get on it," Jack offered, reaching for her mobile phone.

"Ma'am, have a look over here."

Matt was squatting in the far corner of the toilet block, picking at a pile of rubble with his pen.

Karen walked to where Matt was, and looked over his shoulder.

"This looks like dried blood to me Ma'am."

Karen bent down a bit lower.

"I think you're right. This could be where Miguel Victor died. Let's get the SOCOs out here."

Karen stood up. "Right, everybody out, let's not contaminate the scene any more than we've done already."

The detectives filed out of the room.

"While we are here, let's check the rest of the building. There wasn't enough blood in that room to explain how Miguel ended up like he did. Maybe he was butchered somewhere else in the building."

The detectives continued to look for clues in the rest of the property but after another hour they came up empty handed. Billy took Karen to one side as his team filed out of the derelict, former police station.

"This is good work Karen but we're not much further ahead. We need to establish who killed Victor and why? He obviously delivered the goods so why kill him?"

"Maybe he wanted more money?"

"This doesn't make sense though. He played in the golf tournament after he dropped these clubs off. Why would he come back here and then be killed? You'd think he would have been on the first plane back to Spain."

"You're right. This is a mystery."

"How are you holding up. I can see you took quite a whack."

"It still stings a bit, but I'll mend. It makes this personal though. I think it was a message. It will take more than a brick through my window to put me out of the race. We'll get them, boss. Mark my words."

Billy looked at the determination on Karen's face. "I believe you will, Detective Inspector, I believe you will."

He put his hand on her shoulder then followed the rest of the team out of the building.

Karen took one last look around, wondering why people frequented places like this, then left. She spoke to the security guard on the way out, telling him not to let anyone in or out of the building. As she was talking the SOCO team arrived. She told them where the evidence was, and left them to their work.

She had a sudden and desperate urge for a shower.

Scrubbing her hands with hand gel once she was back in the car was all she could do for the time being, to try and wash off the feeling of that place.

"The sooner they pull that down the better," she said to Jack as they pulled out of the car park.

"You're right there, Ma'am. Let's get a cup of tea."

"You're talking my language."

Nothing else was said as they drove back to Southwick North station.

Once the team had reassembled, Karen asked Mick and Cat if they had made any progress with the CCTV coverage. The pair had painstakingly watched the coverage around the town. They had been focussed on the two days after Cat had seen Miguel Victor carrying his golf clubs from the train station.

"No joy, Ma'am. No sign of him so far. It sounds like we'll need to extend the time scale if you think he went back there at some point."

"That's a good idea. Maybe for the two days after the golf tournament."

"We'll get on to it. We did notice something though."

This piqued Karen's interest. "What was it?"

We did spot Prudence Bailey and Phil Brookes leaving the Empire Theatre and walking down Garden Place the day after Miguel walked down the same street.

Karen smiled. "Well, well. We are getting closer to a connection between these two and one of our victims."

She turned to the incident board once again. "It would be fascinating if we saw them walking down the same street as Miguel Victor after the golf tournament."

"I don't want to burst your bubble Ma'am, but they might just have been walking across to the car park after a night out in the theatre."

Karen looked at Jack. "You could be right, but I don't believe in coincidences. They are up to their eyes in this case, and we are going to prove it."

"There's one more thing Ma'am."

"There's more?"

"Yes Ma'am, look who we spotted in the same area the same day that we saw Miguel Victor."

Cat held up a picture. It was of a youth dressed in black with red trainers.

"I take it we still have him in custody?"

"Yes Ma'am."

"Then let's pay him another visit, shall we? Jack, you come with me. The rest of you, get stuck into the CCTV footage with Cat and Mick. See if you can link Prudence or Phil to this location in the days after the golf tournament."

Karen and Jack headed back to Sunderland station where the boys were being held.

It was getting late in the afternoon, but Karen was determined to talk to the boy with the red trainers before the end of the day.

The same Sergeant ushered the boy into the interview room. A duty solicitor had been in the station, and she agreed to join them.

"Have we a name for this young man?"

"His name is Darren, Ma'am," the burly Sergeant replied.

"Well Darren you seem to be in a fine pickle. We have a video of you throwing a body in the River Wear and now we have you on CCTV near the location where one of your victims was last seen with a load of drugs."

"No comment."

Despite the answer, the bravado had gone from the young man's persona. He knew he was in trouble. Deep trouble.

"Have you been dealing drugs Darren?"

"No comment."

"We've found where the drop was made. I would wager good money your fingerprints will be all over the location."

"That's because we go there in the evenings. That derelict building is where we hang out. I don't know anything about any drugs."

"I never said anything about any derelict building Darren."

"No comment." Darren looked even more crestfallen.

"Tell us who you are working for, Darren, and the judge might go easy on you."

"I think my client might need a little more assurance than a might, Detective Inspector. May I have a word with him on our own for a minute please."

"Fair enough. Jack, Sergeant, let's give them some space."

The three of them left the interview room and waited outside. It was just over a minute when there was a knock on the door, and they filed back in.

"I have spoken to my client. Not only will he need assurances that he would not receive a custodial sentence. He also wants protection. The people he is talking about are ruthless and he fears for his life."

"I'll need to talk to someone before we can make such a deal."

Karen looked at Jack who just shrugged. She had no idea how that might work either.

"Sergeant, lock him back in his cell. We've charged him on disposing of a body and we know he was involved with the drug drop we found. We'll talk again, Darren, when I've seen what deal we can offer you."

Karen and Jack left the interview room and headed back to Southwick North. Cat was still at the desk though the others had left for the night. Strangely Billy was still in his office so the two officers went in to see him.

Billy looked up as they walked in.

"Karen, Jack. Have you had a good day?"

"Very good, boss. In fact I think we may have had the breakthrough we've been waiting for."

"Sounds good, take a seat, and tell me all about it.

For the next hour Karen and Jack explained what had happened that day and how they had tied the teenager with the red trainers to the drug drop. While they were talking Cat knocked on the door. Billy waved her in.

"Just received information boss Ma'am that we have Darren's fingerprints at the drug drop in the derelict building and the blood on the floor was a match for Miguel Victor."

"Thanks Cat. Get yourself off now. We'll see you in the morning."

"Yes Ma'am." As she closed the door Karen asked the vital question of the day. "Boss, can we get a deal. We need it for Darren 'Red Trainers' to tell us the information we need."

"I'll have to push that up the line Karen. Given the nature of his first crime, I'm not sure that will be possible. He may yet be the killer."

"We're sure he's not, boss." Jack was keen to get involved in the conversation. "He may be at risk in the cells."

"He can't be in a safer place, surely, Jack. Let's see what I can do tomorrow. I'm not going to get an answer tonight."

"OK boss. We'll sleep on it. Tomorrow is another day as they say."

As she drove away from the office, 'One More Day' from Les Miserable belted out from her car stereo. "One more day", she sang to herself, "then we'll have the killers."

## Chapter Eleven

That evening Karen enjoyed an extra glass of wine to celebrate. She would solve this by the end of the week. She was sure Billy would get the assurances Darren needed and she would find out who employed him to carry out the disposal of the bodies and the drug deals. Two glasses of wine were quickly downed as she enjoyed an Indian take away while watching a healthy dose of Coronation Street. Jinx purred away, contentedly tucked into her side.

She realised some time ago she had turned into her mother, loving all the same things, and behaving just as she used to do. The one difference was the lack of children. She knew her mam would be looking down at her with a frown. "Your biological clock has nearly run out," she would have scolded. "Time to get a man and have a baby, before it's too late."

Karen smiled at the thought. She was flicking through the channels looking for something else to watch after catching up with all the latest shenanigans in Wetherfield, but gave up. "Time for an early night, Jinx? Coming to bed?" The cat looked at her with sleepy eyes then went straight back to sleep.

Finishing the last of her wine she picked the cat up, then carried it upstairs before placing it on her bed. She then went to the bathroom to clean her teeth before climbing under the duvet. Jinx seemed a little put out by all the bouncing about but once Karen had picked up her Kindle and had settled down, the cat happily snuggled back in and went to sleep. Karen's eyes shut as soon as she put down the reader.

*Tuesday, 24th May 2022*

It seemed that as soon as she had fallen asleep the 6.30am alarm was buzzing in her ear. "Alexa, stop." The raucous sound thankfully stopped to be followed by the gentler sounds of Radio 2.

Reluctant to get out of her warm pit, she reached out for the cat, but it had already moved. She knew where it would be. She put on her slippers and walked into the kitchen, pulling her dressing gown tight around her. Sure enough, Jinx was by her food bowl, yowling for some breakfast.

A sachet of food in Jinx's bowl, instantly quietened the animal, which took to devouring the sticky mess as fast as she could. After a quick shower, Karen dressed quickly, then enjoyed her usual breakfast of porridge and fruit. She ate with a spoon in one hand and her phone in the other. As she flicked through the news on her phone the anticipation of the day ahead made her smile.

"The names of the killers will be on my phone soon," she told Jinx, who seemed less than impressed. The cat was more interested in chasing a musical ball around the kitchen than the prowess of her mistress at solving crimes.

Keen to get the day started, she packed her bag. Before she left the house, she kissed the cat, locked it in the kitchen with all its playthings, litter tray and cat basket, then headed out to the car to start her short journey to work.

She walked into the office at 7am. Catherine was already there.

"I'm convinced you sleep here Cat."

"No such luck Ma'am, this place is much nicer than my current digs. The rooms are so damp you could keep fish in them."

Karen laughed. "Oh dear, maybe you should look for somewhere else."

"I will. But they are just around the corner from here, so they are handy for work."

"Any developments?"

"Not yet, but I have been working on the idea that some of the other bodies might have been golfers too. I'm contacting all the local clubs to see if they remember strangers buying clubs just before a tournament started. No joy so far."

"That was a good idea, but maybe they used a number of different methods to get drugs here?"

"That's true."

"I saw an abandoned boat in the Marina when Jack was showing me around. It looked as if it would have been a lovely motor yacht in its day. Perhaps someone brought drugs in by boat, met an untimely end, and now their boat lies abandoned and rotting away. Can you have a look into that too?"

"Will do Ma'am. I'll contact the marina office when it opens and find out who owns it."

"Thanks Cat."

Karen went over to her desk and signed into her computer. She looked at the incident board for a while, wondering how today would pan out, once they had the names of the main players in this case. She stared at Prudence. "I know it's you," she whispered to herself.

As she looked at various CCTV feeds of the area around the drug drop, the members of the team started to drift in. Billy was last, rushing into his office at 9am on the dot.

*****

At the same moment a lawyer entered Darren's cell at Sunderland main police station.

"Who are you, you're not my lawyer?"

The big sergeant locked the door after he'd ushered the lawyer in.

"No, I've taken over. The lawyer you saw yesterday has another case to focus on, so I was recommended."

"Any news on my deal or police protection."

"Not yet, I'm afraid. It was too late last night to contact a judge, but I am sure they'll be working on it this morning. We should hear soon."

"Is there anything you need right now?"

"I could do with a smoke."

"You know this is a smoke free station Darren."

"Maybe there's a smoking area outside I could go to."

The lawyer laughed. "That would be too convenient for anyone looking to escape."

He reached into his pocket and pulled out a small packet of ten cigarettes. "Here, have these. Just make sure you puff the smoke through the bars."

"Thanks, what about some matches or a lighter?"

"Here you go." The lawyer passed his client a plastic lighter. "Just keep that hidden. I could get into big trouble for doing this. Oh, and don't think about setting fire to the bed or something stupid like that. You'll only end up hurting yourself if you do that."

"Thank you." Darren tucked the precious lighter under his mattress.

"Right, I'll be back around 11.30am to see if there has been any progress. Just sit tight and don't get into any trouble." They shook hands. The lawyer knocked on the door and the big sergeant let him out.

Darren waited for five minutes then decided to have a smoke. He took the cigarette packet out of his pocket and retrieved the lighter from under the mattress. He climbed on to the bed to get closer to the window and carefully lit the cigarette, gently puffing the smoke towards the open window behind the bars.

He started to feel a little giddy. It had been a few days since he'd enjoyed a smoke, and he smiled to himself, enjoying the taste of the tobacco. The vertigo seemed to get worse. Darren grabbed on to the bars to steady himself. He still felt good. He smiled again then fell backwards on to the cell floor. As he fell the cigarette landed on the bed and started to smoulder.

After a few minutes, the smoke from the bed caused the fire alarm to go off. The sergeant came running into the cell, quickly smothering the small fire before dragging the unconscious Darren from the room.

Other officers quickly came to the sergeant's assistance.

They checked Darren for signs of life but there were none. The boy was dead.

At 10.15am, Karen's desk telephone rang.

"Detective Inspector Dee, how can I help you?"

There was a pause.

"What? You are joking with me."

The voice at the other end spoke again. Everyone in the office turned to look at her.

"I'll call the pathologist to come over and take charge of the body. Don't touch anything."

Karen saw everyone was staring at her.

"Darren's dead."

"What, how the hell did that happen?"

"No-one is quite sure Jack, but a new lawyer visited him at 9am this morning. I am betting that had something to do with it. Apparently, he was smoking a cigarette when he died."

"The new lawyer must have taken it in to him and poisoned the poor lad." Mick sounded appalled that such a young person should die that way.

"Do we have anything on that lawyer?"

"They are looking for CCTV images of the guy, Jack. They have his name but I'm betting it's false." Karen turned to Cat. Can you check his details out when they get sent through?"

"Yes Ma'am."

"I'll call Dr Rae and get her to meet us in Sunderland station. Jack let's go. You drive, I'll phone Laura while we are on the way."

Twenty minutes later, Karen and Jack were standing over Darren's body. Five minutes after they arrived, Dr Laura Rae joined them.

"What's happened here?"

"We think this young lad was poisoned. Possibly delivered by a cigarette which he was smoking when he died."

Laura bent down to have a closer look at the body. She donned some gloves and carefully opened the lad's eyes, studying them closely. She shone a torch up his nose and into his mouth. She then picked up the box of cigarettes and gave them a cautious sniff.

"Hmmm, I'll need to get him back to the Royal for a proper look, but I'm not sure it was the cigarette. There is nothing in his appearance to give me a clue as to what killed him, which points to something internal."

"Thanks Laura, your help and quick response is much appreciated."

"Anything for you Karen, you know that."

Karen looked at Jack who smiled and winked at her friend.

"I took the liberty of calling the lads with a van. They'll be here soon, then we can clear the scene for you."

Jack thought for a moment. "We need to bag those cigarettes and that lighter. The lawyer may have left some prints on them. We also need to check the external CCTV cameras; we might get lucky with some number plates."

"Good thoughts Jack. Let's get it done. The guys here will be able to help."

Jack rushed off to get some support from the police based in the Sunderland station.

While Dr Rae spoke with the men from the coroner's office, to arrange the removal of the body, Karen bent down to look at the young man lying on the floor. In gentle tones she spoke to the boy, as if he was still alive.

"I'm sorry Darren that we let you down. If only you had told us who you were working with, we may have been able to stop this happening. I'll not rest until we find out who did this. Sleep well Darren."

Dr Rae had spotted the tender moment and placed her hand on her friend's shoulder. Karen stood back up again and looked at Laura with tears in her eyes.

Laura hugged her friend. The feeling of love and strength comforted Karen and the tears eventually stopped.

"Help me find who did this."

"I will Karen, I promise. I'll have some answers within 24 hours."

Jack returned just as they were pulling back from their embrace. "All sorted Ma'am, they'll have everything bagged in a few minutes, then their boys will check for fingerprints. I have given them Cat's details so they can send the results to her."

Jack spotted the redness in her friend's eyes.

"Are you OK?"

"Just thinking about Darren and the life he will never live. What a waste."

"We'll get them Karen. Let's make a pact." She held out her hands and the other women took them, forming a ring. Karen felt that spark again.

"Right here, right now, the Witches of Witherwack declare that we will find who killed Darren and bring them to justice." Jack seemed determined.

"Amen to that."

"Let's do this," Laura added, "and heaven help anyone who gets in our way."

They left the officers from the Sunderland station to their work. Dr Rae gave them both a hug before they left.

When they returned to Southwick North, the mood in the detective's office was sombre. News of Darren's death had preceded them, and everyone knew what it meant to the investigation.

Karen walked across to the incident board.

"First things first. I want another board set up with Darren's name at the top. The murders are linked but I want his killer caught."

"Yes Ma'am, I'll get that sorted."

"Thanks Mick." Karen paused and looked at her team.

"Ladies and Gentlemen. We are up against some clever people. We need to be better than them if we are going to catch them. By killing Darren, they think they are covering their tracks, but all they have done is given us more evidence to follow."

Karen paused while she gathered her thoughts.

"Someone knew we were getting close with Darren. That means we have a leak, or someone talked out of place."

There were a few murmurs around the room.

"I don't mean here. I'd trust you lot with my life. No this either came via the Sunderland station, which I doubt, or the duty lawyer. John, Jordan, can you track her down and ask her to come in. I want to have a word with her."

"Yes Ma'am," John replied, nodding at Jordan.

"What can we do Ma'am?"

Karen again paused before answering Matt's question.

"I still think Prudence is involved somehow, possibly with Phil. Can you and Rachel do some digging into their affairs. Companies they own, financial affairs, telephone records, anything we can get hold of without need of a warrant."

"Yes Ma'am, we'll get straight on it."

"Cat, if you can give them a hand, I would appreciate it but the officers at Sunderland Station will be sending their findings through to you. As soon as they arrive, I want you to drop everything and see if you can track down that bogus lawyer."

"Will do."

"Have I missed anything?"

Everyone shook their heads.

"Great, let's do this people. The boss will be looking for results."

## Chapter Twelve

After lunch the Duty Solicitor, Christine Bateman, who saw Darren first, walked into the Southwick North station. She was asked to take a seat in reception by Tom Moore, who then called Karen to let her know she was there.

Karen and Jack came down from their office to meet her. They all shook hands.

"Thanks for coming in Christine."

"No problem, how can I help you?"

"Hang on, let's find an empty room. Tom, can we use this interview room?"

"Yes Ma'am. Nothing is booked in there for at least an hour."

"Thanks Tom."

The three women walked across to the interview room and sat down around the table.

"I'm not in any trouble, am I?"

"I hope not Christine, but you may be in danger, that's why I wanted to speak to you privately."

"Please, call me Chris."

"I'm Karen and this is Jack."

"Nice to meet you," Christine replied, curious to know why she had been summoned.

"You will remember seeing a young man called Darren, yesterday morning, at Sunderland Station."

"Yes, I do. I was waiting to hear if you had managed to come up with a deal for him. Is that what this is about?"

"I'm afraid not. He was murdered in his cell earlier this morning."

"Oh God." Christine was visibly shocked. "Have you caught the killer?"

"I'm afraid not. A man claiming to be your replacement visited him at 9am. He left him with some cigarettes which we think might have been poisoned. It was a sophisticated hit which needed some intelligence."

Christine thought for a moment. "You don't think I had anything to do with it, do you?"

"No, certainly not, but we wondered if you might have said something yesterday to anyone."

Christine thought long and hard.

"Well, I went back to my office, and my secretary added Darren to my case list. I talk into a Dictaphone, old fashioned I know. Then he types up the notes on each case and files them for me."

"Do you trust him?"

"I do, he's worked with me for years. He's studying now to be a lawyer himself."

"Did you see anyone else yesterday?"

"Only clients. Of course, I wouldn't say anything to them due to client confidentiality."

"What about after work?"

"I went home. Apart from the dogs I haven't seen anyone else."

Jack looked at Christine. "I guess we'll need to talk to your secretary then."

"I'll call him now if you like and get him to come over."

"Thanks Chris, but we'll pop around to your office if you don't mind. Where are you based?"

"I have an office in Fawcett Street." Chris handed Karen a card. "My address is on my card, as is my mobile. Please don't hesitate to call at any time."

"What's his name?"

"Paul Dodds."

Jack took the card and went upstairs to the office. Minutes later John and Jordan left to bring Paul in for questioning.

"Thanks for all your help, Chris. If we need anything else, we'll be in touch."

An hour later John and Jordan brought Paul Dodds back to the station. Karen and Jack welcomed him and found another room to use to talk to him.

"Sorry for calling you in like this, but we need to have a chat with you about a client of your boss."

"No worries."

Paul was smartly dressed and calm. He seemed curious as to what this was all about.

"A young lad who your boss talked to yesterday was murdered this morning and we are trying to establish what happened."

"Was that Darren? I typed up his notes yesterday. We were waiting to see if you guys could come up with a deal for him. That's awful."

"I know, especially as he died in prison."

Jack looked at Paul and thought she noticed a change in his demeanour, like a penny had dropped in his mind."

"Did you speak to anyone about Darren yesterday?"

Paul coughed.

"I may have mentioned something to my boyfriend last night. No names of course. It was just pillow talk."

"What's your boyfriend's name?" Karen was suddenly hopeful they might be on to something.

"Jess."

"Jess what?" Jack sounded frustrated.

"Jess Brookes."

Both the detectives leaned back in their chair.

"Where's Jess now?"

"I don't know, probably at work."

"What does he do?" It was Jack again.

"Well, it's a bit morbid but he works with his dad. They have a funeral business. With some of the stories he tells me, it's amazing I sleep at night."

"Thanks Paul. Your help has been much appreciated. We'll give you a lift back to the office."

"Jess isn't in trouble, is he?"

"I hope not but we'll need to talk to him. Can I ask that you don't say anything to Jess until we've had time to interview him?"

"I won't."

"Thanks again Paul." Karen stood and offered her hand while Jack ran upstairs to ask Jordan to take Paul back to Fawcett Street.

As Jordan and Paul left the office Jack looked at Karen. "You know he'll be on his phone to Jess as soon as he is back in his office."

"I know. Let's get Rachel and Matt to get over to the funeral home and watch what happens. I want to see if we can flush the rats out of their nest. When Jordan gets back, we'll get him and John to go over to collect Jess and bring him in."

"What will we do?"

"I fancy an ice cream Jack. Let's go to Minchellas on the Bents and then we'll park up on Front Street and see if Prudence reacts in any way."

"Sounds good to me. Oh, by the way, your car is in the garage tomorrow to get its blues and twos fitted. A mechanic will pick it up at 9am. Is that, OK?"

"Perfect." Karen was excited to get her Audi all geared up. She had completed her advance driver training six months ago but was yet to put what she learned into practice.

The officers went back up to the office to make sure everyone was busy and to let them know where they were going. The atmosphere was far more positive than it had been when they heard of Darren's death. Now they had their first connection, it had motivated them all to push for answers.

A second incident board had now been installed in the office, and Cat had put a picture of Darren in the centre.

She was quickly put to work tracking down anything they could find on Jess Brookes on social media. Before the girls left, a picture of the young man taken from his social media profile had been added to the board. He had no criminal record.

The smiling bottle-blond baby-faced lad seemed as innocent as a new-born. *I wonder if he knows what's going on,* Karen thought to herself.

Karen and Jack gathered their things and headed out to the car park. They took Jack's car, threading their way through the Roker area before heading along the seafront to Minchellas.

With tubs of ice cream in hand they parked on Front Street where they had a good view of Prudence's house and waited.

As they finished their ice-creams, Karen's mobile rang. The name on the screen identified the caller as Dr Rae.

"Hi Laura, how are things? I am sitting with Jack and I'm putting you on speaker phone."

"Hi fellow witches," Laura replied, laughing her cackling laugh which set the girls off.

"Have you any news for me Laura?"

"Well, I called in some big favours with the toxicology department at the University. The cigarettes and lighter were just cigarettes and a lighter. No poisons present I'm afraid."

"What killed him then?"

"To all intents and purposes, it looks as if he had a heart attack."

Karen looked at Jack before answering. "Is that possible? He was so young and healthy."

"It can happen, Karen, but it is extremely rare which is why I dug a little deeper."

"And what did you find?" Jack joined in the conversation.

"Well, I put all my magic, witch like powers, to that question and thought about how the meeting with the so-called lawyer might have gone. I emailed the lovely Cat to send me any CCTV footage there might be from the cells to confirm my thoughts."

"Yes?" Karen was getting frustrated now.

"I've just sent you the moment the lawyer killed him."

Karen's phone pinged with a WhatsApp from Laura. It was a ten second video of the pair shaking hands.

"They're just shaking hands before he left," Jack said, stating the obvious.

"I know. But look at the boy's face."

They replayed the video and caught the faintest hint of a wince as the imposter shook the boy's hand.

"What happened Laura?"

"This is the scary part. I've looked at Darren's right hand and found a tiny scratch. I still have some tests to do, but it is my guess he was poisoned with a fast-acting toxin."

"Oh my god. Can it really kill that quick?"

"Yes. I had to call it in to the UK Security Agency. Now my place looks like some kind of military scientific secure unit. I think they will be disposing of the body very quickly. They have taken a small blood sample which was rushed away under escort. I am sure I heard Porton Down mentioned. I take it you didn't touch the body, guys?"

"Thankfully not," Jack replied.

"This sounds like a very sophisticated kill, Laura. Am I right in thinking this type of toxin would be hard to come by?"

"Karen, I think you should use the word assassination in this case. Whoever did this will be a trained professional with a support team able to provide the equipment and toxin. He won't come cheap, if he was a hired hand."

Karen shuddered. The thought that they were now embroiled in this level of crime scared her to the bone.

At that moment the front door of Prudence Bailey's house opened and the woman herself walked out carrying her small dog. She seemed in a hurry. A white Porsche was parked in the road below her house, and she climbed in, dropping the dog on the passenger seat.

"Laura, we must go. Thanks for all your help. I hope your mortuary is returned to normal real soon." Before Laura could reply, Karen closed the line and Jack started the engine.

"I take it we'll be following her?"

"Yes Jack, let's see where she goes."

Prudence drove past them towards the junction in the centre of Whitburn Village. Jack did a quick three-point turn and followed her.

At the junction the lights eventually turned green, and the white Porsche turned right, heading towards Sunderland. Jack followed about three cars behind. They travelled in silence wondering where Prudence was taking them, both focussed on her car, ready to react to any move. They crawled through the roadworks opposite the Stack, just making it through the traffic lights in the same group of cars. One of the vehicles between them and the Porsche turned up Dykelands Road.

"Damn, I don't want to get too close in case she recognises us in her mirror."

"I think the only thing she looks at in the mirror is herself."

Jack laughed. "You're probably right."

Another car joined the line of vehicles at the roundabout near the Café Bungalow. They nearly lost her as they crossed the Wear Bridge but spotted the Porsche turning into the St Mary's multi-storey car park.

"There she goes. How do we follow her from here?"

Jack was queuing at the entrance to the car park as Prudence drove in. Three cars were between them and the automated barrier. Prudence headed up towards the upper levels.

"It looks like she's heading into the Bridges."

Jack drove through and parked in the virtually empty bottom section. "Let's walk across the road and see if she comes out the other end of the walkway."

St Mary's car park has a walkway which crosses above the road from level two into the main shopping area.

The detectives ran across the road and made their way around to the main exit from the car park. They popped into a charity shop and pretended to browse while watching the exit.

Half an hour later they gave up. They'd lost her.

"Damn it," Karen muttered as they passed a girl selling the Big Issue. She stopped and bought a copy.

"What do we do now?"

"I don't know Jack. Let's hope the others have had more luck. Let's get back to Southwick North."

## Chapter Thirteen

They were about to pull in the car park when Matt rang Karen.

"Ma'am, Phil Brookes left the funeral home around half an hour ago. We followed him to St Mary's car park, but we lost him. We thought he was going into town."

"Damn it, we must have crossed paths. Phil and Prudence must have met in the car park then left."

Karen thought for a moment. "Can you go back Matt and let me know when he returns to the funeral parlour. I know time is running out for today, but he might go back."

"Will do Ma'am."

Karen hung up the phone.

"Come on Jack. Let's see if we've found Jess."

The women almost ran up the stairs into the office, but Tom stopped them.

"He's in there, Ma'am. We gave him a coffee." Tom pointed to one of the interview rooms.

The girls diverted to the room. Karen paused, shook herself then knocked, putting on her best smile as she walked in.

Jess looked up from the table. He was nursing his cup of coffee while John stood opposite him.

"Hello, you must be Jess. My name is Detective Inspector Dee, and this is Detective Sergeant White."

"Hello," Jess whispered quietly, "am I in trouble?"

"No, we just want to ask you some questions."

"We were talking to Paul earlier. He said he told you about a young man being held in the police cells who was asking for protection."

Jess looked a bit sheepish. "Paul's lovely. Yes, he did mention something about that. Awful to die like that."

"Did you tell anyone about him?"

"No. I could get Paul into trouble. I tell him about the people we work on sometimes but I'm sure he wouldn't tell anyone. It's just pillow talk."

Karen looked at Jack. "Pillow talk?"

"Yes, he's, my boyfriend. I love him."

"Did you spend the night together?"

Jess paused like he had been a naughty boy.

"Yes."

"Thank you, Jess."

"Is that all?"

Karen thought for a moment. "Just one more thing. What time did you start work this morning?"

"I was a bit late. I got in just after 9am. Dad wasn't very happy. I don't think he likes me seeing Paul."

"What does your Mum think?"

"She left us years ago. It's just me and Dad now."

"I'm sorry Jess. John will arrange to take you back to the funeral parlour or home, whichever you want."

"Thank you."

"You're welcome. Come on Jack, let's go up to the office."

The women walked up to the office and hung their jackets on the back of their chairs. They sat down opposite each other.

Karen smiled at Jack. "Did you hear what Jess said?"

Jack nodded. "He knew Darren was dead."

"Exactly."

"Why did you let him go."

"Because we still need to prove that his father is part of all this. It also sounds to me as if Jess is not the innocent wallflower he is pretending to be."

"I think Paul needs to find a new boyfriend."

Karen laughed.

She looked around the office, it was about half full. Matt and Rachel were still out, and John was taking Jess back to who knows where.

"Anyone have anything new?"

Cat put her hand up from behind her big screens.

"I think we've found a couple more golfers who bought new sets of clubs before playing in tournaments. Mick and I are trying to work out what happened to them. It was several months ago and gaining access to records is difficult."

"Good work guys. No news on our assassin?"

"We found him on CCTV leaving the Sunderland police station. We tracked the car to a car park on the Metro near the Beggars Bridge pub. He then caught a train to Newcastle, but we haven't been able to discover where he got off."

"That means he could be anywhere. Have you circulated his picture and MO to our international friends?"

"Yes, Ma'am but we've had no response as yet."

At that moment Billy burst into the room. He looked flustered.

"Good news guys. I've got us some extra bodies. The Sunderland nick were so angry, that they lost Darren in their own station, we've been allocated a half a dozen more officers to help with the investigation. Dee you'll be their boss."

"Thank you."

"Their contact details will be sent over to you."

"Thanks again. I'll be sending details of our assassin over to Newcastle to see if they can help track down his movements. Any help you can give us to get some priority over there would be appreciated, boss."

"I'll do my best. This is getting worse by the minute. Hopefully we'll get a break soon."

"I think we already have something, boss, have you got a minute for me to explain."

"Sure, can you make us a cuppa then we can have a chat. I'm gasping."

"I'll do that Ma'am," Jack offered, annoyed at the way Billy had demeaned Karen in front of the team.

"Thanks Jack."

Karen followed Billy into his office and spent the next half hour explaining the events of the day, and the important lead they had established through their interview with Jess.

*****

The small crowd applauded as the shy Argentinian walked off the 18th green at the Maspalomas Golf Club. He had just shot an excellent 69 on the difficult par 73 course.

He didn't know anyone in the crowd and had pushed his own trolley round the course. No-one was there to meet him when he finished.

A man watched him from the balcony in front of the club, seemed to come to a decision and walked over to shake his hand.

"Well done young man. What an excellent round of golf."

"Thank you, senor." His English was broken but more than adequate.

The man looked at the golfer's clubs. "It looks like you could do with a better set of clubs. These look quite old."

"They do the job, as you have seen."

The man laughed. "My name is Joe Higgs. I have been known to help young golfers like you get up the ladder. How would you like to play golf in England, you could try your luck at becoming a professional?"

"That is very kind senor, but I am due back in Argentina in three weeks."

"That's OK. There's a competition near Newcastle next week. I could get you there and back with time to spare. If you do well, you may be convinced to change your mind."

The young golfer thought for a minute. "And you will pay for all my travel and accommodation?"

"Yes sir. And I will buy you a new set of clubs to take with you."

He thought for a bit longer.

"I need to sign my card and hand it in. Give me an hour to make my decision. Will you be at the presentation later?"

"I will. I'm a member of the club."

"Then I will see you later. My name is Max Candian. I must get going or I will be disqualified. I'll see you later."

Joe smiled and waited until Max was out of earshot. He dialled a number on his mobile. "I think I have a courier for you."

\*\*\*\*\*

That evening Karen sat watching TV with Jinx beside her. She was watching Moana on the Disney channel. She called it brain clearing as she sang along to the hit animation.

A cleaned plate sat on the coffee table in front of her. A jacket potato with baked beans had been quickly demolished when she got home. She felt guilty that she had yet to clean the plates and wash the pan, but she felt like she needed to rest.

Her mobile rang and it came up with number unknown. She answered it cautiously. "Hello?"

There was no reply, but she could here breathing at the other end. "Who is this?"

Still no answer.

She decided to hang up. At the second she pressed the red button on her phone she heard a squeak. It sounded familiar but she couldn't place it.

Moana was forgotten as she sent a message on the WhatsApp group she had with Jack and Laura. The group was called Witches of Witherwack.

Messages bounced back and forth for a while suggesting she get out the house. In the end, they agreed Jack should go around to be with her for the evening.

When Jack arrived, she was carrying a small bag.

"I've brought some essentials so I can stay the night."

"Thanks Jack, you needn't have done that."

"Two heads are better than one." Jack reached into the bag and pulled out a bottle of white wine with a cooling sleeve around it."

"Now that's what I call an essential," Karen laughed, as she turned to go into the kitchen to get a couple of glasses.

The rest of the evening was spent discussing the case and watching movies. Laura kept in regular touch by WhatsApp, just checking in to see if they were all right.

At just after 11pm they decided to call it a night. Karen went up to bed while Jack changed into some pyjamas and curled up on the sofa. Jinx seemed confused for a while and went to curl up with Jack but quickly realised that this wasn't her Mam and ran up the stairs to be with Karen.

*Wednesday, 25th May 2022*

At 2.30am there was a knock on the door.

Jack was up in a flash. She put a small light on in the lounge but made for the kitchen, grabbing the small saucepan Karen had used to cook her beans.

She went to the front door.

Karen's front door had two upper frosted glass panels and Jack could see the top of someone's head through the glass. She put on the outside light just as Karen appeared at the top of the stairs.

A riot of red appeared under the light.

"It's OK. I think it's Laura."

Jack opened the front door and started to speak. "What are you……"

She was stopped abruptly as the clown standing there fired pepper spray in her face and tried to push past her.

Karen was down the stairs in a flash, stooping to pick up the pan where Jack had dropped it. She took a swing at the clown, catching him on the side of the face. He staggered back, stunned by the blow. The clown sprayed more pepper spray towards Karen who turned away to avoid the worst of it. He then ran away, up the short drive, disappearing into the darkness.

Karen helped pull Jack off the floor where she had fallen in the melee, sitting her on the chair in her hall.

Once she was clear of the door she locked and bolted it and helped Jack into the kitchen where they spent some time rinsing their eyes to try and negate the stinging.

"Are you OK Jack?"

"I'm fine now thanks." Jack looked at Karen through bright red eyes. "I thought it was Laura."

"I know. No-one would have expected a clown on their doorstep at 2.30am in the morning."

"Don't tell her I thought she was a clown."

Karen laughed. "I won't."

She checked Jack's eyes again. "Come on, let's get you back on the sofa. We'll be like a wet weekend in the morning if we don't get some sleep."

"Are you going to call it in Karen?"

"No. He'll be long gone now. The neighbours have one of those video doorbells. I'll get the footage from them tomorrow then we can get Cat to work her magic on any CCTV in the area."

Karen was about to walk up the stairs when she turned back to her friend.

"Thanks for being here Jack. That just may put them off in the future."

"You're welcome. What are friends for eh?"

With that Karen went back to bed and Jack turned the light off. She felt something alongside her. The purring gave it away. Jinx had come down to say thank you in her own special way.

## Chapter Fourteen

It took both girls a while to get back to sleep, but both managed to grab a few more hours rest before Karen's alarm went off. After enjoying bowls of porridge and fresh fruit, washed down with large mugs of tea, they drove into work. Karen handed her car keys to the police mechanic who had turned up early. Given the circumstances she checked his ID before handing them over.

Jack had parked around the back of the station, so Karen waited for her before they went inside. It was a beautiful day.

When they walked past the reception desk, Tom Moore looked up. "What happened to you two?"

"We got pepper sprayed by a clown last night, Tom. No damage done though."

"By a clown?"

"Has it never happened to you?" Karen laughed.

"Can't say I remember," Tom replied, laughing too, "do you want me to make a note on the records?"

"No thanks. I think the enemy are trying to wind me up. It'll take more than some random bloke with big shoes to scare me. Besides I caught him a beauty with a saucepan. He'll have a nice bruise on his face, that's for sure."

"Good for you Ma'am, but if you want some boys to keep a watch on your place, I am sure I can rustle up some volunteers."

"Thanks Tom, that's very kind. I'll bear that in mind."

Karen and Jack climbed the stairs, Jack sporting a broad smile.

"What's the matter with you?"

"You more like. Flirting with Tom like that."

I wasn't flirting, just chatting."

"I'll believe you, thousands wouldn't. I'll not tell Laura; she'll be dead jealous."

Karen smiled but ignored the comment.

They walked into the office which was already full. Even Billy was there, staring at the incident boards.

"What the hell happened to you two?"

"A close encounter with a clown at 2.30am in the morning boss."

Billy was visibly shocked.

"This is getting serious. This gang, or whoever they are, must feel they're big enough to try and intimidate the police."

"There has to be a lot of money involved, boss. Most crims would have shied away and kept their heads down."

"You're right Mick. What's the plan for today, Karen?"

"Bearing in mind what Mick just said and the adage, follow the money, let's see if we can get any joy looking at what bank details we can get on Prudence and Phil. See if we can find anything that might connect them."

She paused for a moment.

"Boss, can we get the new guys to keep watch on both Prudence and Phil Brookes to see what they do over the next couple of days?"

"You're in charge, Karen. That won't be a problem. I think we need to get the dive team back in the river too, we've put that off for too long."

"I'll give them a ring boss."

Billy seemed more motivated than Karen had ever seen him before.

"We can also ask them to get more information from those golf courses where those people bought new golf clubs before the competitions. Names, descriptions, that sort of thing."

"Yes boss. Cat, can you send over the details you have."

"The rest of us should stay here and focus on the evidence that is starting to pile up."

"What about Jess, Ma'am?"

Karen looked at Jack. "Do you think we should watch him too? He seems a bit young to be heavily involved."

"Just an itch I have Ma'am."

"OK, Mick can you see what we can find on Jess, check his social media and the like and let's see if he presents us with any gifts that would lead us to including him as a suspect."

"Good stuff people. Let's see what progress we can make today. Karen, my office please."

Karen followed Billy into his office and closed the door.

"This is turning into quite a massive case Karen. Can you handle it? If not, I am happy to call in more experienced officers from Newcastle or further afield if needed. There's no shame in admitting this is over your head."

Karen didn't know whether she should be offended or not but tried to keep her cool.

"It's fine boss, with these extra pairs of hands and our team in full throttle mode we've got this."

"What about the attacks on you. There could be worse to come."

"I've had worse pointed at me than a can of pepper spray, boss."

"Yes, but they might up the ante if they feel we're getting close."

"They'll not get away with this boss. The police are more than just one officer. They can't take us all down. This is just scare tactics to try and put us off the scent. I'm encouraged that they might think we are getting too close."

"OK. But if at any time you feel threatened or you just want out for any reason. Just let me know. There'll be no bad mark on your record or anything like that. You're a good officer, Karen. I don't want to lose you."

"Thanks boss. Much appreciated."

"Right, get back out there before I feel the need to hug you. Let's get those killers behind bars before they do any more damage."

"Yes boss." Karen smiled and gave a military style salute, before turning to leave.

The team were hard at it when Jack announced that the dive team would be back under the bridge that afternoon. They hoped that diving in daylight might help them spot more shopping trolleys and their macabre contents.

Karen decided to pop down on her own, leaving Jack to contact her if needed. On the spur of the moment, she messaged Dr Rae to see if she wanted to join her. It took only seconds to get a reply. They agreed to meet at the National Glass Centre at 3pm and walk along to watch the recovery team.

Karen stared at the incident board. She was starting to realise that her promise to catch the perpetrators by the end of the week was rapidly going out of the window. Short of a miracle there seemed little chance that they would close this case by then.

She had grown to love the team at Southwick North. It would be a wrench to have to leave them so early, but she had made a pledge and she was always good to her word.

As she walked back to her desk, she remembered her last words to her husband before he went on his last tour. *"Just come back safe, I'll be here waiting for you as always."* Those words sat heavy in her heart. She had waited and was still waiting. Gary didn't come home, not even in a body bag. The crevasse had been so deep they were unable to recover his body. There was nothing to bring back.

She sat behind her computer pretending to be focussed on the screen. The tears came again, as they always did when she thought about his death. Her guilt was always close by. She didn't say she loved him as he left. She had rushed to the door, but his car had already backed out the drive.

Karen was sure he knew that she loved him, so much, but the fact that she didn't say it that one time really hurt. They had always said it, first thing in the morning, and last thing at night. Why didn't she say she loved him that day?

Rummaging in her bag she pulled out a pack of tissues and dabbed at her eyes, trying not to smudge her mascara.

"You alright Ma'am," Mick asked, drawing everyone's attention to her. From where he sat, he had the best view of Karen's desk.

"Just something in my eye Mick," she replied, without turning round, "I'm fine."

The silence of the busy returned, broken only by the sound of fingers pressing computer keys.

Cat broke the spell.

"I've found another potential name for the body bags Ma'am. This chap played golf in a tournament last year near Hartlepool and told the organisers he had been forced to buy a new set of clubs the day before the tournament, because his had been lost at the airport."

"Good work, Cat. Flag him up and see if you can find any mention of him anywhere on the system."

Cat gave Karen a thumbs up from behind her computer screens and went back to her research.

Karen was frustrated. The lack of progress irked her. She went over from her desk to stare at the incident boards again.

"Any news on the companies Prudence is involved in yet we can add to the board?"

Mick looked up. "It's still coming in Ma'am but both Prudence and Phil seem to have their fingers in many pies."

"What do we know?"

"Well Prudence has shares in at least half a dozen companies that we know of, so far. We are checking to see if some of her companies are involved with other companies and of course we are also checking to see if she has any offshore interests."

Karen hadn't thought of offshore companies and was impressed by Mick's diligence.

"Phil too has interests in several companies Ma'am. I'll send a list of names to your computer."

Karen went back to her desk as the file from Mick popped up on her screen. She opened it and read through the names, with brief explanations of what each did.

Prudence had a company that looked after her dog breeding business, as they had expected, together with interests in a local fashion shop, a furniture business, a pet food company, a pet supplies company and a hairdresser's salon.

As well as his funeral business, Phil also had interests in the same pet food company and pet supplies company as Prudence. Then in his own right he had shares in a café and a cake shop. He was also listed as a non-executive director of a local charity shop.

Both were noted as great contributors to local good causes, as Cat had already found through the social media pages. Prudence especially being a big name in local dog clubs and charities.

Karen leaned back in her chair. *Maybe we are barking up the wrong tree with these two*, she thought to herself, smiling at her own joke. She felt better now she had pushed through her dark thoughts from earlier. Work to her was cathartic. It kept her going, motivated her, and distracted her in equal measures.

She looked around her team, all heads were down, focussed on the information that was streaming in. Cat had set up a spread sheet to capture all the details and that was now as important as the incident boards. Yet, it was the faces that kept drawing her back. She felt she was a good judge of character and there was something, she couldn't put her finger on – yet.

"Cat, if all these people brought in drugs in golf gear, they must leave the empty bits somewhere. Have a look and see if there are any reports on social media or in the local papers, of people finding abandoned golf equipment."

She was answered with the usual thumbs up.

Not feeling there was anything more she could do at the station, Karen decided to pay Dr Rae a visit.

"Jack, keep me informed if anything crops up, I'm off to see Dr Rae, just to see if there is anything else she can bring to the case."

"Will do Ma'am. If I get time later, I'll join you down by the river. I've got a feeling the divers are going to be in the water for quite some time."

Karen sent a Whatsapp to Laura Rae as she walked down the stairs to the car park. She put her hand in her bag to get her keys and realised her car was currently in the police garage.

"Damn it."

"Trouble Ma'am?"

"Sorry Tom. I forgot my car was in the police garage. I just need to get over to the Royal."

"Do you want me to order you a taxi or I can ask one of the uniform team to pop you over?"

"Thanks Tom, a cab would be great. I don't want to waste the guy's time."

"I'll make that call. They'll be here in two ticks."

"Thanks Tom, I'll wait outside."

Karen smiled at the handsome desk sergeant who smiled back. She went outside and walked up to the top of the drive to wait for the taxi. It arrived just as she got there.

As she sat in the back, she watched her new world going by. Being in the back of a taxi always seemed to put a different perspective on life. The people she watched were all going about their different lives. As she often did, she wondered what each did to survive, why they weren't working or did they work shifts.

*It's all part of life's rich tapestry*, she thought to herself as they drove along. When she arrived at the Hospital, she made her way down to the mortuary to meet Dr Rae.

She was met with a big hug as Laura ushered her into her back room, immediately preparing a coffee for her guest.

"I'm looking forward to another trip on the river."

"I'm not sure I'm so enthusiastic, I am guessing there will be more macabre finds for the divers to bring up."

"Which will come straight into my safe hands. I get excited about dead bodies as you know."

"Me too Laura, but these are in such a state. Doesn't it revolt you just a bit?"

"Not at all. My only reason for getting upset is if I can't identify them, or at least find out something which can help you track down their identity. The only exception is children. I hate finding young people on my slabs." Dr Rae seemed to be welling up, as if recalling some case she had worked on in the past. Karen hurriedly brought her back to the present.

"And how's our cases going? You have several bundles of bones to be going on with."

"That's true, and If we do find more today, I may have to box some of those up before I can take a look at the new bodies."

The women both cradled their cups, thinking about what might lie ahead.

"Still, it's a nice day Karen. Let's enjoy the fact we are out on the river and not cooped up in an office somewhere."

"That's true," Karen looked at her watch, "talking of which we should be going in a few minutes."

"No worries, I'll just pack my boney friends away and get changed. I won't be long."

Laura left Karen to ponder the mammoth task her friend was faced with, amazed at her positivity. In the background she could hear trollies being moved and doors being closed as several sets of remains were locked away. Laura came back in, opened her locker, took off her white coat and quickly put on a woollen jumper.

When she was done, she picked up her car keys and led Karen out to the car park.

"Where are you parked?"

"I've not got my car with me. Can I have a lift with you?"

"Sure, I'm over here."

Laura led Karen over to the staff car park then opened the passenger door for her before going around to the driver's side.

Once they were strapped in, Laura turned the key, slammed the mini into reverse and, with wheel's spinning, pulled out of her parking slot.

Karen held on to the side of her seat as the backward motion, swiftly changed into a rush towards the car park exit.

Soon they were heading down Chester Road towards Sunderland University.

"You know it's 30mph along here?"

"Is it?" Laura replied with her cackling laugh.

"I do work for the police you know."

"Are you going to arrest me?"

"No, but I would like you to slow down. I don't want to be in the car when you are stopped by the police."

"Spoil sport." Laura eased off the throttle as they passed the University, running a few amber lights on the way. Soon they crossed the Wear Bridge and turned down towards the Marina.

Karen had arranged to meet the dive vessel there. She spotted that the black rib was already in place below the Bridge on the way.

The girls were welcomed on board the dive boat. Once again, a temporary structure had been built over the stern of the boat offering protection from prying eyes. A small marquee had been erected on the side of the marina just above the refuelling pontoon. Just in case the team found something. If it came to that, Laura would call vans down from the coroner's office to collect the bodies.

As the boat made its way past the National Glass Centre, Karen admired the scenery. On one side there was the Glass Centre and the University buildings, with the ancient St Peter's Church watching over the river as it had for over 1500 years.

On the other side were the docks, with a large wind farm support vessel moored up, presumably being restocked. She was amazed by it all. This was her new home.

Yet in front of her lay the horrible side of humanity. She could see divers in the water. The skipper of the larger boat explained to the girls that the divers were working in pairs, drawing a long line along the bottom of the river, checking on every snag they felt along the way.

By the time they reached the rib there were six small pink bobbers floating on the river surface. Her heart sank. She knew what they meant. Each little pink bubble floating on that peaceful surface represented another horrendous crime.

## Chapter Fifteen

The process of lifting a total of eight more shopping trollies, on to the boat, took almost all afternoon. It was an awful task. Some of the trollies were almost empty, bags ripped open, and the bones washed away with the force of the river. One trolley held a single skull. Two had just the cable tie, indicating that a bag had once been anchored there.

By 5pm the divers and the recovery team were exhausted.

They volunteered to go down again but Karen made the call. Enough was enough.

Laura was excited by one bag. Compared to most of them it was still intact, and the trolley that held it had some of its original sheen. In her expert eyes, it meant that it was a relatively recent addition to the riverbed. That meant there was a reasonable chance that she could identify the person enclosed.

Once ashore, they arranged for the coroner's vans to collect the remains. Dr Rae was keen to get back to the Hospital to receive the bodies. On the way to the hospital, she dropped Karen off at Southwick North.

When Karen walked back into the station, Tom was holding up the keys to her car. "Here you go Ma'am. All sorted for you."

"Thanks Tom, that was very efficient."

"The mechanic mentioned you had a very nice car Ma'am. The extra switch to control the blues and twos is situated next to your lights control below your steering wheel on the right-hand side."

"Excellent. I can't wait to try them."

"Let's hope it's not too soon, eh Ma'am?"

Karen smiled. She knew what he meant. When those lights went on, it meant bad things were happening.

She went up to the office to check in with the team. Most of them were still working despite the late hour. Only Mick was missing. Apparently, his wife was ill, so he had gone home sharp to check on her.

As soon as she entered the room Cat called her over.

"Ma'am, I've finally had a response from the Marina office about that abandoned boat. It arrived here from Belgium just over a year ago. The owner, or at least the guy who arrived with it, paid a month's mooring fee in advance in cash. He gave the Marina office an address in Ripon Street, then they never heard from him again. They also had a mobile number for him, but it didn't seem to work in the UK."

"Thanks Cat. Jack, we'll check that address out in the morning. Any other progress?"

"We've been putting together a picture of the finances of Prudence and Phil. There are some common areas, and it seems some money has been sent offshore. It looks like there is more money in their coffers than can be accounted for by their normal business activities."

Karen thought for a moment. "Have we investigated her puppy sales, there must be records of where they are sold, happy customers on social media, that sort of thing."

"We'll check that out Ma'am," Matt offered, looking at Rachel.

"Thanks Matt."

Karen walked over to the incident boards and then called for everyone's attention.

"Guys, this case has just become a lot more serious. The dive team recovered evidence of a further eight deaths from the River Wear. Dr Rae is processing them as we speak. Let's call it a day and come back refreshed tomorrow morning. We need to get on top of this sooner rather than later. This will be making the national media soon and I want us to have some answers."

She looked around her team. "I have faith in you, let's get this done."

The team looked serious, this had become a major investigation, the worst any of them had ever been involved in.

On her way back to Witherwack, Karen gave way to temptation. Like a child with a new toy, she had to flick the switch. She looked in her rear-view mirror, nothing was behind her. She flicked the switch and was greeted with the sound of the siren. Pulling over, Karen got out of the car and had a look at the way the blue lights were built inside the front grill.

Impressed, she got back into the car and flicked off the switch for the blues and twos, before she attracted too much attention. Once home she fed a hungry Jinx and settled down to a prawn salad.

With nothing on the television to distract her, Karen began to think about the case. As always, she had a notepad and pen on the arm of the sofa. She picked them up, opening the pad to a blank double page.

For the next hour she set out all the elements of the case. On each page she focussed on an individual, looking for the common denominators. Money was normally the overriding factor in cases like this, but why the body count was so high, baffled her.

As things stood, they faced a simple case of drug importing. Numerous mules had been used, in several different ways. It seems many, if not all, had come to a particularly sticky end.

WHY? She wrote it capitals across the top of every page.

Why kill, the mules? What did they do to deserve such a death?

Her phone buzzed as she mused the question. It was Laura Rae on WhatsApp.

*What are you doing?*

*Watching TV.*

*Fancy a coffee?*

*Where?*

*At the morgue :-)*

*Are you still working?*

*Yep!*

*OK, mine's a cappuccino.*

*I'd have never guessed. You'll be awake all night. Lol. See you soon. x*

Karen gave Jinx a stroke and a kiss. "Sorry my little beauty. I'll see you in a bit, then you can have a treat." She stretched, then got up from the sofa.

Picking up her badge and jacket, she collected her keys from a tray on the hall table, locked up the house and walked towards her car.

It was dark outside. Her security light came on, lighting the way to her car. She noticed that a vehicle was parked across the end of her drive. *Damn it*, she thought to herself as she walked down towards the road.

Suddenly, without any warning, a bag was placed over her head. She tried to shout for help as the darkness overwhelmed her but a strong hand across her mouth stopped her from uttering a sound.

Karen swung her arms to try and tackle her attacker but try as she might, she couldn't connect. "Calm down and you'll be fine," the voice was quiet and menacing. "You're coming with us. Someone wants a word."

Her attacker started to walk her forward. She guessed towards the road. She heard the bleep of an electronic car key unlocking a car door. Putting up as much resistance as she reasonably could, she felt another pair of hands pulling her into a vehicle.

Then all hell broke loose.

A man's voice yelled, "Armed police. Stop where you are."

The hands that were holding her, twisted her around. She was sure she was being used as a shield.

The man holding her muttered an expletive, then nearly deafened her as he yelled from right next to her ear.

"Back off, or she dies."

"There's no escape son, let her go and you won't be hurt."

Karen shuddered, she knew she was in a dangerous position, one stray shot, or sudden movement could end in tragedy.

"What are we going to do?"

The second voice seemed weak and scared.

"Get in the front and start the engine. Be ready to gun the accelerator on my word."

Karen knew this was the leader. He was the one who would trigger whatever was coming next. Yet she could feel his hands shaking; he was nervous too. She thought she would try her luck.

"Come on son. Help us and you could come out of this with a lighter sentence."

"Shut up, you don't know who we are working for. There is no easy way out."

She could feel his grip stiffen. Suddenly she found herself flying forward. Karen put out her hands to break her fall, having no idea where she was going. Behind her she heard a shout, "Drive!"

A car door slammed shut and an engine roared. As she hit the ground with her hands outstretched, she heard the unmistakeable sound of gunfire. The squeal of tyres was followed by the dull thump of a car hitting a wall.

Helping hands pulled her back on her feet, at the same time removing the black bag that had been covering her head.

"Are you OK, Ma'am?"

"Apart from a Foosh injury, I'm fine."

"An ambulance is on its way Ma'am. They'll check you over."

"How did you get here so soon?"

"Your boss had us stake you out, he guessed your enemies might pay you another visit. When we saw that car across the end of your drive, we thought something might happen."

Karen looked at the black car buried in the wall across the road.

"How did they know I would be going out?"

"Maybe they were just hoping you'd see the car and come out to see who was blocking your drive?"

The sound of a siren indicated the approach of the ambulance. She could see armed police surrounding the crashed car. One of the men waved towards her, it was a scything motion across the neck.

"Both dead by the look of it, Ma'am," the officer who was standing with her said, confirming the outcome for her two assailants.

"Damn it, damn them to hell."

Karen could feel the shock and emotion starting to pour out. Another chance to get to the bottom of this case was gone. Two paramedics ran over to her, taking over from the police officer. They escorted her to the ambulance, sitting her down on the back step of the vehicle.

She knew she was in shock; she had experienced it before. Once on active duty when a close friend was killed right next to her and then again when she had been told Gary had died. She let the paramedics do their job without protest. They decided to take her in to be checked over. As the ambulance drove to the Hospital, the paramedic treated her hands, which both had nasty gravel burns. Her left wrist was also badly sprained.

By the time they arrived at the Sunderland Royal Hospital she felt much better, despite the bandages. She insisted they drop her off at the morgue, which caused both consternation and amusement in equal measure.

As she walked in, Laura was working on one of the new bodies. She looked up as Karen entered the room.

"What happened to you?"

Laura pulled off her gloves and ran over to Karen. She put her arm around Karen's shoulder and led her into her inner sanctuary, as she liked to call it.

"I thought you had changed your mind?" Laura was making Karen a cappuccino as she spoke.

"A couple of blokes decided to kidnap me. God knows what they had planned. Unbeknown to me, the boss had my place staked out precisely for this moment. They decided to run instead of giving themselves up. They'll be paying you a visit in a few hours."

"They're dead?"

"An armed response unit was on scene. I didn't see it; I had a bag over my head. An ambulance brought me here."

"Oh, you poor thing. Maybe you should get some rest."

"No. You asked me here, so I want to know what you've discovered. I take it you didn't just want to make me a coffee?"

Laura smiled. "You're not a detective for nothing. Let me show you something."

Laura led Karen out to the morgue where one recognisable body was laid out on a slab, with two boxes of assorted bones.

"This is the newest of the bodies we found, and these two boxes contain the bones from two of the least damaged bags. Have a look at the body first."

Laura pointed to one of the leg bones from the body. There were still bits of flesh on the bones and the smell was not too pleasant, but Karen had seen worse. On the end of the bones, she could see a clean cut, and a couple of gouges which looked like attempted cuts.

"Not saw marks then?"

"Nope, some sort of cleaver I'd say."

Laura reached into the box and took out what looked like a fibula bone. It too had been cut. The same pattern was on that bone and several of the others.

"I hadn't really thought of it before, but the other bodies all had similar cuts."

"You put that in your report after the first set of bodies were found."

"Yes, I did but I've been thinking about these cuts. Wait here."

Laura went over to a metal cupboard and brought out a cleaver and a leg of pork. She placed the meat on the slab and handed Karen the cleaver.

"Are you okay to hold this?"

Karen flexed it in her hand. It stung a bit, but she could hold it.

"It's fine."

"Cut the leg in half."

"What now?"

"Yep, give it a good whack. Try and cut it in half in one go."

Karen eyed her friend then shrugged her shoulders before taking up the challenge.

She swung the cleaver up into the air then took a good hit on the meat. The cleaver stuck on the bone. Annoyed she pulled the blade out and swung again. Once more the blade stuck in the bone. Angry now, she put all her effort into the third blow and was rewarded when the blade passed straight through the meat, impacting on the metal mortuary table.

She was puffing from the effort as she handed the cleaver back to Laura.

"Good effort Karen."

"Thank you. How does this help, apart from allowing me to take out my frustrations on that piece of meat?"

Laura didn't answer, she just pulled out a blade and started to strip the meat back from the bone. The end that had already been cut was cleaned first and there was no evidence of other cuts. When Laura cleared the meat from the end Karen had cut, she could see the similar pattern to the bones that had been found in the river.

"Do you see?"

"I think so. Are you saying it was me who cut up all the bodies?" Karen replied with a smile.

"I'm sure you didn't. But someone like you did. If a butcher had cut the bodies up, they would have all been clean cuts like the cut on the other end of the leg of pork."

Karen thought about the demonstration. She nodded. Laura was right. Whoever did this was not a butcher, in fact they were quite hesitant over their work.

Karen looked at Laura. "An enthusiastic amateur butcher perhaps."

Laura smiled. "I like that description. They knew what they were doing but didn't do it as a day job."

"Is that it? You could have put that in your report."

"But it wouldn't have been so much fun."

"Cutting up meat isn't my idea of fun. I'm a vegetarian remember."

"Oh sorry, I forgot." Laura cackled her weird laugh. "Do you want a lift home?"

"Yes please. I think I need to get my head down."

"You poor thing. You'll be regretting moving here."

Karen smiled. "Not for a second."

"Come on then, let's get you home. Oh, and I found a puncture wound in the neck of the most recent body in this tranche. Once I get the toxicology report back, I'll bet good money he was drugged with the same stuff."

Karen just nodded; she was worn out. As she made her way to the exit, Laura quickly typed a message on her phone and chased after her.

When they got to Karen's house, Jack was waiting.

Karen could barely raise a smile when she saw her friend.

The damage from earlier in the evening was still being cleared up. A breakdown van was struggling to get the wrecked car out of the wall, making one hell of a din. A small crowd was watching the activity. Police tape was everywhere, and an armed policeman stood next to Karen's gate. He nodded as the three women walked past, lifting the tape so they could get into the house.

"She's done in," Laura whispered to Jack, while Karen fumbled for her keys.

The friends followed her in as Karen turned on the lights. There was comfort in the warm glow lighting up the friendly surroundings. Jinx helped to lift her mood too, running up to her and rubbing against her legs. Karen picked up the cat and took her into the living room, plonking herself down on the sofa, totally exhausted.

Jack sat next to her while Laura made tea.

"This isn't good Karen. They are certainly after you."

"I know Jack. I'm trying not to let it get me down but what else will they throw at me? If one of those attackers had survived, we might have got some answers."

"We might yet. We know the car was stolen, it had false plates. Once we've worked out who the two men were, that might give us some leads."

Laura came back with three steaming mugs of tea, placing them on the coffee table in front of the sofa, before taking a seat in the single armchair.

"It's late girls, you get home, and we'll convene again tomorrow."

"If you think we are leaving you on your own tonight, you've another think coming."

"Jack's right. We're staying right here."

Karen managed a weak smile. "Thank you both, but there's no need. I have an armed guard outside as you can see."

"Tonight, the witches stay together. Who knows, we may get some inspiration, something to crack the case." Laura held out her hands and the women formed a circle.

The strange tingle, Karen had felt before, came back, this time stronger than ever. The others seemed to feel something too, by the looks on their faces, but no-one dared say anything.

Almost reluctantly they let the circle break and grabbed their mugs. Jack offered a toast. "The Witches of Witherwack."

"The Witches of Witherwack," the others echoed.

They drank in silence for a couple of minutes, then Karen asked Laura to explain to Jack about the cuts on the bones.

This seemed to galvanise the women as they tossed around ideas based on the enthusiastic, but amateurish way the bodies were cut up.

"Sounds to me like someone has the kit but is not a regular user of a cleaver. Maybe they only get involved when there is a body to dispose of."

"That's exactly it, Jack. But who could that be?"

"It doesn't sound like the work of a funeral director," Laura suggested, finishing off her mug of tea.

Karen was astonished. "Have you drunk that already? You must have a lead lining to your throat."

"I like my tea hot. Always have." Laura seemed almost offended by Karen's remark.

"Unless the funeral director has an interest in a butchery business."

Karen looked at Jack. "What were Phil and Prudence's joint business interests?"

"There were the pet supplies and pet food businesses. That might be relevant?"

Karen held out her hands and the others grabbed them to make a circle. The tingle was there, and they looked at each other. "Are you thinking what I'm thinking?" Karen posed the question.

"Pet food," Jack whispered.

"Oh my god." Laura struggled not to be sick. She might be able to hack open dead bodies and analyse their inner workings, but the idea of feeding human meat to pets. That was a step too far.

Karen broke the circle. "I need some sleep."

"I think we all do. I bag the sofa."

"I'll sleep with you." Laura looked at Karen, spotting the shock on her face. "No funny business. I just think you might need someone close tonight."

Karen was about to protest, then thought, what the hell.

"OK. I'm setting the alarm for six, mind. We've a big day ahead tomorrow."

"You're the boss!" They had a group hug and went to bed. Within ten minutes, and several toilet flushes later, the house was silent.

*Thursday, 25th May 2022*

After a restless night, full of dreams and thoughts of bodies being chopped up for pet food, the exhausted women woke up when the alarm broke their fitful sleep. Jack and Laura left to freshen up in their own homes while Karen showered and prepared for a new day.

Outside, apart from the damaged wall and attendant police officer, everything was back to normal. Karen fed Jinx and locked up. She stood outside, taking in the early morning fresh air. It looked like it was going to be a nice day. She looked at her Fitbit – it was six forty-five.

After having a few words with her guard, she decided that instead of going to the office she would drive down to the National Glass Centre and take a walk along the river. The Wear was flat calm. A few seagulls disturbed the peace while a heron stalked tiddlers in the shallows just below where she stood. The occasional runner and cyclist ensured she wasn't alone until a truck emptying the bins broke the peace and quiet.

She took a deep breath, savouring the salty air. She watched a gull drop a shell on the path, trying to break it to get to the flesh inside. It tried again and again until it finally earned its reward. *Persistence. That's what this job is all about*, she thought to herself as she walked back to her car before driving to Southwick North. She was the first in the office.

As the team arrived, each in their turn asked what had happened to her. By the fourth time of asking, she decided to wait until everyone was present to bring them up to date. Even Billy was in early, keen to know what had happened to her the night before.

She went into his office as he was taking his jacket off.

"Thanks for staking out my house, boss."

"You're welcome, Dee. I had a hunch that whoever was after you might try again. Turns out I was right."

"That's why you're the boss."

Billy smiled. "Come on, let's brief the team on the latest news."

The DCI gathered all the team together in front of the incident boards. He explained about the stake out and the attempted kidnap of DI Dee. The detectives were all visibly shocked. Many looked at Karen. "I'm alright," she held up her hands, "just some gravel rash and a sprained wrist."

"What's on the agenda today?" Mick asked.

With a nod to Billy, Karen took over the briefing.

"We have an idea that there may be a link to the pet food business that Phil and Prudence are both involved with. I want the premises watched to see who comes and goes."

John and Jordan volunteered for that duty.

"Jack and I are going to visit Ripon Street to see if we can find something which might link the abandoned boat to the case."

She looked around at everybody. "I need everyone to be ultra-careful now. They've shown their hand. They're prepared to do anything to protect whatever this criminal business might be. We may even be dealing with an organisation with a reach far beyond our borders, so be careful."

There were nods all round.

"Cat, see if you can dig a bit deeper into the pet food business. Products, clients, financials – anything you can find."

The usual thumbs up and click of her keyboard showed that Cat was already on it.

"The rest of you, keep at the lines of enquiry we are already pursuing. We are due a break. I'm hoping Dr Rae will be able to give us some more information soon. Also, later this morning we will get IDs on the men who died last night. Find out everything possible about them. We'll convene back here later this afternoon."

"Anything I can do Dee?" It was Billy. Everyone looked at him, some not able to hide their surprise.

Karen looked at her boss and smiled. "Thanks boss, just keep an eye on the team for me. I'm sure we will all work easier knowing you have our backs."

Billy smiled and nodded.

"Oh, and if you can get the details about last night's attackers rushed along, that would be perfect."

"Yes boss," Billy mimicked and gave her a little salute.

Everyone laughed until Billy clapped his hands and got them to jump to it.

Karen and Jack got their kit together and headed off to check out the Ripon Street address.

## Chapter Sixteen

Karen insisted on driving, secretly hoping she might get to use her blues and twos. Frustratingly the radio clipped to her belt remained silent. She had to remind herself she was a detective and not a bobby on the beat.

Ripon Street was set amongst a network of streets and alleys in the Roker area of Sunderland. She had no hope of finding the street by herself so let Jack guide her rather than using her Satnav.

The street turned out to be quite long. It was lined with cottages, some with dormers, others with fronts, almost identical to the way they had been built over a hundred years ago. In those days, they provided homes for the men who worked in and around the docks. Just the plastic UPVC doors and windows that most now sported, showed the passage of time.

It was usually out the back where the main changes had occurred. Coal bunkers and outside loos had been replaced with extensions for kitchens and bathrooms. The alleys were lined with roll up doors and shutters.

A few of the cottages still had wooden window frames. One of them proved to be the address they were looking for. It was in a particularly bad state of repair. Many of the properties had nice hanging baskets or flowerpots in front; not this one. The small front yard was full of litter and plastic bottles.

"This one lets the street down."

"You could say that again, Jack. Maybe some little old lady lives here." Karen was pretty sure that wasn't the case but was happy to give the property the benefit of the doubt.

"Shall we?"

"Why not."

Jack opened her door first and stepped through the gap in the wall where a gate once belonged. Karen walked around from the other side of the car.

Jack knocked on the door.

Silence, no dog, no rustle of curtains. Nothing but the faint echo of the knock, hinting at an empty interior.

She knocked again as Karen joined her. The door of the cottage across the road opened.

"You'll get no joy there, pet. No-one has lived there for about a year now. We've called the council, but they've done nothing."

The small elderly lady looked like she wanted to talk, but with only her slippers on, was reluctant to step outside her house. Karen walked over as Jack knocked again.

"Do you remember who used to live there?"

"There was a bloke who used to come and go. There were always people coming and going, often late at night. Not that I'm nosey, pet."

"I understand, you have to be careful these days."

"I think you need to be careful by the looks of you, love."

Karen smiled. "You're right, I've had a few," she paused, "accidents, shall we say, lately."

"Are you the police?"

"Yes Ma'am." Karen showed the elderly woman her badge.

"They make them younger and prettier than in my day," she laughed, showing a set of broken teeth.

"You're very kind. Anything else you can tell us about the people opposite."

"Shady, aye, they were shady."

"Thank you."

"Agnes, pet. Call me Agnes."

Karen pulled out one of her new cards that she had found on her desk the day before, and handed it to Agnes.

"Thanks Agnes, if you think of anything else, give me a call."

Agnes took the card as if it were a great gift. Karen guessed she didn't have many visitors. The chance to chat with a police detective was probably the highlight of her day, or maybe her week.

"Good luck," Agnes looked at the card, "Karen. What a nice name, my daughter was called Karen too." Tears filled the old lady's eyes as she recalled something bad that had happened. Karen had the urge to stop and chat but fought it.

"I have to go but maybe we could have a cuppa one day?"

"I'd like that pet. Just stop by any time and I'll put the kettle on."

Karen nodded and said goodbye, walking back across the road to where Jack stood by the front door. As she did, she remembered her Nan and how she used to sit with her when she was a young girl. Karen had loved those days. The old woman was not dissimilar to her Nan.

She looked back and smiled. Agnes was still framed in her front door. The woman waved and then disappeared back into her cottage.

"No joy?" Karen asked.

"Nothing. Shall we try around the back?"

"Have you tried the front door?"

Jack turned and gave the handle a try, but the door was firmly locked. She looked through the letter box. "It looks in a sorry state in there."

"Let's try around the back then."

The two women walked down the street, counting doors as they went. They were just turning the corner to get to the back alley when two black BMW's with blacked out windows passed them and turned into the alley.

"Call me old fashioned but does that look suspicious to you?"

Jack looked at Karen and nodded in agreement. She took out her phone and quietly walked down to the corner.

Jack pushed her phone around the corner and took a quick couple of pictures.

The two cars were parked at the back of one of the cottages, possibly the one they were trying to access. Two men were chatting next to them as if waiting for something to happen. Despite the rows of green bins, they had a good image of one of the number plates.

She sent the image to Cat with a note to get the owners details.

"Let's walk around to the other end of the alley to see if we can get a picture of the other car."

Karen wasn't sure if she was just being cautious, or if she was just plain scared. She had been the subject of three attacks already during this investigation. If they confronted these men, there was every chance she could be attacked again.

Whatever she was feeling, it didn't matter. Jack agreed with her suggestion and the two women walked around the block of cottages to get to the other side. They were just approaching the end of the row when the cars sped past them. They were so quick, Karen just managed to get a partial plate from the lead car. It ended with LEY.

They continued to the back alley and walked along to where the cars had been parked. Jack looked again at the image. The cars had been stopped opposite a cottage with a black back gate.

To be certain they were in the right place they checked the numbers on the bins. This was the only cottage without a wheelie bin out the back.

The cottage they were interested in didn't have a roller shutter door, just an old wooden door with peeling grey paint. Karen put on a set of plastic gloves and carefully tried the handle. It opened. The swollen wood caught on the step, and she had to lift the door using the handle to get it to open fully.

The back yard was full of rubbish. The only exception was a worn path between the banks of trash which led to the back door of the property. That door stood wide open.

"Call this in Jack. My spidey senses are in overdrive."

"Will do," Jack whispered back, reaching for her radio.

Jack hung back talking rapidly to the duty officer while Karen walked quietly to the open back door. A strange, unpleasant smell, emanated from the property. It seemed to be a mixture of damp, bleach and drains. Karen hesitated, trying to see through the door, but the darkness of the inside gave her no hint of what she might find.

Jack touched her back, making her jump.

"The boys in blue are on their way. I've put SOCO on standby too."

"Good thinking. Do we go in or wait until they get here?"

"Your call boss but I'm right behind you."

Karen smiled. "Come on then. Let's do this."

Karen checked the floor for glass and for booby traps. An old army trait. Carefully she stepped in, trying not to gag as the smell got stronger.

To their right was a galley kitchen with a toilet at the end. The kitchen seemed in reasonable condition, despite being ancient. It was obviously being looked after on a regular basis.

The toilet seemed less cared for. Karen walked to the end of the kitchen and poked her head into the small room. The bath was stained and black. Buckets of water were lined up on the floor, probably to flush the broken toilet. The toilet rolls were cheap. They looked like they were as old as the kitchen. Spider's webs were everywhere.

Karen walked back to Jack who was still standing just inside the back door. She wrinkled her nose. "I hope you don't need the loo. I am guessing by the look of it that only men have been in there for the last year or more."

"Yuk. Let's check the rest of the cottage. It seems deserted. I haven't heard a sound."

"Almost too quiet?"

"Maybe." Jack led the way towards the front rooms. There was a small bedroom with a single mattress off the hall. Then two doors. The first led into a dining room of sorts which had been used recently. There were mugs, beer cans and food wrappers strewn everywhere.

Jack put her finger to her lips and pointed towards the fireplace. On the mantelpiece above, an ash tray made of glass, held a single cigarette. A column of thin smoke signalled that someone was here.

At that moment a police car pulled up outside, the blue light reflecting down the hallway, adding an eerie quality to the building. The girls heard another larger vehicle stop outside and the sounds of sliding doors. That would be an armed response unit.

Jack picked up her radio and whispered into it, advising the controller that they were in the building. Karen edged towards the front door and the door into the front room. A key sat in the front door lock. She intended to turn it and let the support unit in. As she reached for it, a cough came from the front room.

A man was sitting in an armchair with his back to where she stood. The sun shone through the window, highlighting the column of smoke emanating from a cigarette in his left hand. He lifted a cup to his mouth, as she watched, and drank.

"Hello?" Karen tentatively stepped into the room, turning the key in the front door as she moved.

She sensed Jack behind her as she edged closer to the figure in the chair. The women moved either side of the chair as the front door opened. An armed officer entered the room, gun raised. Karen signalled him to stay back.

As they walked around the chair, the person sitting there didn't move. The man's eyes were hidden behind dark glasses. Karen could just make out that they seemed to be unmoving. He simply stared at the fireplace which was laid but not lit.

As Jack walked in front of the window the shadow or movement seemed to register with him. "Who is it?"

"The police. Who are you?"

"Who's there?"

Karen played a hunch and waved her badge in front of him.

The man finished off his drink. Took a big suck on his cigarette then reached for a small glass of water on the table next to his chair. He moved so quickly neither Karen nor Jack had time to react.

He dropped a small pill into the glass which had been secreted in a ring. He drank the glass of water, pill and all, in one gulp.

"What have you done?" Karen asked, frantically grabbing the glass from his hand.

The man took off his glasses. "You were so close, guys."

"Who are you working for?"

The man began to sweat. "Better this way than; well, you know what." He choked as the poison began to take effect.

"Call an ambulance!" Jack shouted at the armed officer. They both knew they were wasting their time. The man convulsed in front of them. Neither of the women knew what to do apart from watch the agony of his death.

Jack turned away but Karen watched until the twitching finally stopped. "This looks like arsenic poisoning," Karen muttered quietly to herself."

She asked the armed officer to check the upstairs but to be careful. Karen reminded them about the potential for booby traps. If these people were willing to kill themselves rather than be captured, then who knew what they were capable of.

Soon the cottage was full of people, searching every nook and cranny for anything which might give them a clue as to what was going on. Even the attic was checked out, though that appeared to be the cleanest part of the house.

Dr Rae appeared as did the SOCO team. Feeling overwhelmed by the activity in such a confined environment, Jack and Karen walked out into the back alley. The bin men were frustrated they weren't allowed down the lane. To ensure nobody missed out on the once-a-fortnight collection, a few officers, and some of the neighbours, wheeled the bins down to the end of the alley for the bin men to empty.

Karen smiled at the cooperation. "People are nice."

"Most of the time. What the hell just happened?"

"I'm not sure. I think he was almost blind, deaf and potentially disabled. His legs seemed quite wizened."

"Was he our boat man?" Jack queried.

"I doubt it. I think he may just have been baby-sitting the house for someone. In payment he probably received drugs and a roof over his head."

"You mean he might have been like someone's pet?"

"I wasn't thinking like that, but you may be right," Karen replied. "Do we know who owns this house?"

"Nope, I'll get Cat on to that right now."

As Jack typed away on her mobile phone, Dr Rae joined them, pulling off her gloves as she walked through the back gate.

"Wow. You guys know how to find trouble. I've never been so busy."

"Sorry," Karen apologised. "Maybe we'll stay in the office in future."

Jack laughed. "Yeah right. You love this. You do too, Laura."

Karen and Laura looked at each other like guilty conspirators.

"Well, there is that." Laura started laughing which soon started the others off.

They were still laughing when DCI Billy Roberts burst through the back gate.

"What the hell people? There's a dead man in there, let's have a bit of respect."

"Sorry boss," Karen replied, trying hard not to smile.

"What happened here, Dee?"

"We've got to work that out yet. I do think we may have broken up something important. If someone prefers to kill themselves rather than talk to the police, whatever is going on here must have been vital to their organisation."

"When we arrived, there were two black BMWs parked in the back alley. They must have been worth more than this cottage. Something goes down here; we just don't know what."

"Jack's right, boss. This place is important to the crims. Let's hope the SOCO boys can find the answers."

Billy's demeanour seemed to soften. "Are you alright, Karen?"

"I'm fine boss. Just frustrated that the case hasn't broken yet. Mind you I think we are getting close. That's why they are getting desperate. I'll not be giving up, that's for sure."

"That's what I like to hear. I need to get back to City Hall. The media are asking questions, and the powers that be, want some answers. I think we need to prepare a statement by the end of the week or at least for Monday."

"Right you are. I'll start putting some details together for you."

"Perfect. I'll see you back at the office later."

With that Billy walked back into the cottage and out the front door. A cordon had been established around the front of the cottage, and a few locals were trying to get a glimpse of what was happening. Some had their mobile phones in their hands and Billy knew this would be all over social media already.

He held his hand in front of his face in a futile attempt to keep his face out of the news, climbed into his car, and drove away.

In the back alley, the women chatted about the case until SOCO gave them the 'all clear' to go back in the house. The coroner's van had been directed down the back alley, and as they walked into the cottage, the guys followed them in, ready to remove the body.

Karen went to have one more look at the man she had watched die. The stress of his death was evident in his face, foam coated his lips, and his eyes were wide, like he had seen a ghost. He wasn't a pretty sight.

By the nasty smell in the room, she also guessed he had soiled himself during his death throws, though she suspected he wasn't used to the benefits of a flannel.

Now she had time to spare, she looked more carefully around the room. It was a mess. The carpet was dark brown and stained with who knows what. Some marks had the hue of blood while others looked like drink spills of one kind or another.

The wallpaper was a florid flower design which harped back to the sixties. In places it was black with damp, and next to the fireplace it was peeling away from the wall. There was a table placed against the right-hand wall of the room with the detritus Karen associated with drug use. Silver foil, spoons, candles, a razor blade, all the paraphernalia she had seen many times before in dingy rooms like this.

On the mantelpiece above the fire was an old clock, the hands stopped at twelve fifteen. Above that, a framed copy of Constable's, The Hay Wain, hung from a rusty nail. It was so badly stained by nicotine that it was hard to make out any detail. In fact, the whole room had a yellow tinge, including the window glass, which looked as if a seagull had taken a dislike to the house, it was so badly splattered.

A small boxy TV sat on a coffee table to the left of the fireplace but whether it worked or not it was hard to tell, it was so old.

A single bulb hung from a central light fitting and yellowed net curtains partly obscured what view there was of the road outside.

Totally incongruous to its surroundings a small potted Gerbera provided a splash of pink from its spot on the windowsill. It was the only thing in the room that looked loved. She looked at the man in the chair again. He certainly hadn't been loved, not for a long time.

She walked back into the hall and took the staircase to the bedrooms upstairs.

As she did Laura and Jack led the men into the front room to collect the body.

The bedrooms were a bit of a misnomer. They had no beds. Instead, each held a bare wooden table with four wooden chairs scattered in various places around the room.

Apart from the odd piece of litter on the floor there were little signs of use. Karen found herself humming empty chairs and empty tables from Les Miserable as she took in the scene. The rooms only had Velux roof lights so there were no views to be had.

A seagull squawked outside the window, and she looked up through the roof light to the cracked chimney pot on which it stood, calling for a mate perhaps.

She sat on one of the chairs for a moment and then was struck by something. Though scattered about the room, all the chairs were angled towards where she sat.

As she pondered what had happened in the room Jack put her head around the door.

"The body's been taken away."

"Thanks Jack. Have a look at this. All those chairs point towards this one."

Jack sat in one of the other chairs and then moved to another. "You're right. A meeting, interview or interrogation perhaps?"

"Is the other room the same?"

The girls moved to the other bedroom. Though the chairs were placed differently, one was the focal point of the other three.

Karen bent down and examined the chair at the focus of the other three more intently.

"Have a look at this Jack. It could be worn from a rope and look, that could be a blood stain."

Jack took a closer look at the back of the chair. "It does look like something has been rubbing the back. We'd need to get that stain tested for blood."

They walked back into the other room. The chair in the same central position had similar marks and stains.

"Maybe someone was held here for a time and tried to break free." Karen sat in the chair again and put her hands behind the back of the chair. "Like this."

"Then people came and talked to them, maybe beat them to get information out of them?" Jack was warming to the idea.

"Before you get excited Jack, there's nothing here to tell us who used this space. I am guessing our guy downstairs was a kind of gatekeeper, keeping watch on the place while the real action goes on up here."

Jack looked deflated. "Perhaps we should do a house to house to see if any of the neighbours can help us out."

"Good idea, let's get uniform to do that."

The bareness of the upstairs rooms and the thought of what might have happened here made the downstairs rooms suddenly seem warmer. Karen shivered, despite the heat in the upstairs room. Sun shone through the sky light, creating a beam of dancing dust motes.

Karen took one last look around. "Come on. Let's get back to the office. Hopefully we'll catch a break today."

## Chapter Seventeen

Back in the office, Karen and Jack drank tea, and stared at their computers. Cat had been busy. Both had several files of information to wade through. These included CCTV files, bank statements and car ownership details. Thankfully, Cat had done her best to summarise all the data in one single file.

The reading was interrupted by the return of John and Jordan.

Everyone stopped to hear how they had got on.

"What?" John looked around the office as everyone stared at them.

"How did it go, you numpty?" Mick spoke for the team.

"Oh, it was fine, nothing happened."

"You didn't see anyone of interest?" Karen asked.

"No Ma'am, it was boring to be honest, so I went into the shop to have a look around. I bought you a present."

Jordan handed Karen a plain white plastic bag. She pulled out two tins of cat food and a leaflet with all the latest offers.

"Thanks guys. What was it like in there?"

"Like any regular pet food supplier, I guess. They had a steady stream of visitors and one delivery truck. It unloaded two pallets of various types of food. Tins, bags, boxes and the like."

Karen studied the tins, which were a normal brand, then had a look at the A4 double sided leaflet. It was headed P & P's Quality Pet Food Supplies. It listed all the food available with the latest prices. It was all standard stuff on the front page but on the back, half the page was dedicated to their own brand exclusive dog food.

She read the blurb. 'P & P's exclusive quality dog food, made from the finest meat available. With supplies limited, please order in advance. Our pet food is the best a dog can get. Half kilo tubs, £30 per tub. Give your pet the best meat money can buy. Be your dog's best friend. Order now at www.pandppets.co.uk.'

The picture underneath was of a plastic Tupperware style tub with P & P's logo on it.

"John. Did you see any of this special dog meat?"

Karen held up the leaflet.

"No Ma'am, but I did see an empty display stand, with an out-of-stock sticker on it."

Karen's mind was working overtime. Jack could see the cogs turning. She leaned across her desk and whispered. "Are you thinking about what we discussed yesterday?"

Karen had been nervous, even frightened to say what she was thinking. This leaflet seemed to endorse the dark thoughts they'd been having. She leaned towards Jack.

"What if the missing flesh from those bodies we've been retrieving was used to fill these tubs?" The fact that she had uttered the words made her shudder.

Jack sat back in her chair, shocked at the thought. She put her hands over her face and rubbed her eyes. "That's sick boss. Do you really think that someone could do that?"

"It could explain why the supply is intermittent."

"Dear God."

The others in the room had noticed the interaction between Karen and Jack.

Karen looked across, noticing that people had stopped working. She stood up to stand next to the incident boards. She pinned the leaflet to the board under the pictures of Prudence Bailey and Phil Brookes.

"Guys, we may have a link. This isn't proved of course and is a bit of a stretch." She paused as if to fully understand the enormity of the situation.

"My thought is that the missing flesh on the bodies we've found might, I repeat, might, be being used to fill this special line of pet food." She pointed to the exclusive offer on the leaflet.

The team all stared at her, thunderstruck by the concept of feeding human flesh to pets.

"Hell Ma'am, that's a bit of a jump and who would be sick enough to do something like that?" Mick asked.

"Maybe these two?" Karen pointed at the pictures of Prudence and Phil.

"I can't believe anyone could be so sick?" Rachel looked as if she was going to throw up.

"It's just a thought right now, an awful one I know. If nothing else, we need to find a way of proving I'm wrong."

"Maybe it's time to talk to Prudence again, Ma'am."

"You're right Mick. Jack let's give her a knock tomorrow. John, Jordan, thanks for the cat food. Jinx will be grateful."

Later that day, on the way home, Karen remembered that she was yet to look at her neighbour's doorbell footage. Subconsciously she had been putting off the moment, knowing it would bring back bad memories.

Mrs Jacobsen was lovely. She didn't really know how the system worked and happily handed over her phone to Karen to check out the footage.

She quickly scrolled through until she arrived at the moment the clown knocked on her door. The system had spotted a black car stopping outside the house, dropping off the clown before it drove off along the road and out of sight. The camera images were in black and white. She watched the clown stand for a second, as if checking which was her house. The clown then walked casually down the short drive to her front door.

The recording ended.

The next one showed the clown running away, turning in the same direction as the car had driven. Something caught her eye at the end of the recording.

She thanked her neighbour for her help. As she left, instead of going home, she followed the same route the clown had taken. Sure enough, as she walked past the next house but one, she caught a glimpse of colour in the hedge. It was the clown's wig.

*Friday, 26th May 2022*

As soon as she arrived in the office the next morning, Karen handed the wig over for forensic testing. She wasn't very hopeful as a close look hadn't revealed any hairs or anything else that might help identify the wearer.

As she took off her jacket, she looked at the incident board.

"Unless the wearer was bald," she muttered to herself.

She looked across at Cat. "Cat, can you check to see if we have any social media pictures of Phil Brookes over the last few days?"

A thumbs up came from over the screens.

Within minutes, Cat had sent Karen a link. It was a social media post from a charity event the night before last. Both Prudence and Phil were there. Phil had been presented with an award and was pictured accepting the prize from a local councillor.

The picture was sharp enough for Karen to zoom in.

She leaned forward to study the image. "Jack, come and have a look at this."

Jack walked around from her desk to study the image.

"Notice anything?"

"It looks like he's wearing make-up."

"Does his cheek look swollen to you?"

Jack's eyes flicked from one side of Phil's face to the other.

"You're right. His right cheek looks more swollen."

"I hit that clown on his right cheek. Maybe the make-up is covering a bruise."

"Let's talk to them both, as soon as we can."

Karen was conscious that her time was running out. She had promised that if she didn't catch the killers by the end of the week she would resign. Today was Friday.

The team were surprised when Billy came into the room, after all it was Friday, and he often took that day off to practice his golf before the weekend.

"Dee, follow me."

Karen got up from her desk and followed Billy into his office.

"Are we there yet?"

"Getting close boss. I think I've identified the clown who attacked us the other night. I also have an idea about the strange way the bodies have been cut up."

"Who's your suspect?"

"Phil Brookes, the funeral director."

"Geez Dee. He's one of the most prominent philanthropists in Sunderland. Why the hell would he be involved in all this?"

"As a cover up for his crimes, perhaps to launder his ill-gotten gains? Maybe he's being blackmailed? I don't know boss, but sometimes nice people do bad things."

"I guess they do."

Billy seemed distracted. "Did you have some news for us boss?"

"Sorry, yes. There's another tournament at Ramside Hall next week. Mostly local players but one name stands out. He's a golfer flying in from Gran Canaria. His name is Max Candian."

"This could be another mule boss. We need to watch him and see what happens."

"My thoughts exactly. Let's not rush this case. This guy might lead us straight to the killers. If we spook them now, they could run, and we'll lose everything we've worked for."

"When does he arrive in the country?"

"He must be landing on Sunday. The practice round is Monday, and they play two rounds on Tuesday and Wednesday."

"When does the flight land on Sunday?"

"There's the rub, it gets in at 2am on Monday morning."

"It won't be easy to shadow him at that time-of-day boss. We'll stand out like sore thumbs."

"I'll sort that out, don't you worry. I'll get some of the Newcastle team to track him. Just be ready on Monday to take over at the golf club. I plan to caddy for him in the tournament."

"What time should we be at Ramside?"

"If you can be there by 10am that would be perfect."

"Just a thought boss. I promised myself that if we hadn't solved this case by the end of the week I would hand in my badge."

Billy leaned forward and put his elbows on his desk. "Don't be stupid Karen. You've got this case. The guys out there love you."

"Thanks boss. I'm just not sure I can do this."

Billy got up from his chair and came round to sit on the front of his desk.

"Karen, you're brilliant at this. Look at the progress you've made so far. Forget handing in your badge, I wouldn't accept it anyway. Just get back out there and deliver these lowlifes into their new lives. Behind bars."

Karen looked up at Billy. She smiled. "Thanks boss. Let's give it another week or two then."

"That's the spirit."

Billy held out his hand and Karen ignored it. She gave him a hug instead. She left Billy in his office, stunned and unsure how to respond. He shook his head and went back to his chair as she closed the door.

Picking up the phone, he called the Newcastle station to make the arrangements to have Max Candian shadowed, when he arrived on Monday morning, at Newcastle Airport.

Karen stared at the incident boards; they were full.

Jack walked over and stood beside her. "Did I see you hug the boss?"

"It was a thank you."

"For what?"

"For believing in me. We all need that sometimes."

"Hell, I believe in you too."

Karen put her arm around Jack's shoulder.

"Thank you." She looked around the room at the detectives working away. "Right, that's enough of that, let's get back to work."

"Mick, can we get another incident board?"

"Yes Ma'am. What shall we do with it?"

Karen looked around the office. The view over the Wear was stunning. It was something they all enjoyed. Many times, she had seen members of the team staring across at the view, mulling over some problem or other, or just daydreaming.

There were three windows in the main office.

"Let's put one board in front of each window. We'll focus on the bodies on one, the suspects we have on the middle one and the drugs evidence on the other."

She looked around. There were no objections.

"Cat, can you arrange the evidence on the boards please."

"Yes boss." Cat gave her usual thumbs up.

Karen seemed lost in thought for a moment.

"Jack, Jinx really loved the cat food John brought back from P & P's yesterday. I think we should pop over and buy some more."

"Ma'am the boss said we shouldn't push the bad guys. What if we are recognised there, they probably have CCTV systems?"

"Then perhaps I should go in disguise. Have you something a bit colourful for me to wear?"

After a quick trip to Jack's home to find some suitable clothes, the women parked up outside P & P's Pet Food supplies in the Hylton Park Road industrial estate next to the river.

Jack stayed in the car while Karen got out and walked over to the pet food store. She was wearing red slacks and a yellow jacket over the white shirt she had been wearing for work. On her head she wore a red Sunderland AFC cap. Her sunglasses were a designer brand Jack loved to wear.

She could see herself walking towards the glass doors. It was quite a change, her reflection seemed to call to her, telling her this is how she ought to be. For a second, Gary walked beside her. It was as if five years had never happened, then the doors slid open, and he was gone.

Tears filled her eyes for a second. Grateful for the protection of the sunglasses she put on a brave face and smiled at the young lad behind the counter.

"Do you sell cat food?"

"Yes, of course." He looked up from his phone and glared at her as if she was stupid. He had the countenance of a typical bored teenager, working for the money, annoyed at being out of bed. "There's a wall full of it over there. We sell dog food mainly, but we cater for all pets, there's even fish food in the corner."

Karen made a note of that. Her fish tank was yet to be unpacked. She made her way over to the cat food, picking up a basket on the way. She placed a week's worth of food in the basket, then made her way over to the fish food, adding a small tub of tropical fish flakes to the basket.

Pretending to browse, she passed the empty stand of P and P's own brand dog food before returning to the counter.

"When are you getting more of your special dog food in?"

The bored teenager was already scanning her purchases as she spoke, keen to get her out of the shop and get back to whatever he was doing before she came in.

"The boss says there may be some coming in next week. It's a bit hit and miss. That'll be fifteen pounds and thirty pence."

Karen tapped her card on the machine and asked for the receipt. Her server tutted as if asking for the receipt was a sin.

"Is the dog food popular?"

"Very, I have a list of people waiting for it. Shall I put you on the list?"

Karen thought for a moment, thinking that might be a good idea but not wanting to give her name. "Yes please, it's Dr Laura Rae."

The lad began writing the name down in a notebook by the till.

"Telephone number?"

"Hang on, I've just got a new phone, let me check." She quickly looked up Laura's number and read it out to the lad.

"Fine, we'll call you when we have some available."

As he finished writing he placed the tins and tub of fish food in one of the shops branded carriers along with a leaflet.

"Thank you."

There was no reply, the lad was already back on his mobile phone.

Karen made her way out of the shop and back to the car.

"Got what you wanted?" Jack asked as she sat down.

"I've put Laura down on the list for dog food. I'd better let her know." Karen started typing on the Witches Whatsapp group.

"It suits you." Jack started the engine as they began their drive back to her house, so Karen could get changed.

"What suits me?"

"Colour. It suits you. You should try it."

Karen smiled then went back to typing. Maybe she would, maybe the time was right.

By the time they got back to the station, Karen had formulated an idea. She knocked on Billy's door and walked in.

"Karen, how's it going?"

"Fine boss, just a bit frustrated that we are stuck in limbo while we wait for the next mule to arrive. I've had an idea."

"Go on." Billy picked up the mug of steaming tea from his desk and sat back in his chair.

"I'm pretty sure there is no need to keep Peter Bailey's remains on ice anymore. Could we release the body to Prudence Bailey? She volunteered to pay for his burial."

"What would be the good of that?"

"Two-fold boss. First, we can see how she reacts when they see the condition the body is in. Second, they might think the investigation is easing down if we no longer need the body."

Billy put his cup down on the desk. Karen could almost see the cogs turning in his head, as he tried to work out if this would in any way compromise the case. He didn't want to scupper the efforts being put in to shadow the potential new mule when he arrived in the country.

"I can't see how it would jeopardise next week's mission boss."

"Are you planning to deliver the news to Prudence?"

"Yep."

"OK then, but be careful, keep information about the body to a minimum and brief your doctor friend. I don't want any hints about the investigation to leak out. When the body is collected the room must be clear, no other bodies lying around."

"I'm sure that will be fine. I'll talk with her to ensure nothing slips out."

"Good. Let me know how it goes."

"Will do, boss."

Karen got up and was about to open the door.

"Oh, one more thing Karen. The Spanish police are watching our potential mule. I thought it would be good to know who is handling him from that end. Apparently, he's been seen spending time with a chap called Joe Higgs who lives out there. Maybe Cat could check if he has any links to the northeast?"

"I'll get her straight on it boss. Good thinking."

"I have my moments," Billy laughed, as he picked up his pen and got back to working on a heavily edited piece of text on his desk.

"If you need any help with anything like that boss, just let me know."

"Thanks Karen, I'll bear that in mind. This is the press release for the media. I'll run it past you when I've finished chopping it about."

Karen smiled, happy to be appreciated and trusted with such a job. She closed the door quietly behind her and went back to her desk.

"Any developments?" The comment was aimed at the room in general.

Cat put up her hand.

"We've had some luck with the car that parked outside your house. The false plates had been spotted in Newcastle and Gateshead. That was on the night of the attack. It seems they came in from over the Tyne."

"Bloody Mags," John muttered.

"They might not have been from Newcastle. They might have come from Scotland for all we know," Karen replied, feeling a bit defensive towards her old patch.

"True, but chances are they came from Newcastle. Maybe they were hired in by the gang here?" Mick suggested.

Karen looked across at John. "Do we know who they were yet?"

"I think there's a backlog with the pathologist Ma'am."

Karen laughed. "Well, we have been overloading her with bodies. I just mentioned to the boss that I'm planning on releasing Peter Bailey's body to Prudence. Jack and I will pop over after lunch. I want us to watch how they react and what they do with the remains. It will mean some surveillance work guys. Anyone got anything on this weekend? Just in case we need some feet on the ground."

"Count me out boss, I'm needed at home."

"I understand Mick. Anyone else?"

Everyone else seemed happy with the idea of earning some overtime.

"Good, I'll let you know if you will be needed. When's the new incident board arriving."

"It is being delivered this afternoon."

"Thanks Mick, you're a star."

Karen looked over at Jack. "Fancy a cuppa with Laura before we head over to Whitburn?"

"Sounds good to me."

"Come on then, let's go."

## Chapter Eighteen

Karen drove this time while Jack messaged Laura to check she would be happy to meet them. She messaged back that she was putting the kettle on, which meant in her case the Barista machine was hot and ready for them.

The morgue looked like they were in a war zone. Bodies were laid out on the table and several sets of remains were in boxes, stacked against one wall. Two trolleys stood along another wall with bodies under white sheets.

Laura ushered the women through to her sanctuary.

Karen explained her plan to release Peter Bailey's body, and asked Laura if she would be comfortable clearing all the other remains away for when the body was collected.

"I can easily hide all the boxes of bones, but they'll expect to see other bodies. The dead guys in the car were in the news so their presence would be unsurprising."

"Fair enough."

Karen cradled her cappuccino in her hands. She always found it chilly in the morgue and that spilled over into the sanctuary. The coffee was warming, forming a barrier between her and the death lying just through the door.

Jack asked the awkward question. "When do you think you'll have some answers as regards the men in the car."

Laura looked down into her drink. "I've let you guys down, haven't I."

Karen and Jack looked at each other.

"Where's that come from? You haven't let anyone down, you've been amazing," Karen replied, trying to reassure her friend.

"I'm keeping you waiting. Time is precious guys. Other things might be happening while we are sitting here. Someone might die and it will be my fault."

Karen reached out and held her friend's hand.

"If something like that does happen, it's not your fault. Bad people do bad things. Our job is to catch them, if that takes time, then so be it. But if they kill again, then that's not on you, or us. That's on them."

Jack stepped in, grabbing Laura's other hand as she watched the tears stream down her face.

"When we do catch them, we need to make sure that the charges stick. You, rushing, might mean that you make a mistake. That could lead to us losing a conviction."

"Jack's right, take whatever time you need, and leave the messy stuff to us. Asking you to do this, will delay you some more, but we wouldn't ask if it wasn't important. Just let us know how they react when they see the body."

Laura looked up through reddened eyes. "I can do better than that. We have CCTV throughout the morgue. I'll send you the video of the collection so you can see for yourselves."

She squeezed her friend's hands. "Thanks guys. I will get you all the information you need. I should have some more details for you by Monday."

"Just don't worry about it. Are you up for brunch again this Sunday? I'm afraid we are all working tomorrow. It would be nice to make it a regular event once all this is over."

Laura smiled at her friends. "Are you sure Karen? I could come in and do some more work on Sunday."

"Laura, we all need a break. Let's enjoy Sunday brunch at Betty's."

"Karen's right. Come on, the witches need to meet. Every witch needs a coven."

Laura laughed her cackling laugh and the mood lifted. They all hugged each other, and, in that moment, Karen felt the tingle she always felt when they were together.

Once they had finished their drinks, Karen and Jack left to visit Prudence Bailey. On the way they stopped at a small café at the centre of Whitburn Village for a bit of lunch.

As they sat, enjoying their toasties and tea, Karen asked Jack how she thought Prudence would react to their visit.

Jack took a bite of her cheese and ham toastie, giving her a few seconds to think about the question.

"I think she'll be ultra-cool. This is a charity job for her so she will take it in her stride."

"Hmmm, I'm not so sure. I am thinking she's probably forgotten all about the offer. This may come as a surprise."

"Guess we'll see. Changing the subject, how did you feel about wearing some colour earlier."

Karen smiled. "It was good. Maybe it's time I changed my wardrobe."

Jack clapped her hands. "That sounds like a good reason to go shopping."

Karen held up her hands. "Hold your horses, Jack. Let me check out what I've got at home first, and by the way I hate shopping."

"You hate shopping? Maybe your type of shopping, you haven't been shopping with me yet. See what you've got and then maybe Sunday afternoon I'll introduce you to shopping, Jack style."

Karen laughed. "We'll see. Come on, let's drink up and pay Prudence a visit."

The couple walked along Front Street as far as the white house. They walked up the short path to the front door and Jack knocked three times.

A young girl opened the door, a different one to the last girl they had met.

"We're here to see Ms Prudence Bailey."

"Who shall I say is calling?" The girl had rehearsed the phrase as her accent was not local and her words were faltering.

"Tell her it's the police."

Before the girl could do anything, Prudence appeared behind her.

"Get out of the way." Prudence pushed past the girl and smiled at Karen.

"So nice to see you again, officers. Come in, come in."

Prudence sent the girl away to make coffee, as her dog padded up to her across the marble floor. Prudence scooped the dog into her arms and led the way to the lounge which looked out over the back garden.

"Please take a seat."

The three women all sat, exactly as they had the last time they were there. The dog snuggled in against her mistress and went straight to sleep. Prudence stroked the dogs head as she spoke again.

"How can I help you?"

"Thanks for seeing us Ms Bailey." Prudence smiled at the correct use of her name as Karen took the lead. "Last time we were here, you offered to help with Peter's funeral if needed."

Prudence nodded, remembering her offer.

"Well, no-one has come forward to claim the body and we have no reason to keep Peter any longer. Would you still be happy to arrange for his burial?"

"Cremation dear, Peter always wanted to be cremated. Of course, I would be happy to help, it's the least I can do. We may not have seen eye to eye, but I wouldn't like to see him abandoned to a pauper's grave."

The girl arrived with the same coffee set on a tray as last time, together with a plate of biscuits. Jack's eyes lit up at the sight of the tasty morsels she had eaten last time they had visited.

Prudence seemed totally unfazed by their presence and began pouring the drinks. "Help yourselves to biscuits," she added, as she poured.

"I have a close friend who is in the funeral business. I am sure between us we can give him a good send off."

Karen lifted her cup as she watched Jack pick up two biscuits and place them on the edge of her saucer. Then she too sipped her coffee.

"That's a good cup of coffee," Jack muttered, as she put her cup down, and started to unwrap a biscuit.

Both Prudence and Karen smiled as they watched Jack attack the biscuit.

"Have you had any more thoughts on why this may have happened to Peter?"

"I'm sorry Detective Inspector, I have no idea why someone would want to kill Peter. I feel so sorry that he has ended up this way. He seems to have had such a torrid time since we parted."

Karen looked around. "And you've done so well in contrast, he must have been quite jealous."

"I was lucky Detective Inspector. My parents sadly died young and left me this house, and a hefty sum of money. If we had stayed together then Peter could have been part of all this."

Prudence sipped her drink. "I'm not even sure Peter knew how well I was getting on; we had no contact with each other."

"You're quite high profile, I am sure he must have seen your picture in the paper at least." Jack spoke with half a biscuit in her mouth which seemed to upset Prudence by the face she pulled.

"Possibly, but he never asked for anything. If he had, I may well have helped him. Arranging his funeral is the least I can do."

"Did you have some good times?" Karen enquired.

"We did, Detective Inspector. When we first got married, he was loving and caring, but gambling and drink took hold and after five years we were separated. There was no way back."

"I am sorry to hear that. I've known some alcoholics in my time. It is a terrible addiction."

All three women seemed to take a moment to gather their thoughts.

Jack decided to change the subject.

"How are puppy sales going?"

"They are all spoken for. In a few more weeks my babies will be leaving their nests and we can start the process all over again. One of the little beauties is going to Norway."

Prudence seemed quite proud of doing her bit for export earnings and sat a bit taller in her seat. The mannerism didn't go unnoticed by Karen, who started to doubt whether the successful businesswoman in front of her had anything to do with the terrible deaths they were investigating.

"I think I should warn you Prudence, that Peter's body is not complete. He has been treated very badly."

Prudence put down her cup. She looked shocked.

"How do you mean?"

"Parts of him were missing when he was found. Perhaps you could warn the undertakers as they might be shocked when they see him."

Prudence seemed shocked, which surprised the detectives. She grabbed a biscuit, and her hand shook as she tried to unwrap it.

"How could someone do that to another human being?"

"I don't know Prudence, but it was a huge shock to us when we found him." Karen took pity on the woman and topped up her cup with the remains of the coffee in the pot.

"Thank you, Karen. I will let my friend know so his men are prepared for what they are given."

"Just get them to call Dr Rae at the Royal Sunderland Hospital and she will arrange a time for the collection."

Jack picked up another biscuit just as Karen made a move to leave. Instead of putting it back she put it in her pocket. Prudence didn't seem to notice, she appeared to be in a state of shock.

"Thanks for coffee and biscuits Prudence, stay where you are, we'll make our own way out."

"Thank you," Prudence said quietly.

The detectives made their way out of the house and walked back towards the car.

"She's either a very good actor or that came as a complete shock."

Jack looked at her partner. "I think it was the latter. Even if she had something to do with his murder, she had no idea how his body was treated. This gets weirder and weirder."

"Let's stay in the car for a bit and watch to see if anything happens."

They had sat in the car checking emails and messages for about half an hour, when Phil Brookes drove up and almost ran up to the house.

Jack unwrapped the delicious biscuit she had stolen from the dog breeder. "Now that looks to me like she has phoned a friend and he has come running."

Karen agreed. "That tells me she is upset and he has come to comfort her. Come on, let's get back to the office."

As they drove back through Sunderland it started to rain. It was only the second time Karen had seen rain since she moved to the city. She had looked up the origin of the name when she was thinking of applying for the job.

Someone had told her the name for the city was derived from Land of the Sun, and up to that moment it had lived up to that name. She now knew different, of course. The real answer was far less glamourous, just like real life at times.

She thought of what her Nan would have said as the rain lashed against the car window, sending the automatic wipers into a frenzy. *'The garden will be thankful for a drink.'* She could picture her Nan speaking the words while looking out at her immaculate garden, which she had maintained until the day she died.

Nan was long gone now. Karen still missed her so much.

They pulled into Sunderland North just as the heavy rain began to ease off. The women ran to the front door of the station to avoid getting too wet, bursting through the door, much to Tom Moore's amusement.

"A bit of rain won't kill you, ladies," he said with a smile.

Karen smiled back. "Maybe not, but sopping wet hair and mascara running down your face isn't a good look, Tom."

"Thankfully I don't have that problem Ma'am." Tom ran his hand over his new buzz cut, smiling as he did.

"It suits you, Tom," Karen added before following Jack up the stairs.

"Stop flirting with the desk sergeant, Ma'am," Jack laughed at her friend who started to redden noticeably. "What with Laura giving you a smacker and the way you are with Tom, you're like a cat on heat."

"Jack, for goodness sake, I'm no such thing." Karen was laughing as they walked into the office.

Billy's office was empty, but everyone was working away until they heard Karen laughing.

The first thing she noticed was the view of the Wear and the Spire Bridge had disappeared. Three incident boards blocked the windows. Cat was putting the finishing touches to the new layout of the evidence they had so far.

"Wow, Cat, good job."

"Everyone helped Ma'am, it wasn't just me."

"Don't listen to her Ma'am, it was all Cat. We did try to help but she knew exactly what she wanted to do. We just got in the way."

"Thanks Mick. Don't be so modest Cat. You've done a great job."

Cat reddened and then rushed back to hide behind her screens.

Karen and Jack perused the incident boards, noting how well Cat had laid out everything they knew so far.

They both stopped in front of the pictures of Prudence and Phil Brookes.

Karen turned to face the team. Everyone was watching to see what news Karen and Jack might have.

"We've been to see Prudence and asked her to arrange Peter's funeral. We warned her that parts of the body were missing, and she was visibly shocked. Jack and I both agree there is now some doubt as to the level of her involvement. We watched the house for a while. Within half an hour of our visit, Phil Brookes rushed in to see her."

"It could be a cover Ma'am, to try and put us off the scent."

"If it is Mick, it was one of the best acting jobs I've ever seen."

"Where does that leave us?"

"Our thoughts exactly, John. Where does that leave us? My gut still tells me they are involved in some way, but even the boss is questioning why they would be involved in such serious crimes."

Everyone seemed disheartened at the latest news. Karen knew it was down to her to gee them up.

"Let's not get our knickers in a twist here guys. We've got a lot of evidence on the boards and there will be more to come. Dr Rae has bodies piling up, yet to be processed and she will be keeping a watch on how Peter's body is collected. Added to that we have a potential mule arriving early on Monday morning. That should provide us with some valuable intelligence."

"What shall we do in the interim Ma'am."

Karen looked at her watch. "Well, it's almost five. Let's call it a day and come back refreshed tomorrow. I'll give some thought to the case over night and then allocate some work streams tomorrow morning. Is that, OK?"

"Sounds good to me Ma'am," Jordan replied for everyone, as the exodus from the office began. "If you need any help just let me know."

"Thanks Jordan, that's much appreciated. Mick, we'll see you on Monday."

Mick gave Karen a thumbs up as he left the office.

As usual the only three left, were Cat, Jack and Karen. Cat was busy on her computer behind her screens as Jack and Karen stood looking at the incident boards, as if waiting for inspiration to come.

Cat put her hand up, but the gesture went unnoticed. She coughed quietly which caused Jack to turn around.

"What is it, Cat?"

"A report has just come in from SOCO Ma'am. It's their report on the cottage in Ripon Street."

"Can you summarise what it says?"

"I've just had a quick scan; I'll work a bit late and circulate a more detailed report tomorrow. In short, they've found evidence of drugs all over the downstairs of the property, especially in the kitchen."

"What about upstairs?" Jack asked.

"There was no sign of drug activity upstairs, but as you guessed, there is blood on two of the chairs and all over the floor. The rooms had been well cleaned but there was considerable evidence of blood splatter. In their words, individuals had been aggressively beaten in both those rooms."

They all paused, taking in the news. Jack asked the question they were all thinking. "But why? And who were the victims?"

"We have some blood samples; I may be able to match them. I'll let you know tomorrow."

"Thanks Cat. Are you sure you are OK working late?"

"I'm fine Ma'am. I enjoy it and, let's face it, I have precious little else to do."

"You could come out with us, Cat?"

Karen looked at Jack. *Us*, she thought to herself. *I don't go out.*

"That would be nice." Cat replied.

"Excellent, we'll arrange a girly night out next week. I'll ask Rachel if she'd like to come with us."

Karen smiled, not wanting to dampen Cat's enthusiasm.

"Right, I'm off." Jack put on her jacket. "I'll see you in the morning. I'm going to the cinema tonight."

"What are you watching?" Cat asked.

"The latest Dr Strange from Marvel. It should be good."

"I like Marvel movies."

"Why don't you come along?"

"Not tonight, I've got all this work to do. Maybe next time," Cat replied while typing on her keyboard.

"That's a date." Jack smiled and made her way towards the office door.

"I'll see you both in the morning."

Karen waved goodbye to her friend and went back to her desk. Instead of getting ready to leave, she flicked her computer on and started to read the Ripon Street report. It ran to well over twenty pages.

## Chapter Nineteen

That evening Karen sat, pad in hand, in front of her TV, trying to work out how best to proceed with the case. A bit of her wished Billy hadn't persuaded her to stay on. At least then it would all be over for her tomorrow; she would be out of danger. She looked at her battered hands, then felt the still raw wound on the side of her head.

As it stood, she needed to push on with the investigation and hope next week they would get the break they needed.

She often thought of her Nan in moments like this. What would she have done in a similar situation? Her Nan had been a Wren in the second world war and spent much of her service time working in intelligence, trying to second guess what the enemy was planning, to make sure the allies were ready for any eventuality.

Karen wished she had inherited her Nan's problem-solving abilities. Right now, she was struggling for inspiration and Jinx curled up on her lap wasn't helping. She sipped her second cup of tea of the evening and flicked the channels on her TV to look for something to watch.

As she often did when nothing took her fancy, she put on a DVD of Les Miserables. She knew DVDs were old tech, but she had a few special discs which she refused to give up.

The harrowing story of Victor Hugo's Jean Valjean both haunted her and uplifted her at the same time. He had committed a crime, so small it seemed ridiculous these days, yet his punishment seemed never ending as he sought to live his life. Despite all that he had to overcome he was a kind and generous man and changed the lives of many people, for the better.

Her mind thought of Prudence, maybe she was a little like Jean Valjean. Maybe pursuing her like they were, was wrong, and they should leave her carry on helping all the charities she supported.

Putting herself in the position of Inspector Javert made her seem inflexible. Yet, like Javert she was driven. She had to get her man, or woman, or both.

Her sleep that night was troubled. Karen had planned to resign, she had accepted her fate, yet tomorrow was going to be just another day. Somehow it didn't feel right.

*Saturday 28th May 2022*

As the alarm roused her from her dreams, she stretched, almost knocking Jinx off the bed. With her wakening, came the doubt that she could lead the team to success with this case. Her body felt heavy as she showered, made her breakfast and prepared for the day.

She reached for her black jacket and paused.

Making her way into the spare bedroom, she was greeted by rows of unopened boxes, including four of the wardrobe type with capacity for storing hanging garments.

Taking a Swiss army knife, which had been left on one of the boxes when she had moved in, she cut the tape of each container in turn then opened them to check the contents. It was like a Pandora's box, full of dresses and jackets of all colours. It was an instant reminder of her old life.

Each garment brought back memories of fun times with her husband. Some Gary had bought for her, others they had bought together when hunting through charity shops, one of their guilty pleasures when visiting new places.

As her hand brushed along a row of jackets, she settled on one, it was pale green. She pulled it out of the box and tried it on, walking into her bedroom as she went.

Karen looked at herself in the full-length mirror built into the back of her wardrobe door. She brushed a fleck of cotton off the jacket. It fitted perfectly. For a moment she saw Gary looking over her shoulder. He smiled and nodded his approval.

She found an old make-up bag which was almost empty. A lip stain seemed still usable, and she applied a bit of colour. The rest of the products had either turned to powder or solidified with the passing of the years. She threw the bag and all its contents in the bin. A trip to the chemist was in order.

It was time for a new start, but that would have to wait, she needed to get to work.

As she walked through the station entrance, Tom Moore looked up from the reception desk and smiled.

"Looking good Ma'am."

"Thanks Tom, thought I'd put a bit of colour on today."

"Special occasion?"

"It's a Saturday. That seems reason enough." Karen was smiling as she headed up to the office.

When she walked into the office the room went quiet. "Blimey Ma'am, you've brightened the place up a bit."

"Thanks John. I decided to open some of the boxes in my spare room. I found this old jacket. I thought I'd give it a run out."

"Suits you Ma'am," Cat piped up from behind her screens.

"Right, everybody, when the DCI comes in, we'll have a briefing session. I want everyone up to speed before the shadowing operation starts this weekend."

After staring at the incident boards for a few minutes, Karen sat down at her desk and fired up her computer. There were a few emails from Cat and Dr Rae.

Dr Rae had identified DNA from two of the bodies recovered from the river. There were no matches on the police database, so Cat was sending the details to international contacts in various forces across Europe.

Cat had also been searching missing persons files with any links to the drug trade. She had identified five people who had gone missing over the last few years with links to the northeast.

Jack looked across from her desk.

"This is interesting. We have a DNA hit on a missing guy from the Netherlands. He was last seen leaving a small marina near Veere in his cabin cruiser on a fishing trip over a year ago."

"I thought our abandoned boat came from Belgium?" Karen replied.

"It could have left Belgium, headed to Veere, then made its way across the North Sea to Sunderland. Or it could have visited Belgium to pick up a consignment before heading back to Veere."

"That's a long old trip Jack. He must have made his way to somewhere like Norfolk then headed up the coast."

"Not impossible. It means he must have had good reason to come here," Jack surmised.

"Like someone looking to deliver a load of drugs."

Jack simply nodded.

Billy burst through the door.

"Happy Saturday detectives. How is everybody?"

"All good, boss," Karen replied. "We were waiting for you so we can have a team briefing before our drugs mule gets here. Is that OK with you?"

"Sounds like a plan. Let me hang up my coat. Nice jacket by the way."

Billy opened the door to his office and threw his jacket on to his chair. He came back and stood in front of the three incident boards.

Karen joined him. "Do you want to go first, boss. Maybe tell us what is happening on Sunday and early next week. Also, anything else you may have picked up over the last few days."

"Thank you, Detective Inspector."

Billy looked around at his captive audience and smiled.

"As you know we have a suspected drugs mule, Max Candian, coming in from Gran Canaria in the early hours of Monday morning. Newcastle have allocated three undercover detectives from their drugs unit to watch out for him and monitor him as he passes through the airport."

After a brief pause to gather his thoughts, he continued.

"Outside there will be two unmarked cars from the fast response team ready to follow him. Obviously, we don't know if he will take a taxi or is being met."

"What time will he be playing golf, boss?" Jordan asked.

"He'll probably play his practice round in the afternoon. I've arranged it so that I am around to caddy for him. I'm hoping I'll get some intel that way."

"And maybe a golf lesson on the way, boss," Jordan suggested.

They all laughed, as did Billy. "You never know it might improve my handicap. But seriously, I hope I can find out why he buys new clubs, if he does, and what happened to his old set."

"That's great, boss. Let's hope we get something useful. I also hope we keep the poor guy from ending up in a shopping trolley at the bottom of the River Wear," Karen replied as she surveyed the room.

Everyone was now focussed on her. Her heart started to speed up as she took in all their faces. These were her team, her friends, her new family, but she still was nervous when she took centre stage.

"Last week I made a promise. I promised that if we hadn't solved this case by Friday, I would hand in my badge. Today I break that promise and make a new one. We will catch these criminals. There's no if, we will solve this case as a team."

Her words were received with enthusiastic nods from around the room.

"We have already hit them hard. We've found their safe house, found the bodies of the people they have killed, they've lost several of their team and above all they know we are close."

"Damn right," Billy added in agreement. Karen continued.

"They have injured and threatened me, maybe they were going to kill me, I don't know. Yet, here we all are, still chasing and ready to finish this off."

She looked at the Boards again then turned back.

"We still don't know who the driving force is, but we believe that Prudence and Phil are involved somehow. Next week we will have some answers. With luck we will solve this case once and for all. This will be a case we will all look back on with pride."

The room erupted with applause, cheers and whoops. Even Billy put his hands together in appreciation.

He walked forward to the centre of the room and called for hush.

"Not so much a briefing but just about the finest motivational speech I've ever heard. Let's get to it guys. I for one don't want to be worrying about these killers for much longer."

"Let's start by getting a brew in. Who wants what?" John offered. After taking orders, he took Jordan along to give him a hand.

Billy put his hand in his pocket and put a £20 note on the table. "The Greggs are on me at lunchtime."

"Heck, I think I've died and gone to heaven." Jack laughed as she spoke.

Everyone else got back on their computers and continued to look for the leads that might break the case. They all wanted to be the one to achieve the ultimate breakthrough.

"Something has been bothering me, Jack," Karen leaned across her desk towards her friend. "We didn't ask Prudence whether she knew about Ripon Street. As a director of the charity that owned it, she should be aware of the property. It might be worth a phone call."

"Definitely worth a call. Do you want me to give her a ring?"

"No, I'll do it. I think she has a thing about rank and may talk to me more than she'll talk to you, no offence of course."

"None taken." Jack smiled at Karen as the DI picked up the phone to make the call.

The number Karen had was for Prudence's mobile, so the call went straight through to her.

"Ms Bailey, it's Detective Inspector Karen Dee from the Sunderland Police, do you have a minute to answer a quick question?"

"Karen, lovely to hear your voice, of course, what do you want to know?"

"Thank you. During our investigations we had cause to visit a cottage in Ripon Street near Roker. Do you know the property I'm talking about?"

"I don't know anyone living around there. What's that to do with me?"

"It's just that it is owned by one of the charities you are a director of so I thought you might know of it."

There was a slight pause at the end of the phone.

"Is that the 'Providing Homes for the Helpless' charity?"

"That's the one."

"I think that charity has around thirty homes around the city. They are principally for people who have fallen under the radar, in terms of benefits. I wasn't aware of that one, but I'm not sure where they all are. I don't play an active role in that charity."

"Who is the main organiser?"

"There is a team that manages the properties and arranges the placing of people in them. You can always visit their office. They have a base in the city. It's in a block of apartments we own and manage. It overlooks Mowbray Park. I'll text you the address."

"Thanks Ms Bailey, you've been a great help."

"Prudence please."

"Sorry, thank you Prudence, if I need anything else, I'll be in touch."

"By the way, I've had a cancellation on one of my pups, can I interest you in a dog."

Karen laughed. "No thank you. I don't think my cat would appreciate a puppy in the house."

Prudence laughed. "Worth a try. Bye Inspector."

The line went dead, and Karen looked across at Jack.

"Let's have another look at that charity Jack. I want to know who all the management committee members are, and let's see if we can find a list of the properties they own."

"I'm on it."

Karen sat back in her chair, and pondered how the links they had, might all fit together.

With everyone hard at work, Karen decided to pop out to Greggs for the lunch run. She took everyone's orders. As the sun was shining, and parking near Greggs was a nightmare, she walked from the station to the Green and stood in the queue for the popular bakery.

She paid for the food with Billy's twenty-pound note and bought herself a pack of stotties to put in the freezer. They were always handy to have if she felt the need for a stottie sandwich.

Southwick always offered a glimpse of the rich tapestry life had to offer. From the beggar outside the bookies, to the housewives, chatting at the bus stop, and much more besides, Southwick encapsulated it all. The impressive war memorial was laden with tributes, and the little café in the centre of the Green did not have an empty table. It was bedecked with bunting ready for the platinum jubilee and looked a joy compared to some of the run-down properties in the area.

Several people said hello as she walked back to the station, highlighting the warm-hearted nature of the people of the northeast. She put Billy's change in the beggar's cup.

Back at the station she handed out the lunch, having given a sausage roll to Tom on the front desk, even though she hadn't asked him if he wanted anything.

More information had been coming in from various lines of enquiries while she had been gone, including a report from Dr Rae on the two men that had been killed in her failed kidnapping.

She passed those details on to Cat who quickly established links to two known criminals based in Newcastle. Cat sent over the full report to Karen who quickly shared it with Jack and the team.

She called over to John.

"John, can you ask the Newcastle station to search their database and see if they can find anything relevant to our case. Give them the details of the two dead guys."

"Aye, Ma'am, will do."

Jack sent over a file from the Charities website. "Here's some information on the charity. There's a picture at the top of their Facebook page which show's all the team members. If you scroll through their page, there's an update every time they buy a new property or house a homeless person. I'm compiling a list of addresses."

"Thanks Jack."

Karen looked at the link, clicking on the photo and expanding it so she could look at all the faces. As she panned through the twenty or so people, she spotted Prudence and Phil at the back. In front of them was Jess, Phil's son. She didn't recognise anyone else.

Her phone pinged as the address for the Charity's office came through from Prudence.

"Jack let's head over to their office this afternoon and find out who all these people are. They should be able to provide us with a full list of addresses, so don't waste any more time on that."

By now the assorted pasties, bakes and sausage rolls had all been washed down with teas and coffees.

Karen and Jack grabbed their jackets and headed out to the car park. This time they drove across the Spire Bridge and turned left towards the city.

# Chapter Twenty

As they approached the address they were given, Karen made a mental note to visit Mowbray Park. It looked like somewhere she would enjoy jogging around. Jack also mentioned it held the winter gardens and the Sunderland Museum. She was keen to learn more about her new home and thought this was probably a good place to start.

Luckily, they found a space opposite the building they were looking for. They got out of the car and dodged the traffic as they crossed the road. A short flight of steps brought them to a front door. Next to it was a small plaque with the name of the charity etched into a square of blue plastic.

"I guess this is the place," Karen muttered as she rang the bell.

A disembodied voice crackled over the built-in speaker. "Who is it?"

"It's the police. We're here to talk to the manager."

"He's not in."

"Then we'll speak to you."

There was a muttered curse from the other end, cut short as the door buzzed open.

Karen and Jack walked into the musty smelling hall, trying to ignore the dingy feeling and obvious lack of investment in the property.

The two women looked at each other. Karen raised an eyebrow. A door at the end of the corridor had a sign stuck on it with those gold and black squares you can buy in all good DIY stores. It was supposed to read RECEPTION, but someone had decided to steal the I and the N.

They knocked on the door and walked in. "Is this recepto?" Karen asked with her favourite winning smile.

"Very funny. If I had a quid for every time someone said that I'd have two quid." The man behind the yellow, old fashioned high counter did not seem amused.

"Not very busy then?" Jack was curious as to why he seemed so jaundiced.

"You're the first people I've seen today and no doubt you're here to make my life a misery."

"Only if you've done something wrong Mr…"

"I'm Brian. Brian Dodds. I look after the place when the Manager is out. He's out a lot."

"Nice to meet you Brian, I'm Detective Inspector Karen Dee and this is Detective Sergeant Jacqueline White. We call her Jack."

Brian held out a hand and they both took turns to shake it.

"I've an office out the back, would you like to come through and have a coffee?"

"That would be lovely, Brian. Lead the way."

Brian lifted a section of the counter to let the officers through into the reception area, which was littered with rubbish. The office wasn't much better, although it did have a basic looking coffee machine.

After offering them seats around a small table, Brian popped into a basic looking kitchen to find two clean mugs, then made them a coffee each, before joining them at the table.

"You're not having one, Brian?"

"You've had the last of the milk. I'll get some tomorrow and bring it in on Monday. That's if my wages go in, let's say I wouldn't call working here a steady living."

Karen eyed him carefully over her mug of coffee. His lank black hair looked in need of a wash and his fingernails looked stained and dirty. His skin was surprisingly pale against his black hair. His eyes were his remarkable feature. They were piercing and a shade of pale blue. They put her in mind of husky dogs for some strange reason.

She was momentarily distracted and almost missed his question.

"So how can I help you?"

"Sorry, yes, we would like a list of all the properties which the charity has on its books, and if possible, a list of all the staff."

Karen showed him the picture from their Facebook page using her phone.

"That's a bit out of date now, I'm afraid. Most of them have moved on and there's not that many of us left. We have a couple of odd job guys who go around and maintain the properties when the tenants report a problem. Other than that, it's just me and Owen."

"Is that the Manager?"

"Yes, Detective Sergeant. He's rarely here. His main job seems to be liaising with our sponsors and making sure we have the funds to keep going. I do everything else."

"Your sponsors?"

"They are the businesses that provide most of our funding." He took Karen's phone and pointed to Prudence and Phil.

Karen nodded. "I understand."

"Except they seem hell bent in buying new properties rather than spend money on the maintenance of the one's we've got. All we ever seem to do is patch up any problems. You can see that this place hasn't seen a paintbrush in a very long time."

"Do you know anyone else in this picture?"

Brian pointed out the two odd job men and then pointed at Jess.

"How is Jess involved?"

"He sometimes brings paperwork in from his dad, and from time to time he has brought in people he has found on the street and asks us to home them in one of the properties. I'll print out a list of them for you now."

Brian went over to an ancient looking computer and called up a file which he sent to an equally ancient looking printer.

"I'm surprised Jess is involved in housing people," Jack whispered.

Karen looked at Jack, then at her phone. "Maybe he has a bigger role in all of this than we thought?"

The whirring of the printer put an end to that conversation, as a piece of A4 gradually emerged from the machine. It had lists of text which filled the page from top to bottom.

Brian pulled out the piece of paper and handed it over to Karen.

"Here you go."

Karen scanned down the page until she spotted the property they knew about.

"This one in Ripon Street. Have you ever been there?"

"When it was bought a few years ago I went to check it over. It was a nice little cottage if I remember correctly. An old lady had lived there and had kept it clean and tidy."

"Have you had any issues with the property or the tenant recently?"

Brian looked Karen straight in the eye. His gaze sure and steady. "We put a disabled and virtually blind guy in there two years ago. I've not heard anything from him or about the cottage since."

"Where did you find the tenant?"

Brian, looked to the ceiling, sitting back in his chair, trying to recall the detail requested. Then he remembered. "He was one of Jess's. He found him begging near Keel Square and decided we should try to help him out. He's been a good tenant, quiet as a mouse."

"Well, your good tenant just killed himself when we went round to see him." Karen fell short of giving Brian all the details as she wanted to see how he reacted. The shock of the news hit him hard.

"Flaming heck. Why would he do that?"

"That's what we are trying to find out, Brian. Make a note that the property is a crime scene, please don't try and gain access. We'll let you know when you can have it back. Is that, OK?"

"Understood. The poor man."

Karen made to leave, and Jack joined her. "Thank you for the coffee, Brian, and good luck with getting paid. If you think of anything else that might be relevant, just get in touch." Karen handed him one of her new cards.

Brian looked at it, with blank eyes.

"Maybe I'll spend some time next week going around all the properties to check if everyone is OK."

"I wouldn't do that just yet. We'll be knocking on doors next week, so just relax, and let us do the work for you. If we see any problems, we'll let you know."

Brian seemed puzzled and looked like he wanted to ask more questions, but he decided against it. He just nodded his acknowledgement and watched as the two detectives let themselves out of the building.

He sat at the table in his office and looked at Karen's business card. Brian was worried, not too worried, but he knew there were difficult times ahead. He picked up the phone. He had to warn Owen.

Karen and Jack dodged the traffic to get back to the car. Once seated Karen looked at the list of properties. The page had come from a spreadsheet so she could easily see there were thirty-four properties on the list. They were in alphabetical order, with fields to cover their address, date purchased, purchase price and current tenant.

This was gold dust for their investigation.

As soon as they were back in the office, she gave the list to Cat to feed into their system, creating a database of their own, which they could interrogate, and add to, when each property was visited.

Karen looked at her watch. The day was almost done. There was precious little chance anything interesting would happen this late on a Saturday afternoon, so once Cat had added the spreadsheet to their internal network, she decided to call it a day.

She stood up and walked to the centre of the room.

"Thanks for all your hard work, guys, it's been a productive week. We've just obtained a list of all the properties that are owned by the charity that owns the Ripon Street property. Next week we'll be doing some door knocking to see if there are more dens like Ripon Street out there."

There was a quiet groan around the room.

"I'll get uniform to help, don't worry. There are far too many for us to handle, and anyway, we are going to be busy around the golf course at the beginning of the week. Get some well-earned rest and I'll see you all bright and early on Monday."

"Coming for a swift half, Ma'am?" Jordan asked as he headed for the door.

"When this case is done. I've got a few things I want to look at before I leave, but you go and enjoy yourselves. Maybe this time next week, we can all raise a glass to a job well done."

Jordan smiled. "Sounds like a plan. Have a good weekend Ma'am."

"You too Jordan."

As the detectives filed out of the office, Karen looked again at her list. At least two of the properties were in the Southwick and Witherwack areas. She decided to at least have a passing look at them before Monday.

"Don't forget brunch at Betty's tomorrow," Jack shouted from the hallway, as she was swept along by the other detectives.

"I wouldn't miss it for the world Jack. Have a good evening and I'll see you in the morning."

\*\*\*\*\*

While the detectives had been working, Max Candian was having a great time. He had been invited down to the Marina at Mogan, in Gran Canaria, to a party on the boat owned by Joe Higgs. It was a fabulous boat, with a huge deck out the back which had been covered with tables, each containing food or alcohol. Champagne seemed to be the order of the day.

Once everyone was on board, they sailed out of the Marina into the flat calm waters surrounding Gran Canaria on that beautiful spring day. Dolphins seemed to be everywhere, although all but Max seemed completely uninterested by the antics of the beautiful creatures that surrounded the boat.

Finally, about three miles from the harbour the boat stopped, and some brave souls donned their bathing suits and jumped in for a swim.

Max watched enviously. He wasn't a great swimmer.

"Not going in for a dip?" It was Joe Higgs. He had spotted the young man standing on his own and had come over for a chat.

"Not for me Senor Higgs. I am not a good swimmer."

"Joe, please. I am glad you could come along today. We felt it would be nice to give you a bit of a send-off before you head to England for the golf tournament."

"You have been very kind to me, Joe. I will never forget what you have done."

A momentary look of sadness seemed to cross Joe's face.

"It's nothing Max. Just enjoy the moment. You never know when it might be your last."

Joe handed Max a new glass of champagne.

"Let's hope that won't be for a long time," Max replied, clinking glasses with the big Englishman.

A man dressed in black came up from below decks at that moment. Max thought he looked so out of place amongst all the scantily dressed partygoers.

As he watched, the man looked his way and smiled. He smiled back, raising his glass, before taking another refreshing gulp of the champagne.

He staggered slightly, grabbing hold of the boat rail.

"I think I have had too much of this fizz, Joe. I'm feeling a bit, how you say, woozy."

"I think we all are Max, it's the heat, the motion of the boat and the champagne. Don't worry, you'll be fine. Maybe we'll go downstairs where it is cooler, and you can have a rest."

"Thanks Joe."

Joe helped Max below deck and let him sit on a white leather couch. He took the glass from the young man's hand and placed it carefully on the shiny table which sat in the centre of the extravagantly decorated room.

"Close your eyes for a bit Max. Have a sleep."

"I think I will Joe, thank you," Max replied drowsily. Within seconds he was unconscious.

The man in black came down the steps and into the room.

"Is he out?"

"Sleeping like a baby, boss."

Joe got up and knocked on a door at the back of the room. Two men came out and immediately got to work. One pushed a needle into the side of Max's neck, while the other started to undress the lad.

"He was a nice lad. Seems such a shame."

"Such a waste too, but this is the only way," the man in black replied, taking off his own shirt and trousers.

He put on Max's clothes, which were a good fit, while the others stripped Max naked then put some bathers on him.

One of the men stripped off and got into a set of matching bathers. The other studied the young man, then made sure the man in black's hair was brushed the same way as Max.

Happy with their work they all stood up.

"We need to do this as quickly as possible."

Joe and the man in bathers picked up Max between them and began to walk him outside. The other man went around to the front of the boat. The man in bathers, jumped into the sea, taking Max with him.

The cool water seemed to have an effect on Max, and he started to stir. Towing him around to the front of the boat, the man supporting Max grabbed a rope, which was passed down by the second man from the front deck. He dove under the water and tied it around Max's leg.

By now Max was splashing around, wondering what was happening. Still heavily sedated, he was unable to shout, but deep inside his foggy brain he knew he was in trouble.

The man on the deck looked down at him, no feeling in his eyes. He was joined by the man in black who was now wearing his clothes.

The new Max waved at the old Max, as he rolled a fender, which was attached to the other end of the rope, into the water.

For a split second, Max saw hope. He could hold on to the buoyant fender. He was being rescued. That hope was quickly dashed as the fender, filled with concrete, splashed heavily into the water and dragged him down.

He tried for one last time to scream, but the water was already filling his lungs. The bright blue skies rapidly turned into the pitch dark of the ocean depths. Max Candian was gone.

The new Max walked around to the back of the boat and picked up a glass of champagne. He went and stood on his own, watching the swimmers. A half smile crossed his lips.

*****

Not all the detectives had packed it in for the night. As ever, Cat was still at her computer, clicking away at her keyboard, trying to track down people through social media or police records.

"Don't work too late, Cat."

"I won't Ma'am. I'm just checking a few of the names you found today on that list you gave me. I've also had a look at Brian Dodds, who works in their office."

"Anything interesting?"

"Well, most of the people on the list are men. In fact, there are only two women. One of them lists her 'partner' as Brian Dodds."

"So, he lives in one of the houses owned by the charity."

Cat nodded. "And, the chap who lived in Ripon Street, he has a list of offences after his name. He was considered a fine example of a reformed character and was given a job by a certain funeral director a couple of years ago."

"What was his job?"

"The local media produced an article about his transition to the right side of the law. There were no pictures, but he was described as a pall bearer and grave digger."

"The man we saw wouldn't have been able to do anything like that. How weird? We need to follow that up next week. Thanks Cat, good work."

Karen studied the young woman whose eyes were already glued back on her computer screen.

"Do you fancy fish and chips, Cat?"

Cat looked up, completely surprised.

She stuttered for a moment, Karen thought she was looking for an excuse not to go but then she blurted out. "That would be lovely."

"Come on then. Get your jacket."

They took Karen's car as it transpired Cat bussed to and from work every day. Cat seemed amazed with the tech in the Q2, especially the satellite navigation system.

They drove down to Roker Beach and parked behind the RNLI building. It was a nice evening, so they strolled along to the chippie at the end of Roker Pier. They each ordered fish and chips. They found an empty bench just before the pier gate and sat in the sun to eat their meal.

Two gulls decided to investigate, hoping they might get lucky. They stood in front of the two women waiting in hope for a dropped chip.

As they ate, children played on the beach and in the playground. Parents fussed around their charges, building sandcastles, kicking balls or simply filling buckets of water for their children to splash in. A few hardy souls braved the cold waters and a couple in wet suits, dragging marker buoys, swam across the calm waters inside the pier heads.

Others, not so brave, yet still keen to keep fit, jogged up and down the pier. Fishermen made their way down towards the lighthouse for an evening of fishing. Couples strolled in the sun, students and pensioners alike.

It looked idyllic, yet if you looked closely there were a few indications that all was not well with the world. Empty bottles and beer cans were prominent amongst the detritus left after a long day. Alcohol played a heavy part in the lives of many of the locals. It didn't have a positive effect.

As the women ate, and chatted, while people watching, Karen warmed to the shy young lady who was such a key part of their team. The show of friendship had brought out her character, and Karen learned more about her life in that hour, than she had discovered in the previous two weeks.

It was nice.

Karen also realised how important it was to involve herself with the team. Apart from Jack and now Cat, she knew precious little about the men and women she worked with. It was time to get out there and enjoy their company, find out what drives them and what interests them. Only then could she learn their strengths and weaknesses. Only then could she employ them to the best of their ability.

Once they had finished their meal, they picked up a hot chocolate from Love Lilys and walked along the beach. A young lad was desperately trying to get his kite in the air but seemed unable to understand that he needed to run into the wind.

Karen had learned a lot about Cat. Her parents had split up when she was quite young, her father had been an alcoholic. That trauma had given the lass a fear of men which she struggled to overcome. It seemed she had a soft spot for Jordan but was too afraid to even talk to the lad.

Cat also liked to play Pokemon Go and showed Karen how to spin PokeStops, fight in PokeGyms and catch the myriad of creatures which inhabited the landscape all around them.

She shared a love of cats with Karen and for exercise played table tennis with her mum. She didn't think she was good enough to join a club. Karen urged her to consider it as she might meet some nice people.

After dropping Cat home, Karen mused about her evening as she drove back to Witherwack.

Once in the house, she fed Jinx, poured herself a glass of wine and settled herself down on her sofa to watch Casualty, one of her favourite programmes. For a few hours the case had been forgotten. Her time with Cat had been fun; she needed more fun. She looked at the photo of Gary and smiled, mouthing the word 'cheers' to her soulmate before taking her first sip.

When she worked in Newcastle, she had been nicknamed the Ice Queen. Always dowdy, she had been totally work focussed and never socialised. It had taken its toll. On more than one occasion she had considered that she was suffering from depression but had always shied away from talking to anyone about it. Yet, here in Sunderland, life seemed to be taking a different turn. She had made friends, good friends.

It was time to live again.

# Chapter Twenty-One

*Sunday, 29th May 2022*

Karen was awake as soon as the alarm went off. When she opened the curtains, she was greeted by a grey damp landscape of wet roofs and puddle filled roads. She had found a new exercise regime on her phone, and spent fifteen minutes doing star jumps, planking and sit-ups, before taking a shower.

Wrapped in her towel, she headed straight for the spare bedroom, and started rooting through her boxes of clothes to find something brighter to wear. Once she was dressed, she headed for the kitchen.

Knowing she was going to enjoy a big brunch, she settled for a glass of orange juice, and an apple to start her day.

Jinx was rubbing her legs as usual, waiting to be fed. After filling the cat bowl, she sat at her small kitchen table and pondered about the case, and what the week ahead might bring.

She couldn't wait to hear that Max Candian was in the country, and safely under observation. The next few days would be very interesting indeed. The scraping of the cat's bowl on the tiled floor, woke her from her thoughts, as Jinx tried to lick the pattern off the bowl.

"Still hungry?"

The cat looked at her as if to say, 'isn't that obvious.'

Karen shook a bag of cat treats, which she always kept handy, and the cat leapt on to her lap. She tipped three of the crunchy pieces into her hand, and Jinx devoured them in seconds, then looked at her, demanding more.

"That's enough piggy wiggy. You'd eat the whole packet if you had the chance. I wonder what they put in these things?"

She gently stroked the cat, which, purring loudly, made to settle on her lap.

"Oh no you don't. I've got a date with brunch."

She picked the cat up, took it through to the lounge and placed it gently on the sofa. "I'll see you later."

Karen put on her coat, and made her way out into the damp, flicking the hood of the coat over her head. She locked the door and walked out into the drizzle, to walk around to Betty's Café.

Dr Laura Rae and Jack were already there, sitting in a corner of the café, watching her walk in from their prime spot in the window.

She took off her coat and hung it on a coat stand, behind the door. There were audible gasps from her friends.

"Wow, you look gorgeous," Laura said, with a little too much enthusiasm for Karen's liking. Jack simply smiled at her friend.

She had chosen to wear some yellow trousers with a pale blue top. "I'm supporting the Ukraine."

"I can see that, what a brilliant choice of colours and what a difference. I like this new friend of mine."

"Thanks Jack."

Karen took her seat just as Betty walked over.

"My, my, what a ray of sunshine on such a grey day," Betty smiled at Karen. "What can I get my favourite witches this week?"

"Brunches all round please, the veggie one for me, with three teas." Karen looked at the others to make sure they were all in agreement.

"Anything else?" Betty asked.

"Do you serve frogs and puppy dog tails?" Jack joked.

They all laughed, as Betty walked back to make up their order.

Karen held out her hands and they formed their circle. The usual tingle filtered up to the back of her neck, as the little hairs located there, stood-on end.

"Have we all had a good week?"

Before anyone could reply, the café door opened, and two girls walked in.

"That's my old school mate Jessica. Jessica, Jess!" Jack shouted.

The table seemed to buck, as she said the words, and the salt and pepper pots fell over. Jack broke the circle and made to get up to see her friend.

"Careful Jack, you've knocked everything over."

"I didn't touch the table Laura, I thought you must have hit it with your knees?"

"Not me." They both looked at Karen.

"Not me either. That's strange. Go and see your friend, Jack, before the tea arrives."

As Jack went off to speak to her friend, Karen and Laura inspected the table.

"That was weird, maybe the table was propped on something, or settled in some way."

"Or we had an earthquake. Are there any old mine workings around here?"

"There are mine workings everywhere around here, Karen, but I don't think it was that. We would have heard crockery breaking or other people commenting if the building had moved."

"Very strange, one of those unsolved mysteries, I guess. Not enough of one to make a documentary about though."

"I'm not sure about that. They make programmes about everything these days."

Laura laughed that cackling laugh of hers, and soon Karen was laughing too. Jack returned to the table. "What's so funny?"

"Karen suggested they might make a documentary about our moving table."

"Well, they make programmes about everything these days."

"That's exactly what I said."

The friends all burst out laughing again just as the tea arrived.

"You lot are upsetting my regulars. Keep the noise down please."

"Sorry Betty," Karen apologised.

"That's alright pet. I'm just joking with you. It's nice to hear laughter in the place. It can be a bit like a library in here some days, if you know what I mean."

The friends all smiled as Betty handed out the teas.

"I'll be mother," Karen offered, and began pouring tea into the assorted cups from the huge teapot. The meals arrived just as Karen had filled all the cups, and the friends began to eat.

They all started to talk about their week from a social perspective. Jack was amazed Karen had taken Cat out for chips the previous evening. She was pleased that her new boss was gradually easing herself out of the dark hole she had been in since her husband had died.

Meanwhile, Jack's week seemed to be filled with endless nights out, while Laura had apparently spent the whole week working late.

Most of the time was spent eating, as the friends simply enjoyed being in each other's company. Jack seemed happy to regale the others with tales of the escapades, her and her friend Jess, had at school. The mention of the name made Karen think. It was when Jack's friend was mentioned that the table moved. Jess was also a person of interest in the case.

A coincidence? Karen didn't believe in coincidences.

When their brunch was over, Laura excused herself as she wanted to get back to work. Jack persuaded Karen to go with her into town in search of some new make-up.

The rest of the day seemed to fly by. At the end of the afternoon, laden with several bags of make-up and new clothes, Karen was dropped back home by the tireless Jack. She needed a cup of tea and invited Jack in. Jack declined as she was meeting some friends in town later and wanted to go home and rest before the action started.

Jinx was waiting for Karen when she unlocked the door.

Having had enough excitement for one day, Karen settled down for the evening with cheese on toast, a bottle of wine and a packet of biscuits.

At just before 10pm she received a WhatsApp message from Billy. Their target had checked in and was on his way. She went to bed happy, with Jinx curled up alongside her.

*****

The new Max Candian, complete with expertly forged passport boarded a plane to go to England. He had only just arrived in Gran Canaria a few days earlier to make the arrangements. He usually travelled in a better class of plane than this, but he had a persona to maintain.

Despite the problems he was experiencing with the Police and the incompetence of some of the people he had trusted, there was a slight thrill about this trip. He would be playing in a Northeast Qualifier for the British Open. He reminded himself he had to focus on the problems in hand and not get carried away by the golf.

*Monday 30th May 2022*

His flight to Newcastle was on time, and though tired, the adrenalin was pumping.

He had checked in his new golf clubs; he knew the Spanish police were watching his every move and was keeping true to the original plan that had been sold to Max Candian. Joe Higgs had provided him with some cash and all his expenses would be covered, just in case some financial checks were carried out. He would be met at Newcastle Airport. From there he would be taken to his hotel.

A practice round had been arranged for the Monday afternoon and the tournament would start on Tuesday.

The new Max had always been able to sleep, wherever he was, and, within minutes of take-off, he had dozed off. His head rested against the wall of the cabin next to a window.

Some turbulence disturbed his slumbers, and as he woke from his deep sleep, he could see the orange lights of towns and cities far below him. As they commenced their descent into Newcastle Airport, he began to spot traffic on the roads. Low level scattered clouds occasionally obscured his view.

The captain announced that the cabin crew had ten minutes to landing. A stewardess smiled at him as she checked he had his seatbelt on. This was it; he would soon be back in England and playing his favourite sport. He had a lot of business to conduct but he resolved to try and enjoy the next few days. In a few months' time, he could be playing in the British Open. Life couldn't be much better.

As the jet touched down, he felt a sense of relief that he had arrived. It didn't seem possible that so much had gone so wrong with his operation in such a short time. Some of his top operatives would be joining him in Sunderland. He trusted them with his life. Between them, they would get the business back on track; and that meddling detective would get her just desserts.

He popped to the toilet while he waited for the bags to be offloaded. When he returned to the carousel everyone from the plane was waiting. It seemed to take an age but eventually the bags started to come through. His seemed to be almost last to appear. He grabbed his rucksack and then his golf bag and headed through the exit.

When he emerged into arrivals, a tall man waved to him. He was holding up a sign with Max written on it. The man smiled and waved him over.

"Welcome to England, Max."

Max hadn't been that fluent in English, so the new Max had to maintain that façade. He pretended to be unsure, for the security cameras, then walked over to the man who was sporting a broad smile.

"Thank you."

"Here, let me take your bag. My name is Stu and I'm here to help you in whatever way I can." The big man took the golf bag off Max's shoulder. "Let's get you to your hotel, I bet you are looking forward to some sleep."

Again, Max pretended he wasn't a hundred percent sure what was being said but he followed along.

"Thank you very much, Senor."

As they walked out to the car, a man on a ride-on floor cleaner watched them pass. As they walked out, he spoke into a hidden microphone tucked inside his jacket lapel.

Outside a large black car was waiting for them, engine running. The golf clubs and Max's rucksack were stowed in the boot and the big man opened the back door and ushered Max inside.

The man climbed into the passenger seat, checked Max was OK and then told the driver to head for Sunderland.

A radio played quietly in the car as they headed South, driving through Newcastle, then across the Tyne before heading to Sunderland.

Max stayed glued to the window. He pretended to be engrossed by the passing scenery despite the late hour.

The driver seemed to know what he was doing, despite not being part of his normal team. In less than half an hour they were approaching Sunderland. At that time of night there were hardly any cars on the road. One car did overtake them, driving like a mad man, but apart from that little of note happened during the journey.

When they reached Sunderland they headed to the centre of the city, pulling up outside a Premier Inn.

They got out of the car, Stu lifting out Max's rucksack. Max went to pull out his golf clubs, but Stu insisted he leave them in the boot, until he needed them tomorrow.

There was a room booked in Max's name. Stu helped Max by filling in his details on the welcome form. The receptionist gave Max his room key and told him where breakfast would be served.

Stu escorted him to his room and made sure he knew how everything worked. He promised to collect him at 11am the following morning to take him to the golf course.

After Stu had gone, there was a knock on the door. Max opened it and let the two men in. One had blonde hair and the other was short and stocky. For the next half hour, they made their plans, before the man in black went to bed.

He was asleep as soon as his head hit the pillow. It had been a busy couple of days.

*****

Billy had been monitoring the operation from the moment the plane landed. He had observed, on CCTV in Newcastle's police station, as Max collected his bags. He then watched as his escort collected him, and then drove Max away, in a black Mercedes.

He had made sure they had the best possible image of the man who met him, and an expert was already checking it for possible matches on the police database.

Unmarked police cars had successfully followed Max to Sunderland and had watched as he was deposited in the Premier Inn, minus his golf clubs. Billy was convinced that was the last they would see of those clubs.

One of the unmarked cars was assigned to track the Mercedes back to Newcastle, while others watched the Hotel until Billy's team could take over. John and Jordan were in place at four thirty.

The only bad news of the night was that the black Mercedes had been lost on the return journey, soon after they had left the hotel. Billy was gutted, as he felt it may have led them to where the golf clubs were dismantled. He put into operation a massive check on road cameras to try and find where it went.

At five in the morning, he went home and got to bed. He had to be at the golf course before lunch and needed to catch up on some sleep. The last thing he did before turning the lights off was to send a message to Karen, to let her know what was happening.

Karen had struggled to sleep, so when her phone vibrated, she was awake instantly. She read Billy's note and climbed out of bed. Jinx was annoyed at being disturbed so early, but after a stretch and yawn, the cat went straight back to sleep.

The early hour didn't seem to bother Karen. She was all business as usual, as she had a quick shower, grabbed some fruit and yogurt for her breakfast, then made a sandwich. Always be ready for a long stint, had been drummed into her over the years. The importance of keeping herself fed and watered, to maintain her peak performance, was uppermost in her mind. She had experienced deprivation in the army. It wasn't pleasant.

She slung her battered bag over her shoulder, grabbed her keys and headed down to the Southwick North Station. When she arrived, it was the night shift on the desk. She nodded to them as she rushed up to the detective's office. Flicking the lights on proved a problem as she hadn't been there in the dark before, but with the help of the torch on her phone, the place was soon awash with light.

She messaged Jack and Cat, deciding to keep Rachel, Matt and Mick in reserve, in case the day turned into a late session.

Both arrived together. Jack had picked Cat up on her way into the office.

Cat soon found the same CCTV feeds that Billy had watched, which provided Karen and Jack with their first view of Max Candian. The young, tanned Argentinian had seemed tired and nervous at the airport, which would have been understandable given his journey and the strange environment.

Jack checked in with John who was watching the Hotel from a position across the main road. There was nothing to report.

Cat worked on checking traffic cameras to see if she could find the black Mercedes which had been lost in the early hours. After a while she was confident it hadn't left the city, as all the feeds, covering the roads the car could take back to Newcastle, didn't show any hint the black car had gone in that direction.

Eventually she did find it crossing the Spire Bridge. It turned down towards the river and disappeared amongst the industrial and retail units. She called Karen over.

"Good work, Cat. Jack, do we have anyone in that area?"

"I think the units down there are serviced by a private security firm; we don't usually patrol those estates."

Frustrated, Karen thought for a minute. "Do you fancy a run out?"

"Heck, we'll stick out like a sore thumb down there at this time of day."

"I know, I know, but the pet food outlet is down there, and I'd love to know if that's where the car is parked."

"The funeral parlour is down there too. OK, but let's get some back up."

"No Jack, whatever we do, we can't scupper this operation. We have to be in and out like shades. Let's think about this. We could walk from here and observe from the bushes that run along the path by the river."

"Sounds like your cup of tea, I'll follow you. Phones on silent."

"There, you're thinking like a soldier already. Cat, you're manning the fort. If we get into any bother, I'll let you know."

"Right, you are Ma'am."

A thumbs up from behind her computer screens added to her acknowledgement of her orders. Both women put on police issue stab vests and black jackets before heading downstairs. They told the duty desk sergeant where they were going, just in case, but added they should keep all patrols away from the area unless they called for assistance.

The two detectives walked out into the dark. There was a strip of light in the sky away to the East, hinting that dawn was on the way, so they didn't hang around. The cover of darkness was their best friend.

Crossing the main road was easy at that time of day, there wasn't a car in sight. They made their way down to the river side and followed the path along towards the industrial units.

Their eyes gradually adapted to the dark as they walked along, trying their best to be quiet. An early morning jogger nearly bumped into them at one point, which gave all three of them a shock.

After what seemed like an eternity, they neared the part of the industrial units where the Pet Food Supply business was based. In the gloom they could just make out the P & P's logo over a roller door. The entrance was also protected by a similar door. There was no sign of life.

It was another half a mile to the Funeral parlour, but with nothing else to do, they carried on along the river path. The darkness gradually started to lift. Once again, they were disappointed. There was no sign of a car, and the roller shutters, which were everywhere in the city, showed not a chink of light.

In fact, the only activity they saw was around a small bakery which was already busy, producing bread for outlets across the region.

They decided to break cover and walk back along the road which supplied the entrances to many industrial parks along the Northern side of the River Wear.

Amongst the various units was a set of offices which could be let out individually. From the road they could see some light leaking out behind a set of blinds. Curious, they walked down to the entrance to the units. There, parked below the entrance to the various suites, was the black Mercedes.

Karen took out her phone and took a picture of the units so she could work out which one was being used at that unearthly hour. It flashed.

"Damn it."

"Quick, let's get back to the road," Jack suggested as she turned and started to walk quickly away. A torch shone on them, blinding them both.

"Oi, you two. Stop where you are."

As the two women held up their hands to shield their eyes from the bright light, a security guard approached them. Karen noticed someone twitching the blinds from the occupied office, trying to see what was happening.

The security guard walked right up to them. "I've noticed you two hanging around, casing the joint, are you?"

Karen discreetly pulled out her ID. "Police, and yes, we are casing the joint, but if anyone asks, we were two young scrotes who should have been tucked up in bed. If I hear you've said anything else to anyone, you'll be out of a job."

"OK pet, no need to be so harsh."

"Well, this is important. Make out you're chasing us away. Happy to play along?"

"Got it. I'll turn around, then you start running."

The guard looked back towards the offices and industrial units and the girls legged it. The guard turned and started to run after them, shouting for them to stop. They didn't, and he soon gave up.

Once back on the road the women slowed down. Jack was a bit puffed out. Karen's superior fitness showed as she hardly broke sweat.

As they walked back to the station, Karen checked the image she had captured. It wasn't the greatest given the bad light, but she was sure it was the same car.

Once back at the station, they brewed up to help warm them up. It was cold down by the river. There was precious little they could do, as it was so early, so Karen busied herself checking out the office block, where she had seen the car. She found the units online and noted the telephone number to ring, once reception was open. She would have to wait until eight.

As dawn broke, it looked like they would have a good day for the golf tournament practice round. Karen decided she should dress more appropriately and decided to head home and get changed into something brighter. She suggested Jack do the same.

It took them both less than an hour to get home and back. They were both sitting at their desks at just after six thirty. Cat was still beavering away and reported that the team outside the Premier Inn had not seen any action.

Cat was also keeping an eye on traffic feeds around the industrial units in case the suspect car moved away. She couldn't get a direct view on the vehicle, which Karen suspected was deliberate.

It was just before eight, while Karen and Jack were on their third cup of tea, that Cat yelled from behind her screens. "They're on the move."

Both Karen and Jack rushed across to watch the camera feeds. The black car was on its way towards the Stadium of Light, merging with the early morning traffic heading into the city.

They watched it enter the St Mary's Car Park and followed it up to the second level. It circled all around that level, despite there being loads of empty space, and then it headed back down and out of the car park.

From there it headed towards Seaburn; parking up near the Bungalow Café. Two men climbed out and went into the Café, after pausing for a quick chat by the door. They seemed to be pointing out towards the lighthouse at the end of Roker Pier, as if they hadn't seen it before.

Matt walked into the office just as the men disappeared. Karen ordered him straight back out again to watch them. She wanted to be sure the detectives knew where the men went after their breakfast.

As soon as Rachel arrived, she was sent out to give Matt some back up. They both took a bench along the road, about 50 yards from the café. They looked just like a young courting couple.

In fact, as Karen watched them on the traffic feeds, she began to wonder if they were just play acting. She made a mental note to ask Jack, when they were alone, if she was missing out on some gossip.

At eight o'clock sharp Karen rang the admin office at the office rental hub. It took her ten minutes to get through. She wasn't impressed.

However, the friendly staff more than made up for it, by helping her identify the office that she had seen being used the night before. It was being rented by a company that wasn't on their radar, called NECharityHome. When Mick arrived, Karen sent him on a rare outing. She asked him to search the office by the river, to see if he could establish what it was being used for.

She asked Tom Moore to give him some support. He leapt at the chance to get out of the office and went straight out with Mick, as soon as he had arranged cover for the front desk.

By ten o'clock the car was on the move again. This time the car went to the Premier Inn where Max, was waiting for them.

He got in the car, carrying a small bag. From there the car left Sunderland on its way to Ramside Hall. John and Jordan shadowed them to make sure they didn't take any diversions.

Karen called Billy to let him know they were on their way, then, together with Jack, they too headed towards Durham.

On the way she received a call from Mick. The office was virtually empty. Just a set of broken golf clubs, in a ripped-up bag. He was arranging for a SOC team to check for any traces of drugs.

She stopped him. "No Mick, get out of there and make sure the admin office keeps quiet about your visit. I don't want to spook the crims."

"Will do Ma'am."

They pulled into the car park at Ramside Hall and were lucky to find a parking space in front of the Spa. It was extremely busy with golfers and their supporters. A few early starters had already completed their practice sessions while others were just making their way towards the course for their allocated start times.

Karen spotted the DCI's car in the car park. They made their way towards the professional's shop as Billy had suggested. Players were milling around, some practicing their putting or simply warming up on the range. They spotted Max on the putting green; Billy was with him.

It looked like they were building quite a friendship. A golf bag was alongside where they stood. It looked the same as the one she had seen him collect at the airport.

Billy waved at her and walked over, after having a quick word with Max.

"I told him you were my sister. I offered to caddy for him, and he has accepted. He was pleased to have someone local on his bag."

"How is he?" Karen asked.

"He seems fine, amazed at the excellent treatment he has been given."

"Did he have to buy a new set of clubs?"

"No, everything is OK, it's his usual bag, with lucky ball marker."

"It's not the same bag boss. We've found the one he collected from the airport, in bits, in an office down by the river, along with a broken set of clubs."

"That's weird, he seemed very familiar with the bag, like he'd owned it for years. I'd better get back, though I think this is going to be a waste of time."

"Enjoy the round boss. Keep a close eye on him!"

Billy gave them a thumbs up and went back to help Max practice his putting. Karen sent a message to Mick. She had an idea.

Keeping a discreet distance, and trying not to get in the way, the two women watched Max play his round of golf, with Billy carrying his bag. It was almost four hours later when they finally walked off the course.

Max wanted to get back to his hotel, and with no black car waiting, took the offered lift from Billy, who delivered him to the Premier Inn.

As he left the car park, he made sure someone was watching the hotel. Just in case the man who had met him at the airport, who he now knew was called Stu, came back for the young Argentinian. From the hotel he headed straight back to the office to give a briefing on what he had learnt.

When Billy walked in all the team, apart from John and Jordan were present. He didn't bother to take his jacket off.

"OK people. I've spent the day with Max, and I am confident that he is an innocent party in all of this. He is a great golfer, well compared to me. It seems they changed tack a little this time and swapped his clubs for exact replicas." He looked at Karen.

"Yes boss. Mick found the set of clubs he travelled with at a rented office down by the Wear. We know they are his clubs because we've matched them to the CCTV footage. The bag didn't hold any waterproofs, balls, etc., the clubs looked like they've never been used."

Karen looked at Billy. "Do you think you should tell Max what is happening?"

"Good idea. We could offer him immunity from prosecution and protection, in exchange for his help with the case?"

Karen smiled. "I was hoping you'd suggest that. It needs some thought though. He might run a mile or panic in some way. If we lose him, he could end up at the bottom of the river."

"Let me have a think. I've got to know him quite well today and we have him on our radar, so there's no mad rush to do anything. We are teeing off at ten thirty tomorrow morning so we should make our decision before I go to the course. I'll talk to him after the round. I don't want to put the guy off his golf."

Mick put his hand up. "I've just heard back from SOC boss, there was cocaine inside those clubs. It was also woven into the fabric of the bag. Unfortunately, we don't have any fingerprints or evidence we can use to identify these guys."

"All I've got is the name Stu, but that could be false," Billy added. "Anyone else have any ideas?"

Karen looked at the three different incident boards and spoke up.

"I'm beginning to wonder if there isn't another person involved in these crimes. This seems too big for a local funeral director and a dog breeder to engineer. We have people being moved internationally, bodies being chopped up and disposed of, and cocaine trafficking."

She looked around the room, most people were nodding in agreement.

"All we have had so far are mysterious people in black, driving black cars. Let's call our mysterious person Black for now and let's keep an open mind as to who they may be. Chances are they may not even be based in the Northeast."

"Good call, Karen." Billy replied.

"Anyone else?"

Cat, slowly put her hand up. "Yes, Cat."

"I've been studying the footage of the black car in St Mary's car park. I think I know where they made the transfer."

Billy and Karen went over to look at Cat's super-sized screens.

"If you watch, the car simply seemed to drive up to level two and then down again after circling the level without stopping. But if you watch closely, they pass a woman who has her boot open, as if she is loading her shopping into her car. We can't see from this angle, but as they pass the car with the open boot, they seem to slow down slightly. I think they threw something in the back of her car."

Karen made Cat replay the footage several times before she stood back. She looked at Billy. "I think she's right."

She froze the picture on the boot of the car and read out the car number. "The car was reported stolen three days ago, Ma'am."

"What about the woman?"

Karen zoomed in on the best image they had. She looked, ordinary, in her late thirties or forties maybe. "Face recognition?"

"I'll run it, Ma'am."

Billy walked across and looked at the incident boards. He pushed the images of Prudence and Phil down the board and pinned up a blank sheet in the centre of the panel. Picking up a marker, he wrote BLACK across the top of the paper. He circled it.

"This, ladies and gentlemen, is our nemesis. He or she is behind all this, and we need to bring them down."

Several of the detectives, slapped their desks.

Karen's phone buzzed. She answered it.

"John has eyes on the black car. It's back at the Premier Inn."

"Let's hope they don't take Max. He was planning on having a meal at the hotel and resting before tomorrow. I'm due to pick him up at eight thirty." Billy looked concerned.

"I'm going over there, tell John and Jordan. I'll offer to take him out for his supper."

"Is that a good idea boss? They might smell a rat."

Billy was already heading for the door. "I don't want to lose this guy, Karen. He's not involved and I'm going to do all I can to keep him safe."

With that Billy ran out the door and Jack telephoned John to let him know the boss was on his way.

There was a feeling of high tension in the office. Karen had to think of something to refocus the team. "OK guys. Let's focus. I want everyone looking for that car that collected the cocaine. I want to know where it went after it left St Mary's this morning."

She picked up her phone. "I'm going to call Dr Rae to see if she has any updates for us. Jack, see if you can isolate an image from the guys in the black car and put that through face recognition."

Cat put her hand up. "Yes Cat?"

"Ma'am, shall I see if the faces on the charity website are on the system? We never did check them all out."

Karen was annoyed at herself. She should have obtained more detail from Brian. She had just accepted that the faces on their Facebook page were just old employees.

"Good idea Cat. See if any of their faces ring bells."

Karen looked around the room, everyone was busy. On a whim she forwarded the link to the charity Facebook page to Dr Rae, asking if any of the recent bodies could be people in the group photo.

Her phone buzzed at almost the moment she sent the email. It was a Whatsapp from Dr Laura Rae.

*I'll see what I can do. How are you? X*

She replied – *All good thank you.*

She thought about adding a kiss and decided not to tempt fate.

Karen sat staring at the image. There were people in that photo who could potentially fit the profiles of the men in black they had encountered during the investigation. She looked again at the tall man at the back, standing just behind Jess.

She got out her phone and, using her camera, zoomed in on the tall man. Once the picture was taken, she used her photo editing software to circle the man she was looking at, and then sent the image to Billy. It was a bit grainy, but she was happy with the result.

At the hotel, Billy was just knocking on Max's door when his phone buzzed. He ignored it. Max answered the door, smiling at the familiar face of his caddy.

In the background, Billy could see two men in the room. One was sitting on the bed, looking at his phone.

"Hi Max. I was going to offer to take you out for a meal, but I see you have company."

Max looked towards the man on the bed. "Would it be, OK?"

"Who is that?"

"He is my caddy. We'll be talking about tomorrow and how to play the course."

The man on the bed shrugged. "That's OK. What's your name mate?"

"Billy Cooper. And you are?"

"We're employed by Max's sponsors. Just making sure he has everything he needs. We'll leave you to it. Don't get him drunk."

Billy laughed. "No chance of that. I want him fit and raring to go tomorrow. Maybe he'll qualify for the Open and then I can caddy for him there. I'll collect him in the morning if that's OK with you?"

"Whatever. Good luck tomorrow, Max. We'll be watching."

The two men brushed past Billy as they left the room and went back to their car.

Max put his shoes on. "I don't like them, Billy."

"Neither do I Max, now come on. I'm starving."

Billy and Max walked into town to find a restaurant, passing John and Jordan in their car. Jordan got out and followed at a discreet distance while John stayed in the car to watch the hotel.

Cat was focused on the local traffic camera network and spotted the black car drive the short distance from the Premier Inn to St Mary's car park. She called Karen over to watch what was happening. Two men got out of the car and walked into town, one of the men was Stu, the man who had met Max at the airport.

When Karen saw who they were, she decided to head into the city. It would be a late night.

## Chapter Twenty-Two

It turned out Max loved Indian cooking, so they paid a visit to the Spice Empire, which was located virtually opposite the Empire Theatre. Billy was partial to a Tikka Masala, so he was more than happy to oblige the young man.

Jordan stopped at the theatre, making a show of reading the billboards and what shows were coming to the city in the next few months. As he stood there, the two guys dressed in black, turned into Church Street and checked that Max and Billy were in the restaurant. One of them took a picture through the door of the restaurant, presumably to get an image of Billy.

They then walked a little further up the street and waited.

Jordan walked a little further into town and called Karen.

"Ma'am, the two guys ferrying Max about are waiting outside the Spice Empire where Billy and Max are having a meal. I think they've just taken a picture of the boss."

"Damn it. If they identify him then there could be a ruckus when they come out. Maybe we can get them picked up?"

"What for Ma'am. We haven't got anything on them, yet!"

"Maybe we can engineer something? Leave it with me."

Karen put a call in to uniform and a plan was put in place.

Half an hour later four officers were walking to the entrance to the Empire theatre. They saw Jordan, who had received a phone call from Karen, outlining the plan.

Suddenly Jordan made a break from the officers and sprinted towards the Indian restaurant. As he approached the two guys watching Billy, he stumbled and ran straight into them. One of them fell over while the other made to grab Jordan.

"Oi, you three, stay where you are," the lead police officer shouted, which inspired the two men to scramble to get away.

The four police officers barrelled into them and in the melee, all three of the men were arrested. Several police cars arrived, and despite their protests, all three were taken away in separate cars.

Jordan was dropped back to Southwick North, while the other two were taken into custody in the Sunderland Central station. Their belongings, including their mobile phones, were confiscated.

Despite the late hour, Karen and Jack went over to the city to see if they could get any information from the phones and other bits and pieces.

Both men had been isolated in separate cells, which meant the police now had a great opportunity to identify them. They had not been formally arrested yet, so there were no photographs, but Karen got a good look at both the men through the small window in the cell doors.

Though the photo from the charity Facebook page was a few years old, she was pretty sure one of them was in the photo, possibly both. She had the link she wanted. That was suddenly verified when she finally received a reply to the photo, she had sent Billy. He was convinced Stu was the tall man in the picture.

Karen advised the duty sergeant in the station that he could release the men. But before she left, she took Stu's mobile phone, threw it on the floor and stamped on it. "Tell him it got damaged in the fight and he should submit a claim for a replacement."

The sergeant laughed. "Yes Ma'am. What shall we tell them about the incident."

Karen thought for a moment. "Tell them someone in the restaurant saw the whole thing and confirmed they were just innocent bystanders."

"Will do Ma'am." The sergeant winked at Karen and left to pass on the news.

"Let's get out of here, Jack. I don't want them to see us."

The women left Sunderland Central and headed back to Southwick. It was getting very late, so once they were in the office, they agreed to call it a day. By now, Billy had delivered Max back to his hotel and a new team had taken over watching the place from John.

Nothing was likely to happen overnight, so everyone headed home.

Jinx was desperate for food by the time Karen got to her house. Karen was hungry too and settled for cheese on toast after feeding her cat. Her priorities were clear.

A glass of wine also appeared as she settled down to watch anything but the news. Her phone rang as she was taking her first sip. It was Dr Rae.

"Karen, I have been looking at the bodies from the car wreck outside your house. They were pretty banged up. You could say they would make a good advert for wearing seatbelts." She laughed her cackling laugh, although it wasn't really funny.

"I've done a bit of reconstruction and am pretty sure I can match them to two of the youngsters in the photo. I'll send over a copy of the image with the two guys marked. If you can get names, you have your attackers."

"Thanks Laura, you're an angel. Get yourself home. I'll be buying brunch on Saturday."

Karen hung up on Laura and immediately rang Jack. They arranged to pay Brian Dodds at the Charity office, a visit the next day, while Billy and Max were on the golf course. They needed names and she hoped Brian would have the answers they needed.

She finished her glass of wine just as a random edition of QI was finishing. She thought about pouring another but opted for bed and a book instead. She was tired.

As she lay there reading, with Jinx curled up alongside her, sleep took her. The Kindle she was reading fell on the floor. Karen was so tired; the noise didn't wake her.

During the night she woke with a start. *Where did Max get the golf clubs he used in the competition?* The random thought kept her awake for a few moments, but tiredness soon dragged her back into a deep sleep.

*Tuesday. 31st May 2022*

Karen woke feeling refreshed and excited. This could be the day they would start to put all the pieces of the jigsaw together. The people involved all seemed to have a link to the housing charity. It could be that they had been looking at the mysterious Mr or Mrs Black, as Billy had named them, all the time.

A quick shower was followed by fruit and yoghurt. Jinx was fed with barely a second glance. The cat was left staring at the door as Karen almost ran to her car. She was in the office at eight on the dot.

Jack appeared soon after and they decided to visit Brian at the office of the charity just after nine. There was no point sitting in rush hour traffic, there was too much going on.

She checked the overnight reports. There had been no further activity at Max's hotel and Billy was on his way there to have breakfast with the young golfer on his big day. There had been no sign of the two men after they had been released. John had suggested they might have lost interest in Max and Billy, given they had the drugs.

Karen was not so sure; the crims had invested too much money in Max just to let him disappear back to the Canaries. She surmised they might have something further planned for him, not that she could think what that might be.

With Billy on the golf course for most of the day, it was down to her and the team to push the investigation along.

They managed two cups of tea before they set off for Mowbray Park and the offices of the charity, Providing Homes for the Helpless.

Parking just outside, they rapidly climbed the steps and walked into reception. A young girl looked up and took some chewing gum out of her mouth. "What do you want?"

"Charming!" Jack muttered. They both showed their badges. The girl seemed less than impressed.

"Is Brian available?" Karen asked forcing a smile on her face.

"Who?"

"Brian Dodds."

"Never heard of him." The girl turned away and put the chewing gum back in her mouth.

"Excuse me, we met him here just a few days ago. He manages the Providing Homes for the Helpless Charity. This is its office."

The girl looked at them as if they were stupid. This time she didn't bother to take the gum out of her mouth.

"We've just rented this place. It was listed as vacant last week. We're going to set up an Arts Café here. My friend has just popped out to get some supplies. I've never heard of that charity."

Karen and Jack looked at each other.

"Can we have a look around?" Karen wanted to see for herself.

"Fill your boots, but there's nowt to see." The girl didn't even bother to look up from the magazine she was reading.

The two women lifted the counter and went out to the back of the office where they had spoken with Brian. It was completely empty, apart from some dubious artworks leaning against the wall in one corner.

"I think we've been played." Jack kicked the wall in frustration.

"Maybe we misread Brian. Perhaps there's more to him than meets the eye?"

Jack just nodded in agreement.

"Let's check the rest of the building, maybe someone else here knows something."

Jack followed Karen out of the office. The girl barely acknowledged their passing. As a thought Karen asked her a question.

"Do you know who is in the rest of the building?"

"No idea. We have the ground floor; the rest is in flats."

Karen didn't bother to thank the girl, she just headed up the first flight of stairs. On the small landing there were two doors, numbered two and three.

They knocked on Flat Two, with no response. The door to Flat Three opened. "That one's empty. Can I help you?"

A young man stood in the doorway, with the palest skin Karen had ever seen. In fact, his pallor was more grey than white. It didn't look as if he had shaved or even washed for a few days, his hair looking long and greasy.

The women took out their badges and walked across the landing.

"Did you know Brian Dodds, from the charity which used to be downstairs?"

The young man dropped his eyes and looked at the floor.

"Not really, I know there was a charity based there as they placed me in this flat, but I don't know any names."

Karen pulled out the picture from the charity Facebook page. "Do you recognise any of these people?"

He took the picture and gave it a good scan. "I recognise this one. He found me begging in the city and took me in. My parents had thrown me out of their house."

Karen looked at the person the young man had identified. It was Jess.

"Thank you. Why did they throw you out?"

"Drugs. I became addicted to cocaine when I was sixteen. I'm trying to get clean now and having this place has made a huge difference."

"What's your name?" Jack asked.

"Joshua, Joshua Kettering."

"Thanks Joshua. How does the Charity work?"

"How do you mean?"

"Do you have to pay rent or anything like that?"

"Nothing. They just said they would check in on me every now and again. I moved in about six weeks ago. The rooms were completely kitted out with everything I need, which was great."

Karen looked at Jack and they turned to leave.

"Oh, just one last thing." Joshua was about to close the door but stopped when Karen turned around.

"Do you know what happened to the person who lived opposite?"

"I don't really know; he was like me, but I think he must have done something bad as they evicted him."

"The Charity?" Jack seemed incredulous.

"Yep, I heard a barney one evening and peeked out. Two guys all dressed in black were physically dragging him out of his flat. It's been empty ever since."

"Did you know his name?"

"I just knew him as Jimmy."

"Thanks Joshua. You have been very helpful."

Joshua simply nodded and closed his door. The sound of bolts echoed around the empty hall.

The women looked upstairs but thought better of going any further.

"Let's get a crew in here to get us into that flat. I'd like to know who Jimmy is, or was, and who else had been in that flat."

Karen took out her phone and rang the charities phone number. It went straight to an answer machine. She didn't leave a message.

"Come on, let's get out of here. This place gives me the creeps."

"You don't have to ask me twice. I've just got a bad case of the shivers."

The two women took a deep breath when they reached the pavement. The sun was breaking through the clouds and provided some warmth on their faces. Karen called the station and asked for uniform to send a team over to break into Flat Two. They had thirty minutes to wait.

"What are you thinking Karen?"

"I'm thinking we should have solved this case a week ago. Brian is either the organiser, behind all this, or knows who it is."

"That's if he's still alive."

"What do you mean?"

"Perhaps he knew too much, maybe he was silenced after he spoke to us. There are several options."

They were still discussing whether Brian was involved when two police vans parked up alongside them. Eight police officers got out, all wearing stab vests. A couple wore face protection, and another carried a red battering ram.

Karen led them up the stairs to Flat two. A sergeant told them to stand back. The constable with the enforcer waited for the go ahead. The two guys with masks stood behind him.

The sergeant looked at Karen who gave him a nod. "OK lads, as we practised, on three. One, two, three."

The constable swung the ram and the lock on the door shattered, taking some of the door frame with it. The two police officers with masks ran into the room and quickly checked the small flat for any sign of life. It was empty.

"Was that necessary, sergeant?"

"You never know what you might find, Ma'am. Anyway, it's good practice."

"Thank you, sergeant."

Karen walked over the splinters into the empty flat. Jack had called a forensics team over, but Karen thought she would still have a look around.

The place looked bare. There was a table and four chairs in the kitchen diner. A bed frame, minus a mattress, stood in the single bedroom. The bathroom was old, but it looked as if it had never been used.

She put on a pair of blue gloves, and carefully opened a few of the kitchen draws. There was a full set of cutlery in one draw and several pots and pans in another. The flat was basically ready to move into.

"I don't think we'll find much here Jack."

"I think you're right. Someone has been very thorough. but you know the golden rule, they'll always leave a clue."

Karen smiled at her friend.

"I admire your faith in forensics. Let's leave them to it and make our way over to the golf course. I also want to catch up with the office to see if there have been any developments."

Ramside Golf course was much busier than the day before. People had come from all over the region to watch a field of over a hundred hopefuls, all looking to grab the solitary Open Golf qualifying place on offer.

There were a few other prizes available, thanks to local sponsors. But no-one really cared about those. The chance to play at St Andrews in the 150th Open was all that mattered.

Max had just teed off, which meant the women would have little opportunity to talk to Billy. They managed to get close to the green on the third hole, and Billy walked over to them as Max and his fellow competitors paced around the green.

Karen told Billy about the disappearing charity office and of their suspicions about Brian Dodds.

Max managed to sink a long putt for a birdie, so Billy had little time to talk. The girls decided to head back to the office. At least they knew Max was safe while he was playing golf in front of so many people.

Back at base they caught up on all the latest news from the team. Cat had separated all the faces associated with the charity Facebook page and was starting to put names underneath each photo. She was using facial recognition software. A surprising number were known to the police.

It looked as if the whole of the criminal network might have been captured in that photograph. The one person that wasn't in the picture was Brian himself.

*Maybe he took the photo,* Karen thought to herself. *Or maybe he deliberately left himself out of the shot, to make sure he wasn't identified.*

Whatever the reason, Karen decided to try and record a photofit of Dodds, so they could add something to the incident boards.

That took about an hour. Despite all her efforts, and that of the photofit expert, she wasn't impressed by the results.

## Chapter Twenty-Three

On the golf course Max was playing a blinder. Billy was in awe of the young man's abilities, having seen nothing like it, beyond the golf he had watched on the television. He wasn't on his own though, this was a quality group of golfers. By the end of his first round, Max was sitting two shots behind the leaders, firmly in the top ten.

He would have everything to play for, the following day.

Cat continued to put names to faces, and by the end of the afternoon almost half the men and women who supposedly 'worked' for the charity had been identified. Some of them had extensive records, some of them were dead.

Karen forwarded the information on to Dr Rae. She reviewed the bodies they had found against details from their police records. Several were a possible match.

The detectives considered what this meant. Their collective conclusion was that this was a criminal network, with a unique, macabre and violent punishment regime. It seemed the only explanation.

There were thirty people in the picture. Many were still to be identified, their role in the charity revealed, and most importantly, whether they were alive or dead. They needed someone from inside the organisation to identify everyone. They needed Brian Dodds, or whoever was behind all this.

Karen and Jack, with the backing of their DCI, set up a massive operation for the following day. Teams of uniformed officers were sent to a dozen addresses to try and pull in some of the people Cat had identified.

It was seven in the evening by the time Cat left the office. Jack had gone home a few minutes before, and Karen had just spoken with Billy. He was spending the evening with Max, frustrated to not be in on the action.

When Karen returned home, she enjoyed a quick plate of pasta, then fed Jinx. Once she was happily ensconced on the sofa, she called to talk to both Jack and Laura. Both agreed the conclusion they had reached about the role of the Charity in these crimes, seemed the logical one, although Laura pointed out some of the bodies she had in her morgue, were not good matches for the people in the photograph.

They agreed to meet up at Southwick North the following day to discuss how the operation was proceeding.

Karen tried to relax for the evening. Two glasses of wine helped, as did the company of her beloved cat. It would be an early start in the morning.

*Wednesday, 1st June 2022*

At just before five o'clock, Karen joined a team of uniformed officers outside a property just off the Newcastle Road. She had chosen this raid because the woman in the picture had been standing near the centre of the group, just to the right of Jess Brookes.

The woman's name was Arianna Picton. She went by the name of Anna. She lived in the house with her husband and son. She had a criminal record as a small-time drug dealer, though had nothing against her name for the last five years.

The electronic hands on her watch hit five. Karen gave the team the nod and they smashed open the front door. At the same time, teams across the city were doing the same thing. Jack was out there somewhere, as were all the other detectives in her team.

As the front door shattered, specially trained officers burst into the house, shouting at the top of their voices, doing everything they could to disorientate the occupiers.

The house was clear downstairs, so the team moved upstairs. Karen followed them in, noting the trappings of a normal, well to do family. As she walked over to the mantelpiece, above the expensive looking electric fireplace, she noted a set of family photographs.

Anna was there with her husband and their son. She picked up the picture as the shouting upstairs intensified. The man in the picture wasn't Anna's husband. It was Brian Dodds, the man she had met at the office of the Charity.

There was a scream from upstairs and the sound of a window breaking.

"He's getting away," one of the officers shouted.

Karen rushed towards the back door, struggling in her hurry to turn the key. Outside she could see a man, dressed only in boxer shorts, drop to the ground, just as a uniformed officer walked in the back gate.

There was a single shot, and the officer fell to the ground. The man jumped over him before disappearing into the darkness of the back lane. She had never even considered they might be facing armed criminals.

She ran to the officer shouting for someone to call an ambulance. Karen could see in the light emanating from the house that he had been shot in the shoulder. She shouted for help, pushing her hands against the wound to try and stop the flow of blood. Within minutes the siren of an ambulance could be heard as other members of the team helped her to support their wounded colleague.

She kept reassuring the man that he would be fine.

"I've got you, just keep strong. The ambulance is on its way."

"It hurts like hell, Ma'am."

She looked down at the young officer. He couldn't have been more than twenty years old.

"Think of the kudos with your mates. You'll be the only one with a bullet wound."

The lad managed a faint smile. "Should be worth a round at the pub Ma'am."

"That's for sure, and I'll be first in line to buy you a pint."

"I'm sorry I couldn't stop him."

"Don't be daft. He had a gun; you didn't even have time to pull your taser."

A hand on Karen's shoulder told her that the paramedics were here.

"Look after him, guys. He's a brave lad."

Karen left them too it. In the distance she heard a motorcycle start up. She went back into the house. The scene was quite chaotic. Police were combing the house for any information they could find about the man who had shot their colleague. Anna was wrapped in a dressing gown, sitting on the sofa in her lounge, with her son cuddled up alongside her. She was in an obvious state of shock.

Karen sat down in the armchair opposite her.

"Sorry about this Anna. We're following up on all the employees of the Housing for the Helpless Charity." She reached into her pocket and showed Anna the photograph.

Anna took it and studied it.

"That is you in the picture." Anna just nodded.

"Was that Brian Dodds, who just escaped out of the window?"

Anna looked at Karen, fear etched across her face. She kept quiet.

"I know you're afraid Anna, but you are up to your armpits in this, whatever it is. If you want to stay with your son, I need you to help me."

The boy seemed to understand and snuggled in closer, Anna kissed him on the head.

"He'll kill me," she whispered.

"We'll protect you. Give you a new life."

Anna shook her head. "You can't protect us. I can't talk to you."

"Can you at least tell us who all these people are?"

Anna looked at the photograph again, shook her head and handed it back to Karen.

"Then we'll have to take you in I'm afraid, to be formally questioned." She looked around and grabbed the nearest officer. "Sergeant, can you please arrest this woman on suspicion of murder, I'll call social services to come and take the lad into care."

Anna looked up, stunned by what she had just heard.

"Murder? I'm not involved in any murders. It was just some harmless drug dealing. I'm not a murderer."

"Drug dealing is not harmless, Anna. We have several bodies linked to this organisation, and whether you knew it or not, is something we intend to find out."

Anna just burst out crying and pulled her son in tighter still.

"I'll leave you with him until social services arrive, but then you are coming down to the station with us."

Anna looked distraught, as Karen left her to see what, if anything, had been discovered. As she walked upstairs, the young constable was taken through the house on a stretcher to the ambulance and driven away.

On the upper level of the terraced house, officers were working their way through the three bedrooms. One was being used as an office and was getting special treatment. Two computers were being bagged up ready to be taken away, while all the drawers and cupboards were being searched.

The boy's room was relatively untouched, and Karen went in and sat on the bed. It had a red and white Sunderland AFC duvet and pillowcase set. On the wall was a framed signed Sunderland shirt. There were various toys around the room, a tablet for computer games, no doubt, and a few pictures. The bed was all crumpled from where the boy had jumped out and ran to his mother.

One of the pictures attracted her attention. It was of the boy and Brian, if that was his real name, sitting on a large motorcycle in a garage. They were laughing and looked as if they were having a good time.

*Where is that garage?* Karen thought to herself.

She had noticed a pile of boxes in the background, behind the bike. She needed to know where that lock up was.

Karen took the photo and frame and went back downstairs. She showed it to Anna.

"Where is this garage, Anna?"

Anna took the photograph and started crying again. "I don't know. He never took me there. He called it his man cave."

Karen looked again at the photograph. She could see the door of the next garage in the row and hoped that might trigger some sort of recognition by someone in the force.

She gave it to one of the police officers after taking a picture of the image with her phone. Outside the night was starting to give way to dawn as Karen climbed the stairs again to look in the other upstairs rooms.

The main bedroom was as the couple had left it. Apart from all the drawers and wardrobes which were now open with some of the contents emptied on to the floor or bed. The window hung open where Brian had made his escape.

Karen looked out to see where he had jumped. Beneath them was the roof of the kitchen extension and from there it looked like he had jumped down on to a small lean to store before making his escape.

Given the speed of their entry into the building, she knew he would not have had time to get dressed, managing at best to grab the gun and maybe a wallet or a few small items he could carry.

She wondered if he had an escape plan and knew exactly what he would do in these circumstances.

Karen was about to walk back downstairs when she saw the open bathroom door. She popped into the bathroom and opened the unit above the sink.

In there was the usual bits and pieces, including toothbrushes, toothpaste and some tablets. She looked down at the floor. It was beautiful, with grey and white patterned tiles. The white bath had a shower over and a bathmat was in place ready for those using the shower.

It was slightly askew, which offended her need to have everything in place. Without thinking, she went to push the mat back in place, but noticed a few scratches on the tiles near the end of the bath.

She pushed the bath panel. It rattled.

Karen called for some help. One of the officers came in and took over. He got down on his knees and played with the bath panel for a while. Eventually the officer managed to pull the panel away from the bath, revealing a dark void.

Getting her phone out, she turned on the torch function and shone it under the bath. In the far corner were a pile of small bags. The officer reached in and pulled one out. The small black backpack style bag was dusty and had some cobwebs across it, yet it seemed new.

Karen carefully opened the bag and shone her torch inside. Through the small gap she could see it was full of money. The policeman pulled another five bags out from under the bath. Four were full of money, the fifth was full of drugs.

Taking one of the bags of money, Karen walked back down to talk to Anna, just as a representative of social services appeared on the scene.

Karen showed Anna the bag. "Have you seen this before?"

Anna looked inside at the rolls of cash. She shook her head. "Where was that?"

"Under your bath."

"I've never seen that before."

"There were drugs there too Anna. A lot of drugs."

"I'm sorry, I never knew they were there."

Karen was frustrated but not surprised. She smiled at Anna to try and reassure her.

"I think we are just about done here. This gentleman will take your son into care until this is all sorted out. An officer will take you down to the station and your house will be secured for further forensic tests."

Anna just hugged and kissed her son. In the end the police and social services had to drag the boy away from his mother. It was traumatic, one of the most traumatic things Karen had ever witnessed.

Once she had ensured all the money and drugs were safely processed, she headed back to Southwick North to find out how the others had fared.

The office was a hive of activity as the detectives returned from their respective raids. She called for everyone to be quiet. One by one she had each detective recount the details of the person they had apprehended. Cat worked frenetically to gather all the information provided by each detective.

When everyone had reported in, she recounted the details of her raid. All were shocked that a firearm had been used.

The upshot of the early morning raids were the arrests of six of the people on that image. All had criminal records involving drugs yet claimed those days were long past.

As Karen listened to the reports, she was struck at how petrified all of those arrested had been. It was a common thread.

The office had quietened down as each of the detectives wrote up their reports. She watched as they started to come through. The first from John Phillips seemed particularly frightening as the man they had apprehended had tried to kill himself before he could be restrained.

John reported the fear in the man's eyes. He had been babbling when he was carried into the car that 'Nero would kill him' or at least that was the best John could interpret from the terrified rantings.

The next three reports just noted how afraid each person had been. Each refusing to cooperate with the police for fear of their lives.

Jack's report was the last to come in. The woman she arrested had been afraid, yet seemed to carry an air of arrogance. The woman had said that they, the police, wouldn't hold her for long. 'Nero would save her'.

Karen sat back in her chair.

"Jack, did you find out who this Nero was? Your target mentioned the name as did one of the others who was arrested."

"Afraid not. I thought she might be referring to a god of some kind that would save her."

"The man John arrested was petrified of what 'Nero' would do to him. It looks like we might have a name for the centre of our incident boards."

Karen called Mick over. "You're the font of all knowledge, non-computer based, Mick. Have you ever come across the name Nero?"

Mick looked at Karen, the cogs obviously whirring. "Well, aside from the obvious, I've not heard of a criminal going by the name Nero."

"What's the obvious?" Jack asked.

Mick smiled the smile of the older and wiser towards the youngsters, yet to learn the ways of the world.

"Nero was an Emperor of Rome, said to be mad, he allegedly fiddled while Rome burned. I personally think he was a victim of bad press."

Jack seemed unimpressed.

"What might be more interesting Ma'am is that the word nero is Italian for black."

They all looked at the board which featured the word black in the centre.

"What's the betting our Mr Black, Nero and Brian Dodds are all the same man?"

"I'd go with the first two Ma'am but the third might be a stretch. Brian could be Nero's right-hand man. It could be that Nero is not even based in this country."

Karen stood, walking across to the incident boards. She called everyone to attention.

"Guys, we have a name. Two of the people we arrested mentioned the name Nero. One seemed to fear Nero, the other believed he or she would be their saviour. Cat, check all the police records to look for any mention of the name. When you've done that, try our European colleagues to see if they have a Nero on their wanted lists."

She looked around at her detectives. They were the cream of the crop as far as she was concerned. Her faith in them was complete even though she had known them for less than three weeks.

"Once you have completed your reports, grab a tea or coffee then go back to interview the detainees. Ask them the question, who is Nero? Watch their faces. I want to know exactly how they respond."

The chorus of "Yes Ma'ams" pleased her.

Karen returned to her desk and continued to write up her report. She hated this side of police work but knew how vital it was. This aspect of the job was the bread and butter which fed the investigation. The time it took was her bugbear.

In the excitement of the moment, she had almost forgotten that Billy needed to be informed. She picked up her phone and sent him a message. *Call me when you can. We have a name. Does Nero mean anything to you?*

## Chapter Twenty-Four

DCI Billy Roberts stood on the first tee at Ramside Hall, waiting for Max. He had left him in the changing rooms to get ready, while Billy made sure all his kit was in order. He must have checked the number of golf clubs in the bag a dozen times, as well as ensuring he had waterproofs, towels, balls and all the minutiae of the game he loved.

He looked at his phone and read the message from Karen.

This looked like real progress. He just had to ensure the young golfer got through the day, then he would take him to the station. That would just be a precaution, for his safety more than anything. Billy suspected his charge knew nothing about the crimes he was unsuspectingly involved with.

He looked at the time on his phone, then checked his watch. Max was leaving it a bit late. Billy used to have recurring nightmares about being late on the tee box. At his level in the sport that seemed ridiculous compared to what Max was potentially going to lose if he missed his tee time.

Then a switch in his mind went from, concerned caddy, to DCI in charge of an important person in the case. He started to walk back to the clubhouse, breaking into a run.

As he searched the locker room and the toilets, he kept asking everyone of they had seen Max. No-one had seen the young golfer. He looked at his watch again. In desperation he ran to the range. Max wasn't there. He checked his watch again. They had ten minutes before Max's name would be called.

Now panicking, Billy ran back to the tee box. He was hoping, beyond hope, that he would find Max waiting by his clubs. He was.

Billy had been about to call Max in as missing. He took a deep breath and walked the last few yards over to his charge.

"Where have you been?" Max asked.

"I just needed the loo one last time before we teed off."

Max looked at Billy and smiled. He looked the picture of innocence. Max took his mobile phone out of his pocket, switched it off, then slipped it into the top pocket of his golf bag.

"Let's win this thing." Max held out his hand to Billy who shook it. The hairs on the back of his neck stood up. Something in the young man's bearing had changed.

Billy smiled back. "It's in the bag."

Max took out his driver and walked over to the tee box as the starter called his name. Billy took the bag and followed him. Max confidently thrashed the ball down the first fairway towards the distant green.

As they walked down the middle of the fairway, Billy let Max walk ahead. He took out his own mobile and sent a quick message to Karen. *Not sure Max is kosher. Keeping an eye on him. Send some cover.*

Back at the office, Karen looked at her phone.

"Jack, fancy a cuppa?"

Jack looked across at her friend. Without question she got up and followed Karen down to the canteen.

They made a cuppa, their third of the day. Karen showed Jack the message. "Who should we send?"

"Rachel's raid was a bust, there was no-one home. I'd send her with Matt. He's finished his report and they work well together."

"You'll make a great DI one day Jack. They were my picks too. Is there something going on between those two?"

"Not sure, they are always together. Could well be."

Karen took a sip of her tea.

"Do you think Max could be involved?"

"It seems a bit of a stretch. There's been no clue from his journey to hint that he might have anything to do with the murders. He seemed to be just a clueless mule."

"A confident, clueless mule, by Billy's estimation. I think we are at a tipping point in this case Jack. I've also got an unanswered question, niggling at the back of my mind. Where did he get his golf bag from? Billy seemed to think it looked like his regular bag. How can that be, when we know the clubs he brought here were broken up to get to the drugs?"

"Are you thinking his regular clubs were already here?" Jack queried.

At that moment Mick popped his head around the canteen door. "They've found that garage Ma'am."

"Great work Mick. Come on Jack let's get over there."

The women quickly downed their drinks and followed Mick back to their office to get the address. They collected their jackets and bags, then headed out to the car park.

Jack drove as Karen used her phone to direct her to the location of the garage.

When they arrived, a police cordon had been established around the entrance. Someone had already opened the door. They showed their badges to the police sergeant in charge of the scene, before ducking under the police tape to have a look at what the garage contained.

A single strip light lit the dim interior. There was a gap in the centre of the garage where the motorcycle had been stored. Drops of oil stained the floor where the bike had stood. To one side was a work top, covered in tools. The paraphernalia of a motorcycle enthusiast.

The rest of the walls of the garage were lined with cardboard boxes.

"We haven't opened any of them, Ma'am, we decided to wait until you arrived."

Karen put on a set of rubber gloves. She looked at the worktop, spotting a Stanley knife. She picked it up and walked across the garage to the first pile of boxes. Casting her eyes over the pile she couldn't see anything which might constitute a danger. After the shooting she was being ultra-cautious.

She gingerly lifted the top box from one of the stacks, placing it carefully on the garage floor. It was sealed with brown parcel tape. Karen slid the knife down the centre of the box, then cut along the edges to free the lid, which she then pulled open.

Jack bent down to see what was in the box.

"Photographs," Jack exclaimed. She sounded exasperated.

Karen reached down. Shuffling the photos about. She grabbed a handful of the prints, placing them on the floor. She dug into the box and took out another set, noting that they were general shots. Not one of them had images of individuals.

Two more handfuls were strewn over the floor before she stopped.

"Aha!"

Karen sounded triumphant as she lifted out a bag of money. More followed, as well as bags filled with drugs.

"Bingo!" Jack almost danced with excitement.

Karen called the uniformed officers in. Together they methodically worked through the pile of boxes, discovering more and more drugs. She estimated they had discovered several million pounds in cash as well as a pallet load of drugs.

A police van was called to take the haul away. A SOC team arrived to search the garage for clues, so Karen and Jack moved outside to take stock.

"This is more drugs than a few golfing mules and a boat could have brought into the country."

Jack looked at Karen. "What the hell have we stumbled on here?"

A pale blue van with black wheels pulled up at the end of the street. It was impossible to see who was driving through the smoked-out windows. Whoever it was, they barely paused before driving off.

Karen spotted the passing van.

*Just a passer-by or someone looking to reclaim their property?* She thought to herself.

It was not exactly an inconspicuous vehicle. She resolved to ask Cat and Mick to try and track down its movements using the local traffic cameras.

With nothing more they could usefully achieve, and the garage full of people in white overalls, Karen and Jack headed back to the car and drove back to Southwick North.

\*\*\*\*\*

Brian Dodds drove away, smacking his hands on the steering wheel as he went.

"Aaargh," he screamed. "Bloody police."

He thought frantically, not sure what to do next. His family life was gone, his future was gone. He was trapped between a rock and a hard place.

Everything he had risked, all the plans he had made, the life he had dreamed of; all lost in the blink of an eye. He would have his revenge. He didn't know how or when, but he would kill that detective. Karen Dee would pay for this.

Now he needed time, he needed to regroup. Above all he needed help.

With that in mind he drove out of town towards Newcastle. Slotting in with the rest of the traffic on the A184 he put the radio on. Classic FM blared away, trying, but failing, to lift his mood.

## Chapter Twenty-Five

Back at Southwick North, the detectives were buzzing with excitement. They had taken a real step forward in their investigation, seizing the spoils of the terrible crimes that had been committed, provided them with a real boost.

All were convinced Brian Dodds was their man.

At the request of Karen, Cat had searched for and picked up the van leaving the city. Traffic cams had followed it all the way to Newcastle. They lost it close to St James Park in a spot where camera coverage was low.

The Newcastle police were called to scour the area, to no avail.

Wherever Dodds had gone, he knew how to disappear.

*****

The blue van had barely left the road before it was swallowed by a non-descript rusting garage door. Inside, it was pitch black. As the garage door rattled shut, bright strip lights illuminated the vehicle, temporarily blinding Dodds.

As his eyes grew accustomed to the glare, shadowy figures approached his vehicle, opened the door and helped him out. Another opened the back door, quickly checking if there were any contents, before closing it again.

The van was completely empty.

Brian was ushered into a back room, which was less harshly lit, then tied to a simple wooden chair. He didn't struggle, he knew there was no point.

A dark-haired man in an immaculate dark blue suit walked into the sparse room and sat at the table, flanked by two others, similarly dressed. Brian's chair was the opposite side of the table, facing the three men.

"What are you doing here Brian?" It was the man in the centre of the three who spoke. He looked deadly serious.

"Hello Owen, the police were chasing me, I needed to disappear." He immediately regretted using the words. Quickly he continued. "I need somewhere to hide."

"Of course, we can help with that. Where is all the merchandise and money you were keeping safe for us."

Brian looked to the floor. "The police have it, that Detective Dee found my lock up."

"How did she do that?"

"I have no idea. She's very clever."

"Too clever for you Brian?"

"I got away didn't I. So not that clever."

"Yet you have lost everything. All that you have accumulated for us is gone."

The three men looked at each other.

"What are you worth to us now? You have nothing, the police know who you are, they are searching for you, and you have brought them one step closer to us."

Brian felt bile rise in his throat. He had to think fast.

"I know this business; I can start again, somewhere where the police don't know me."

There was a pause. Brian could feel his hands shaking behind his back. This was the moment that would decide his fate.

"Brian, you have been a trusted supporter, you have done well, up until now. I am sure you could start again somewhere, but as you say, you know our business well. If you were caught you could tell them all about us to reduce your punishment."

"No, I would never speak…"

"Shut up when I am talking." Owen slammed the table with his fists.

"Your only value to us now is your body. Take him away."

Brian screamed. "NOOO!"

Two men had been standing close behind him. One, with bottle blonde hair. grabbed his arms, while the other put a cloth over his mouth and nose. His wild eyes gradually closed as the chloroform took effect.

Brian was bundled into the boot of a black car, that had been in the back of the large garage. After checking the road was clear, the vehicle was driven out by the blonde-haired man, heading quickly back towards Sunderland. It headed towards the industrial estate on the banks of the River Wear. In the growing darkness, the car pulled up behind the Funeral Parlour.

The limp form of Brian Dodds was carried into the back door.

Later that evening Karen received a text. It was from P & P's Quality Pet Food Supplies. Laura had forwarded the message on to her. The shop had received a new supply of their premium dog food. There was a link to their website to enable her to place an order.

The message sent a chill down her spine.

She ordered a kilo of the meat for testing purposes, in Dr Rae's name.

Karen sent a Whatsapp to Jack and Dr Rae to let them know what she had done. She was convinced their search for Brian Dodds was now in vain. It was still early, so she invited the women over for a cup of tea. Laura was there in five minutes; Jack took a bit longer.

With the TV volume turned down, and Jinx settled on Laura's lap, the three women discussed the events of the day. Karen explained she believed the new stock of dog food was very likely to be from the body of Brian Dodds.

"How much meat would you get from a man's body?"

Dr Rae looked at Karen. "There's a question you don't get asked every day." She took a sip of her tea. "How much do you think he weighed?"

Karen looked at Jack. "Around 13 stone?" Jack nodded in agreement.

"Then I reckon you could get anything up to 100 pounds of meat, that's 45 kilograms in new money."

Karen did some quick mental arithmetic. At £60 a kilo, that makes the body of Brian Dodds worth around £2700, if that's where the meat is coming from."

The women went silent for a moment, each contemplating the gruesome process of turning a man into dog food.

Karen reached for the chocolate digestives.

"Help yourselves fellow witches. There's plenty more where these come from. I've ordered a kilo of the dog food. I'll pick it up tomorrow."

"If you let me have the sample, I can get it tested. We should be able to see if it is human. I am guessing it will be cooked in some way before it is put in the tubs."

"Will that cause a problem with the testing?"

"No Jack. There are some fancy pieces of kit out there these days. This will be done using a DNA sequencer, which can tell us the origin of the meat."

"Will it take long?"

"Everything has to be done yesterday for you guys," Laura smiled, as she sipped her drink. "No, it won't take long. I have some friends who can do this for me. I might even be able to get you an answer tomorrow if you get the sample to me early."

Karen looked at Jack. "I'll pop over on my way into work tomorrow. I'll ask Cat to look at CCTV cameras around the Pet food shop to see if she can spot where the delivery came from."

"Sounds like a plan, boss." Jack picked up her third biscuit.

"Don't you get fed at home," Laura joked, laughing her cackling laugh.

"It's not good etiquette to leave food on a plate Doctor. You should know that." The three friends laughed. Comfortable with the company they were keeping, happy to know each would have the other's back if they were in any sort of danger.

"Any news on the other bodies we found yet?"

"Well, we have had an interesting development, just today. We have done some of our own DNA work on the bodies. Most don't tell us much but one, a body that has been in the water a long time, came back with a strong European link."

Karen was curious. "Can you tell where in Europe they came from?"

"It's not an exact science, Karen, but there is a strong chance they were Dutch or German. The genetic markers pointed to that area of Europe as a likely origin for that person."

Karen thought about the boat in the Sunderland Marina.

"That could be our sailor, Jack."

"Sounds plausible."

"Thanks Laura, I know it has been a difficult time. We really appreciate all that you are doing for us."

"The Witches of Witherwack need to stick together." Dr Rae held out her hands and the three women linked, forming a circle of sorts.

Karen felt the usual tingle. Jinx suddenly let out a squeal and leapt from Laura's lap, rushing out of the room towards the kitchen.

"That's weird. I'd better check she's OK." Karen let go of the other two and followed Jinx into the kitchen. The smell wasn't very pleasant. Jinx was in her litter tray.

"Tummy trouble little one?" Karen asked the cat, which looked decidedly unhappy. She rubbed the cats head then opened a drawer to get out a cat litter bag to dispose of the rather large poo the cat had left in the tray.

"Do you want some more tea?" She shouted back towards the living room.

"Yes please," Jack and Laura shouted back in unison.

Karen filled the kettle and flicked it on. She looked at her watch. It was just before 9pm. She went to the cupboard and brought out the rest of a packet of chocolate digestives and took them into the living room.

"Is Jinx, OK?" Laura asked.

"Tummy trouble. I wouldn't go in the kitchen for a while."

At the same moment, Jinx put her head around the front room door, peering in cautiously.

"What's the matter with you?" Karen asked the cat before picking her up and dropping her back on Laura's lap.

"She looks like she's had a shock," Jack observed, leaning across to stroke the cat's head.

"So would you if you'd just produced what she has," Karen laughed, as she went back to the kitchen with the empty cups to make the tea.

"Do you get a tingle when the three of us link hands?" Jack whispered the question to Dr Rae.

"Yes, I do. I thought it was just me."

"I'm sure Karen is feeling it too."

Karen reappeared with a tray of drinks.

"Tea all round."

Jack took her cup and looked at her friend. "We were just saying we get a sort of tingle when we link hands."

Karen had just picked up her cup, cradling it in her hands, enjoying the warmth.

"I've always had it, since we first held hands in Betty's Café. I thought it was just me."

"Maybe it's some sort of static?" Laura suggested.

"Or maybe we really are witches," Jack laughed, and the others joined in.

Jinx almost ran off again, but Laura managed to hold her down. "Every witch needs a cat, Karen," Laura cackled.

"That's me then," Karen smiled, reaching over to stroke her cat. "Traitor, why do you always sit on someone else, when we have visitors?" Jinx looked at her but went straight back to sleep, purring away under the head strokes and tickles she was enjoying from Laura.

Jack tried to bring the discussion back to the case in hand.

"Karen, any thoughts on who might be behind all this?"

"I'm not sure yet, but I think this is beyond Prudence and her boyfriend." She sipped at her tea. "I think there's someone else we haven't factored in. Dodds wasn't the tip of the iceberg; he was just a cog in the machine."

"Maybe the apex of the organisation isn't in the UK, maybe it's organised from abroad."

Karen looked at Jack. "That's possible, but I believe there is a UK kingpin. Someone here is calling the shots. They may be in Sunderland, or they may be in Newcastle; I'm not sure which, but I feel they are close."

The women put down their cups and instinctively held hands again. The familiar tingle played through their hands and up their arms.

They glanced at each other, then Karen made a suggestion.

"On the count of three, all say where they think the UK boss of this criminal organisation is based. One, two, three."

"Sunderland." They all gave the same answer at the same time.

"OK, that's creepy," Laura remarked.

"I was thinking Newcastle before I blurted that out."

"Me too Jack. What were you thinking Karen?"

Karen broke the circle.

"I was thinking Sunderland. I just wanted the answer to be in our patch."

"Maybe your thoughts influenced ours in some way."

"Who knows Jack. Let's not worry about that now. I'm tired. Let's get a good night's sleep. We have a lot to do tomorrow."

As she went to bed, she suddenly thought. *I wonder how Billy got on today. I thought he would have been in touch.*

\*\*\*\*\*

In the early hours of the following morning, a shopping trolley from a nearby supermarket was thrown off the Spire Bridge. The two youths, dressed in new black tracksuits, who had done the deed, laughed as they ran off towards the South end of the bridge.

In the dead of the night, no-one saw the remains of Brian Dodds splash into the River Wear and sink to their final resting place.

# Chapter Twenty-Six

Billy had been amazed at the skill of the young golfer he was caddying for. Max had played the first nine in four under par, then started back with a birdie on the tenth.

At that point he was tied for the lead and had the momentum to carry him forward to win the tournament.

What he couldn't account for was the skill of the other golfers. Despite his best efforts he was pipped to the post by a teenager from Durham. Max was gutted. In fact, he was furious.

Billy had never seen him so angry.

The presentation was a strange affair. Despite picking up the runners-up prize and a nice cheque, Max wouldn't smile. He glowered at the camera, when he had his picture taken, and snatched the cheque away from the sponsor. Billy applauded politely, but there was a level of awkward embarrassment in the room.

Max drank too much, and spent too much time on his phone, given the importance of the occasion. Some of the conversations he was having seemed intense. They only sufficed to make him angrier.

At one point he stared straight at Billy while talking. Averting his eyes before continuing his conversation. Billy felt uncomfortable and headed outside for some fresh air. He took out his mobile with the intention of calling Karen.

A four iron across the back of his head put paid to that. He slumped to the floor, his phone fell from his hand and slid across the tiled patio. In the gathering darkness, it lay unnoticed as Billy was bundled into the boot of a black car and driven away.

*Thursday 2nd June 2022*

At 8am Karen was standing in a queue outside P & P's Pet food suppliers. She was about tenth in line.

As soon as the doors opened, people filed in. Those who had booked the dog food headed to a special counter to collect their orders while others fought to fill their baskets with the meat.

Karen paid £60 in cash and pushed her way out of the shop through the throng of people jostling to buy the dog food. The car parks around that part of the Industrial Estate were chock a block with vehicles. One flashed at her. She walked over.

It was Laura in her mini. She wound the window down to let Karen pass her the dog food.

"Take care of this, its precious stuff. They'll be sold out in minutes in there."

"If only they knew what they were buying."

"I think they'd quickly go back to their old dog food."

"You'd hope so. But some of that lot, don't care where it comes from. They just want to feed their dogs the best."

"More money than sense. I'll get this lot to the DNA Lab as quick as I can. I'll let you know later what the results are. Then you can shut that shop down."

"It will be my pleasure. I'd best get over to the station now. I have a few things to do today."

Laura drove away, wheels spinning, as Karen walked over to her car. Ten minutes later Detective Inspector Dee was parking around the back of the Southwick North station.

She walked into the office. Everyone stopped and stared.

"I like the new look," Rachel smiled across at Karen.

Karen had forgotten she was wearing the same disguise as she had used the last time, she visited the shop. Hanging her cap on the lamp on her desk, Karen walked across to the incident boards.

"Cat, can you check the traffic cams around the Hylton Park Road Industrial Estate. I want to see if you can spot any late-night deliveries."

"On it, Ma'am." The customary thumbs up from behind the screens indicated that Cat was already working on Karen's request.

"The rest of you. We need to bring in Prudence and Philip. I want to hear what they know about all this. Apart from you Mick, I need you to do some research for me. Look at the finances of the Pet Food Shop. I want to see where the money is syphoned off to," she thought for a moment, then added. "Look out for sums of money going out of around two thousand pounds."

She looked around. "Has anyone seen the boss?"

"No Ma'am. Not yet, but it is still early," Mick commented without looking away from his computer.

Karen went back to her desk and sent a message to her DCI. There was no reply.

*****

Billy found himself tied to a chair in a room, just like a room he had seen before. He was on his own. His head hurt like hell. The side of his face felt sticky. He was sure it was blood.

Unlike the last room he had been in, this one had no windows. There was a chill in the air. He guessed he was in a cellar.

The three chairs on the other side of the table were empty. He wondered how long they would stay that way.

*****

Karen was worried. She talked to Jack. "I think we need to get over to the Golf Club and see what happened."

"You're right. It's not like him to be quiet, especially about golf. I wonder how Max got on?"

Cat must have heard. "He came second, I saw the result last night on the internet."

Karen walked over to Cat. "Were there any pictures?"

Cat flicked through a few pages on the Golf Club's social media site. "Here you go."

Karen looked at the photos. "He doesn't look very happy, does he?"

"Nope, he caused a bit of a fuss and left early."

"Did the boss feature in any of the photos?"

Cat flicked through the pictures. "There he is."

Karen looked at the photo and could just make out Billy applauding at the back of the crowd in the club house.

"Well, we know he was there at around 7pm last night. Come on Jack, let's get over there and see if anyone saw him leave."

The pair made their way down to the car park and took Karen's Audi to make the drive to Ramside Hall. When they arrived, they went immediately to see the club professional. He remembered seeing Max and Billy the day before but didn't see them leave. He suggested talking to the Club Secretary.

On the way across, Karen noticed a security camera on the outside of the clubhouse.

Once in the club they quickly found the secretary's office. The name on the door read, Tony Stewart, Club Secretary. They knocked and walked in.

Karen quickly asked if he had seen Billy the night before. Tony had seen Billy but had been so busy organising the presentation that he didn't see him leave. The man mentioned that Max had seemed very agitated when he picked up his prize.

Karen asked if they could check their CCTV camera system. Tony was happy to help.

The pair watched the film from the previous evening. They started at 6pm and let the film roll from there, fast forwarding sections when little was happening. Then they spotted Billy. They could make him out in the crowd at the presentation and then saw him move outside at around 7.30pm.

The camera feed from outside picked up the DCI at the back of the clubhouse standing on his own. He was on his phone as someone walked up behind him and hit him with a golf club.

Both Karen and Jack jumped at the force of the blow.

Another man joined the assailant. It was Max.

Together they dragged the unconscious form of DCI Billy Roberts towards the car park.

Karen rewound the tape to the moment of impact. She had spotted Billy drop his phone.

They quickly checked the other cameras and saw Billy being loaded into the boot of a car before being driven off. Crucially they could make out a registration number.

After thanking the club secretary, the two detectives made their way out to where Billy had been hit. They soon spotted blood on a paving slab, then Jack noticed his phone under a bush which was overhanging the patio area.

Karen picked it up and placed it in her pocket.

"We've got to find him Jack. Let's get back to the station. He is our priority now. We find Billy, we solve this case."

They walked quickly back to the car.

As they drove back Jack asked the question that had been nagging at her since they saw the CCTV footage.

"Do you think Max is the person in charge of the whole operation?"

"That's the way it's looking, Jack."

"Where do you think they took him?"

"We'll get Cat on the case. In fact, call it in. Also get Mick to check on that list of properties owned by the charity. My money is on them taking him to one of those."

Jack dialled into the station as they were heading back down the A690 to Sunderland.

Back at the office both Prudence and Philip were in separate interview rooms waiting for Karen to return.

After a quick briefing where Karen arranged for Cat to involve all the team in the search for the car, Karen and Jack headed down to the interview rooms to the two Ps.

"Ladies first," Karen suggested, and they walked into the interview room where Prudence was waiting for them, with a lawyer.

"Hello Prudence, nice to see you again."

"I wish I could say the same. What's the meaning of this?"

"I'm going to be straight with you Prudence. I think you can help us with a very serious case we have been working on for the last few weeks."

"Of course, if I can help, I will."

"Now I must caution you, that we believe you may be complicit in this case. You might not know that you are involved, but we must consider you a potential suspect at this stage."

Prudence looked a bit shocked.

"I understand," she replied carefully, glancing at her lawyer. "I have nothing to hide."

"Thank you. Then let's begin."

Karen reached for her phone and produced a photo of Max when he was receiving his trophy. "Do you know this man?"

Prudence took the phone. She stared at it for an uncomfortably long time. Tears seemed to well up in her eyes.

"I'll need protection if I answer your questions."

"We'll do everything we can to keep you safe."

"That's not enough Karen, I need a promise."

Karen looked at Jack, then back at Prudence. "I promise we will keep you safe." She knew it was a promise that would be difficult to keep. With Billy's life at stake, it seemed the words were worth saying.

Prudence handed the phone back to Karen.

"His name is Nero. He controls our lives. He controls everything."

"Do you have a surname?" Jack asked.

"His name is just Nero. I have only met him once. You only need to meet him once. He asked us if he could use our premises as a front for his business. I say ask, that's a euphemism for demanded with menace."

"Have you profited from the arrangement?"

Prudence looked down at the desk. "He paid us what he called a rent for the use of the premises and a commission on sales. I don't know what he was selling."

"You don't know what he was selling? Don't give me that. You know exactly what he was selling. He was selling human flesh."

Prudence looked at Karen, as horror swept across her face. "No."

"Yes Prudence. Human meat."

"We were told he would get the occasional highland bull from a local heritage herd." Prudence began to cry. Her lawyer looked as if she was about to be sick.

Karen reached across and squeezed Prudence's hand.

"I know this is hard Prudence, but this Nero has our boss, and we need your help to find him, or he will be processed in the same way as all the other victims."

Prudence took a deep breath. Looking around the grey room all she could think of was the idea that she might be spending some time in a cell like this if things went against her. The life she had enjoyed, her dogs, her business interests, status and lovely house were all about to disappear.

With a look at her lawyer, who nodded to reassure her, Prudence told Karen and Jack all she knew.

She began with how Nero had come into their lives. Philip had been asked to arrange Nero's mother's funeral. She remembered it so well, as it had been a massive affair and Philip had asked her to help with the arrangements.

Philip had still been married at the time, and Prudence had been having an affair with him, which Nero somehow picked up on.

They had visited his house which overlooked Roker Park. It was a very grand house she recalled. Nero's father had died several years before which had left his mother in charge of the family business. Nero never told them what that was, but when the day of the funeral came, there had been some very dodgy looking characters paying their respects.

Some of the guests had come from around the world, and Prudence compared it to a mafia funeral. She smiled half-heartedly as she recalled how most of the guests wore sunglasses, despite it being a grey October day.

The first inclination of trouble came when Nero called Philip to ask if they could use his funeral parlour. Philip had declined but Nero was insistent, saying he knew about his affair with Prudence and would tell Philip's wife, if he didn't give them the keys.

Philip had no idea why they wanted to use the premises, however in his heart he knew it wouldn't be good. He gave the keys to one of Nero's men and let them get on with it.

Next, he called Prudence and offered to her a range of exclusive dog food to sell through her shop. Again, he used the threat of telling Philip's wife about their affair if she didn't comply.

For a while all had gone well, then Nero started sending them invitations to posh events, their status in the community began to grow and soon they were offered the chance to get involved in a charity Nero was running.

They couldn't say no.

Philip's wife had become suspicious of the couple, then one day around four years ago she was found dead in her car alongside the A19.

The day after, Philip received a call from Nero. He told Philip that his worries were over. Him and Prudence had nothing to fear. He had also told him that he was employing Jess at the Charity, so he could keep an eye on him.

They both felt it was clear that somehow Nero had engineered her death. Employing Jess was something else he had over them. They knew if they did anything wrong, or said anything, Jess would be killed, and they would be next.

For the last few years, neither Prudence nor Philip had heard from Nero. Then Karen and Jack had knocked on her door and she knew their house of cards was about to fall.

Nero had telephoned Philip to order him to try and put Karen off the scent. The upshot had been the clumsy clown attack. Prudence believed that Nero had then taken it upon himself to get rid of Karen.

Karen asked Prudence if she remembered where Nero's mother's house was. She gave Karen the address.

They had a much shorter conversation with Philip who corroborated all that Prudence had told them. He too asked for protection. Karen left him hanging. An assault charge would have to be considered in his case. One nugget they did get from Philip was that his son Jess was missing. He hadn't seen him for several days.

That would have to wait for a while. Jess was listed on the police database as a missing person.

Back in the office, Karen walked over to Mick's desk to look at the list of properties linked to the charity Brian Dodds had been involved in.

All had been visited by the detectives over the last couple of weeks. None had given rise to any concerns. The occupants had all been grateful tenants who had been taken from the streets and given a roof over their heads.

Time was running out. She made her decision.

"Jack, let's visit the house in Roker Park Road. John, Jordan you come with us to provide backup. Mick can you arrange an armed response unit to be ready in the area in case we run into trouble."

She looked around her team. Everyone was focussed and keen. "Matt and Rachel, can you go to the Funeral parlour. I want it cordoned off as a crime scene. Be careful though, we may be too late, the boss might already be there. Is everyone up to date with their firearms training?"

Everyone nodded in response.

"Right, vests on and gear up. This might get nasty."

As everyone dressed ready for action, Karen called the uniform team to warn them about what was happening. They offered to put officers in the area, which Karen gratefully accepted.

She looked at her watch. It was just after 10am. Time to go.

Within ten minutes they were parking their cars in Park Gate Road. The police presence was subtle but obvious to the detectives. Two vans could be seen in the vicinity of the park, one in Side Cliff Road and another parked up in Roker Park Road itself.

More support was being driven to the area as Jack and Karen got out of their cars. Karen adjusted her bullet proof vest, pulling her jacket around her. Jack went to the boot of her car and pulled out the heavy red enforcer.

She walked around to the front of the house, with Karen taking the lead. Together they walked up to the red front door of the imposing brick building. The windows looked dark and unlived in. Upstairs the curtains were closed. Karen knocked on the door, then let her hand rest on the Glock 17 pistol in her jacket pocket. She carried it there rather than in her holster. It was an affection she had developed a few years ago.

There was no answer.

She tried again. After a few more seconds she gave Jack a nod.

Summoning all her strength, Jack swung back the enforcer, but Karen grabbed her arm before she could smash the door down. Instead, Karen tried the door handle.

The door creaked open. Karen scanned the empty hallway in front of her. Her expert eyes caught a glint of light on a trip wire, fixed across the hallway. The wire didn't seem to be attached to anything nasty. It was fixed to the wall on one side, and a small hall table on the other. Perched on the table were two old vases. Enough to make a loud noise if the wire was pulled, causing them to topple on to the tiled hall floor.

Karen crept in, stepping over the wire, making sure Jack avoided the trap. She pulled out a penknife and carefully cut the wire. Slowly and methodically, they checked each room on the ground floor. The place looked bare and unlived in. Jack followed behind; her gun drawn.

When they reached the far end of the house, they found the kitchen. There were three dirty mugs in the sink. That sent a tingle down Karen's spine. What remained of the liquid in the bottom of the cups was still wet.

"These are fresh Jack," Karen whispered.

Her mind flashed back to the room with the three chairs.

John and Jordan walked into the room. Karen put her finger to her lips. She spoke to them in hushed tones.

"John, Jordan, check upstairs, we'll check the garden and have a look around to see if there are any rooms we may have missed."

As John and Jordan headed upstairs, Karen and Jack opened the back door and walked down into the garden. It was a jungle. Whoever had been there was not interested in gardening.

A white plastic garden table with three battered chairs sat on a small, paved area next to the back wall of the house. A full ash tray, and some abandoned beer cans pointed to recent use.

The detectives looked around the table. Jack spotted a worn strip of grass leading to a corner of the house. Almost hidden behind a bush was a wooden door. It had a brand-new padlock fitted. It was unlocked.

Karen whispered to Jack. "We've been stomping about in the house. There's a chance they might know we are here."

Jack nodded. "The boss could be down there. We need to look."

"There might also just be a very rusty lawn mower, piled on top of a broken hedge strimmer."

Jack smiled. "I'll go first, you watch my back."

"The hell you will. This is my case, Jack. I'll take the lead. Besides, I'm ex-military, this is bread and butter to me."

"If you insist. After you."

Using her foot, she edged the door open. It was pitch black inside. She pulled a torch from her jacket pocket and shone it down the steps into what looked like the entrance to a cellar. There was a door at the bottom of the steps.

Taking the lead, Karen carefully walked down the steps. Now she was close, she could see the door at the bottom was slightly ajar. A light shone through the narrow slit. Crucially she could hear voices.

She turned to Jack, putting her finger to her lips.

Carefully she pushed the door an inch further open. As she did, Karen pulled the gun out of her pocket and adopted her favoured weaver stance which she used when not on the range.

From her position she had a good view of the room. There were two men sitting in chairs in front of a plain wooden table. The layout was the same as the cottage they had visited earlier in the investigation. She couldn't quite see the other side of the table, but guessed Billy was sitting tied to a chair. A strip light provided the illumination.

One of the men at the table looked like Max, or Nero as they now called him. She couldn't be sure because the second man was sitting between him and her position.

The question in her mind was whether there was another person in the room. That third chair had been pulled back.

There was a muffled groan from further in the room. It was time to go in. Her heart rate had elevated, and she could feel her hands shaking.

She turned to Jack. Karen mouthed, 'on three.'

## Chapter Twenty-Seven

Just at that moment, the door at the top of the stairs opened and Jordan shouted down. "The house is clear Ma'am."

All hell broke loose.

Karen burst through the door. "Armed police, stay where you are."

In that split second, time in the room seemed to stand still.

Billy was tied in a chair opposite to where the men were sitting. Behind him stood a blonde-haired man dressed in the same uniform black as the others. He had a bunch of Billy's hair in his hand and had just pulled the DCI's head back. Billy couldn't see what was happening.

Jack followed her in, gun at the ready.

The man behind Billy reached behind his back and pulled out a gun. With Billy in the way, Karen hesitated to take a shot. The blonde-haired man fired just before she did. She felt the bullet clip her left shoulder. It didn't affect her aim.

Pulling the trigger, she shot the blonde-haired man in the head. There wasn't time for niceties. Both Nero, and the man sitting next to him, were now on the move. Nero turned away from the action while the other man ran at Karen, rugby tackling her to the floor.

It was only then, when she hit the floor, that she realised Jack was on the floor next to her. The fall knocked the gun out of her hand.

She felt hands around her neck. Struggling for breath, she tried desperately to shift the man who was on top of her. Desperate thoughts started to race through her mind, as she failed to shift the heavy bulk of the stocky man, who had her pinned down. Her eyes were wide open, as the man's head exploded in a burst of red mist, his blood falling across her face.

Jordan stood over them. "Sorry Ma'am."

"Get this man off me. Where's Nero?"

"He left through that door over there." It was Billy's voice.

Jordan pulled the dead body off Karen who stood up and looked around, taking stock.

John was bending over Jack who was looking up at him.

Karen shouted. "Are you OK boss?" The sound of the shots was still ringing in her ears.

"I'm good. Get after that bastard. We can't let him get away."

Karen looked down at Jack. The wounded detective just smiled up at her. "Go," she whispered. "I'm fine."

Karen turned and ran through the door and up a set of wooden stairs. The door was closed at the top, but she was on a mission. Karen turned the handle and smashed her shoulder into the door, in one fluid motion, bursting out into the hallway of the house. The door had been a secret door, with no visible handles or hinges on the house side. The perfect bolt hole.

The front door was wide open, and she raced outside, just in time to see Nero run into Roker Park.

Without hesitation she ran after him. Police were running towards her from both sides, as she ran across the road. She pulled her radio from her pocket.

Breathing hard she gave her position and ordered all the teams available to surround the park.

With officers behind her, she ran down past the old Lodge and the Victorian bandstand. Nero was some fifty yards ahead of her. People scattered out of the way as the two ran past.

At the end of the path through the park, a gate leads out on to the promenade and then to the beach. Three round wheeled pods were situated there. One was open, serving teas and coffees to people walking the promenade or taking a stroll on the beach.

There were three couples sitting at the small bright tables as Nero ran past.

He went to run on the beach but with the tide in, there was nowhere to go. He looked down the promenade to see police officers running in his direction. Looking back the way he had come he could see Karen running towards him with more officers behind her.

Nero ran back to the tables, grabbing one of the women, pulling her away towards the sea. He pulled a gun from his pocket and pushed it against her head, backing up until he was against the railing and could go no further.

The sun shone down as the sound of the waves became the dominant noise in that small corner of Roker seafront. Karen stopped some thirty yards away from the man she desperately wanted to arrest.

Seeing the fear on the woman's face, she holstered her gun and walked a bit closer. The woman's husband made to run past her, but she stopped him. "Leave this to me."

Karen looked over to the man who was her prey.

"Let her go, Nero, it's over."

"It's never over, Dee," he virtually spat her name with contempt. "I want safe passage out of here or she dies."

"No-one needs to die, Nero, just drop your gun."

"You need to die, Karen. You have done this; you have caused this mess. Everything was fine until you came here. I should kill you now."

Karen took a glimpse around, noting there were now firearms officers amongst the police surrounding Nero. One caught her eye and with the faintest of motions, pointed up. Karen didn't need to look, she just nodded and turned back to Nero.

"No-one wants to die, but I would happily change places with that woman. She is an innocent bystander here, let her go."

Nero looked around, for the first time she could see the glimmer of fear in his eyes.

"You're wrong about me. I'm not the boss here."

"Then who is?"

"He would kill me if I told you. There is no future for me here."

"Tell me his name."

Karen held her hands wide making a motion for the firearms team to hold off.

"You'd like that. This is bigger than you, this is big business."

"Give me a clue, it will stand you in good stead in court."

"Prison isn't for me. Get me safe passage and I'll give you a name."

"You know I can't do that, Nero."

"Then she dies, and then you die."

The look on Nero's face seemed to change. Then his face disappeared. A single shot taken from high above her ended the man's life in the blink of an eye. The woman screamed and Karen rushed forward to grab her. As she held her in her arms, Karen looked up to the top of the small cliff above where they stood.

Billy stood next to a police sniper. He simply nodded to her and turned away.

Karen escorted the woman back to her frantic husband who had been restrained by the police. Police officers ran in to make sure Nero's lifeless body wouldn't magically awaken. The gun, which was still held in his lifeless fingers, was made safe.

It was over. Karen's thoughts turned back to Jack.

Turning, she ran back up the hill to the House in Roker Park Road.

There was an ambulance parked outside the house. The paramedics were nowhere to be seen. Karen rushed inside; a feeling of dread weighed heavy on her heart. She was almost reluctant to find out how her friend was.

She was just about to go down into the basement when the door swung fully open and a paramedic appeared, dragging a stretcher into the hall.

John was with the stretcher which was being pushed by the second paramedic. He was holding a drip bag above the person they were taking out to the ambulance. It was Jack.

Her jacket and vest had been removed and the bullet wound to her right shoulder had been heavily strapped. There was a lot of blood across her chest.

Puffing from the exertion, Karen stopped the paramedic and looked down at her friend.

"How is it?"

"It hurts like hell, but they tell me I'll be alright."

"You'd better be."

"Did we get him?"

"We got him. Bullet to the head. No more Nero."

"Thank god for that."

Karen squeezed Jack's arm. "I'll visit you in hospital. I just need to see how the boss is doing."

"I'll see you later then. Let Laura know what's happened."

Karen smiled down at her friend as the paramedics took her away. John went with her to the hospital.

Karen watched as the ambulance drove away. She was framed in the doorway of the big brick house. As she was standing there, Billy limped around the corner from Side Cliff Road. He looked shattered, battered and bruised.

As he approached, she started to notice the damage that had been done to him. His clothes, those he had left, were torn, ligature marks were on his wrists, one eye was badly swollen, and his neck showed signs of strangulation. He was limping quite badly too.

"Do you need an ambulance boss?" Karen asked, once he was close enough to hear her.

"I'd have needed a hearse if you hadn't shown up. Or a shopping trolley."

She was amazed at his attempt at humour despite the trauma he had experienced.

They both sat down on the front step of the house.

"I'll be fine. A medic gave me the once over. Nothing is broken. I've just been told to rest."

"If we smoked this would be the perfect time to light up."

"Aye, good job we don't smoke, eh? I'd settle for a pint right about now."

"Just stay there for a sec, boss." Karen got up and walked into the kitchen at the back of the house. She had noticed a fridge when she had walked through the house the first time, and having seen empty cans in the back garden, she wanted to check the contents. Her hunch was rewarded.

She walked back to the front of the house and sat back down, handing a can to Billy while pulling the tab on her own.

"You're an angel Detective Inspector Dee." He pulled the tab on his own can, then they clinked cans before he took a deep swig of the amber liquid.

"Arrrgh," Billy sighed. "I thought for a while there I had drunk my last beer, until you showed up. How did you know where to find me?"

"Prudence met Nero, or Max as you know him, sorry knew him, here a few years ago. We got lucky."

Billy drank again from the can. "Good detective work, Karen. I knew you would be an asset to the team."

"What were they after, boss. Why did they give you such a beating?"

"They wanted to know where we had taken all the drugs you found in the lock up. They also wanted more information about you. It seems they were intent on killing you, and any family members you might have."

It was Karen's turn to take a big swig from her can. "Nice to know I managed to get under their skin."

"You did more than that, you degraded their business until they lost their ability to operate. Those three were apex players in the crime syndicate."

"Do you know their names?"

"No idea, that blonde guy was the cruellest. They called him Diablo. Nero called the other one Carniflex for some reason."

Karen pulled out her mobile and looked it up. "That's Latin for Butcher."

"Nice," Billy drank the last dregs from his can. "Were there any more of these?"

"Two more."

"I'll get them."

"You stay where you are, you need to rest remember."

As they sat drinking their second cans, a scene of crime team arrived to go over the property. They were quickly followed by Dr Laura Rae, whose job it would be to ascertain the cause of death for the inevitable report that followed every time the police discharged their weapons.

"Drinking on the job Karen? And before lunchtime." Laura laughed her cackling laugh which made the two detectives smile.

"I would call it a well-deserved reward for a job well done."

"Well, I am hoping this is the end of it, my morgue is full of bodies. It was almost empty before you turned up. I need a rest." She laughed again.

She squeezed past them then turned back. "Coffee Saturday morning?"

"You bet. Have you heard about Jack?"

"No, what's happened?"

"She was shot, took a bullet to the shoulder."

"Dear God, no wonder you're on the beers. I'll check in on her when I get back to the hospital."

With that, Laura headed down into the basement to evaluate the dead bodies before they were removed to her morgue.

A small crowd was starting to gather behind the police cordon, amongst them were a reporter and a photographer.

"I think we had best get inside boss. The paparazzi are here."

"Good call, Karen." Billy stood up and gave Karen his hand to help her up. As he pulled her up, she winced.

Billy looked at her and realised she had a bullet wound on the top of her left arm.

"What the hell Karen, you've been shot."

"It's nothing boss, it was the bullet that hit Jack."

"You need to get that seen to. I'll call a car over to take you to the Royal. You can check on Jack while you're there."

"Thanks boss."

Then Billy pulled her in and gave her a hug. He whispered in her ear. "Thank you for saving my life. I'll never forget what you did for me today."

Karen was surprised at the tenderness of the embrace. As she pulled away, he went to kiss her. She pulled back in shock.

"Sorry Karen. I don't know what I was thinking."

"You're not thinking boss. You nearly died. Take some time off. I'll watch the shop until you get back."

Tears started to stream down Billy's face. His body started to shake. Karen waved an officer over. She recognised shock when she saw it. It had been ever present in her life in the army while they were in active service.

"Look after him constable, I'll get an ambulance to take him to the hospital, I think we both need to be looked at."

Karen went back out into the street and made a phone call. Within five minutes an ambulance appeared. As she was standing waiting, the reporter in the crowd shouted across to her.

"Detective, Detective, can I have a word?"

Karen walked over to the police cordon. "What do you want?"

"Can you tell me what's happened today. I've heard reports of shots being fired and several fatalities."

"What's your name?"

The young reporter looked shocked at the question, as if she didn't expect the detective to give her the time of day. Fumbling to find her ID tag, she blurted out. "Emma, Emma Jones from the Echo."

Karen looked at her watch. Noting a new scratch across the face. "Come to the station at 4pm and we can have a chat."

The girl seemed excited. She handed Karen her card. "Thank you, who should I ask for?"

"Karen, Detective Inspector Karen Dee."

## Chapter Twenty-Eight

Shortly after lunch Karen and Laura stood each side of Jack, as she lay in her hospital bed. Her complexion was almost white, indicating the ordeal she had just been through.

The good news was that she was awake, and the doctors predicted she would make a full recovery, with no lasting physical damage. Karen was more worried about her mental condition. Post-Traumatic Stress Disorder was not confined to the military. It could result from all manner of shocks. What Jack had been through could leave deep mental scars.

The three women held hands. The tingling sensation seemed stronger this time. Jack smiled up at her friends, taking strength from their touch.

"Betty's tomorrow?"

"That would be lovely. I think you deserve a cream cake. Mind you I'm not sure the Doc will let you out that quickly."

At that moment the Doctor came into the room, followed by a nurse.

She checked out Jack's vital statistics. "How are you feeling Jack?"

"I'm feeling good Doc. Especially now my friends are here."

"You have been remarkably lucky young lady. The bullet missed all your vitals. If it had hit your left-hand side you would be dead."

"I guess I should buy a lottery ticket."

"Too late for that, you've used up enough luck for a lifetime."

Jack smiled. "Can I go now?"

"Not today, I'm afraid. We'll keep you in tonight and keep an eye on you. If you are OK in the morning, we'll let you go as long as you have someone to keep an eye on you."

Karen didn't hesitate. "You can stay with me. Jinx will be pleased to have some company."

"Thank you."

Laura squeezed Jack's hand. "I'll pop in later to check how you are, then I'll pick you up in the morning."

"Excellent. I'll leave you in your friend's capable hands," the Doctor stated with a smile.

The Doctor and nurse left.

Laura turned to Karen. "I need to get downstairs, I have a few more bodies to process. I'll come and get Jack tomorrow at around ten, and then I'll meet you at Betty's with Jack at 10.30am. You can take her back to yours, after we've had cake and a chat. Is that OK with you, Jack?"

"Sounds like a plan," Jack replied, sleepily.

Karen stood up. "I need to get back, I have a journalist coming to see me at 4pm. I'll see you in the morning. Take it easy Jack."

Karen leaned forward and kissed Jack on the cheek.

With that, the friends both left, leaving Jack to rest. Her eyes closed before they had even left the room.

Karen had suffered little more than a scratch. She walked into the office, seemingly as good as new. As she walked through the door, the detectives burst into applause.

There were lots of whooping and hollering as she walked to the front of the room, standing in front of the incident boards. Karen called the room to order.

"Guys, today is a cause for celebration. There will be no more bodies in the river, the drugs network in the Northeast has been shattered and the people who were coerced into working for this criminal network, have no need to be afraid anymore."

She looked around the room at the smiling faces. Mick, John, Jordan, Rachel. Even Cat had moved out from behind her screens and looked happier than Karen had ever seen her before.

"Jack will be OK, and the boss should make a full recovery, although he may be off work for a week or two."

She smiled at her team.

"Tonight, we celebrate. On Monday we write up these reports and put this case to bed. I have a reporter to see. As soon as I am done, I'll meet you in the pub." She reached into her pocket and pulled out a credit card. "The first round is on me."

The detectives made their way out of the office as Karen looked at her watch. It was 3.50pm. She went down to reception. Tom Moore was on duty, so she whiled away the minutes, telling him about the case and all that had happened earlier in the day.

He was very impressed and seemed very interested.

She looked at her watch again. Twenty minutes had gone by. Emma was late.

She took Emma's card from her jacket pocket and pulled out her phone. She started to dial the number when a Whatsapp came in.

*Don't be late Ma'am. My glass is almost empty.* It was from Mick.

She smiled and put her phone away.

"Tom, if the reporter from the Echo turns up. Tell her it will have to wait until Monday now."

"Will do boss. Well done today. It's an honour having you at Southwick North."

Karen smiled. "Thanks Tom. I love working here."

With that she left the station to join the others at the pub.

# Epilogue

The next morning Karen was up bright and early. Jinx was fed and watered, before Karen went out for a run. She felt free, as if a huge weight had been lifted from her shoulders. Every tree seemed greener; the sky seemed bluer; the world was a better place, now that Nero was gone.

Her reverie faded for a moment as she watched again in her mind, how the man had died. Life was so fragile. That could have been her in the cellar, but for the grace of God.

When she arrived back at the house, she showered quickly, then changed into a clean pair of jeans and a turquoise t-shirt. It felt good to be in fresh clothes.

Stepping outside her front door, she took a deep breath, then walked around to Betty's Café. She sat at the table by the window and waited. She was on her second cup of tea when Laura's mini pulled up outside.

It wasn't her usual reckless driving. Laura had a fragile load on board and didn't want to cause any damage.

Karen watched as Laura climbed out of the car, running around to the passenger door to open it for Jack.

Jack took Cat's arm for support as they walked up to the café. Karen rushed to open the door for them. As soon as they were sitting down, Betty brought over tea and cream cakes.

"You witches look like you need this. Thank you, for keeping us all safe."

*****

Across the city, a group of children were playing in Mowbray Park. At the bottom of the Jack Crawford statue a tramp was asleep in a sleeping bag. One of the tinkers kicked their ball at the sleeping figure. They hit the silent form square on the head.

Instead of waking up, the figure rolled off the plinth, falling out of the sleeping bag.

One of the children screamed.

The lifeless eyes of Emma Jones stared up at the blue sky as the kids ran to get help. On her chest was pinned a note.

## DISCLAIMER

The Witches of Witherwack is a work of fiction. Any resemblance of the main characters to persons living or dead is purely coincidental. The dialogue and situations are a product of the author's imagination. The events portrayed are based around the City of Sunderland during the spring of 2022 and incorporate real places and real events, but the storyline is completely fictitious and does not in any way represent real people or real events.

All rights to this novel, and any subsequent novels, are reserved.

No part of this publication may be copied, reproduced, stored, or transmitted in any form or by any means, whether electronically, mechanically, by photocopying, recording or otherwise without the written permission of the author, except as a brief quotation used for critical articles or reviews.

### Film/TV Rights

If you would like to discuss film or television rights, then please email the author on tonybrassell@gmail.com

## ABOUT THE AUTHOR

Tony's serious writing started with his Guernsey trilogy. Ten Days One Guernsey Summer was the first in the trilogy. It tells the real story of how his grandparents left the Island just before it was invaded by Hitler's armies in the summer of 1940. To produce a novel based on their story he had to fictionalize the timeline a little, and add the story of a German Pilot, who was involved in the bombing of Guernsey, just before the invasion.

Journey Home and then finally the Battle for Guernsey quickly followed, both complete works of fiction, the latter falling under the genre of Alternative History.

He then turned to his favourite reading genre, science fiction, and started the Warriors of Sol series which has evolved over the years. It has been influenced by his interest in Roman History. Project 75 was the first book, with A New Future following quickly in its wake.

He suspended work on the third book in that series to focus on The Kangaroo Ace.

That book started as a short story for a writing competition for the BBC, but as an indie writer he was not allowed to enter. That drove him to fully develop the idea into a novel. Tony loved the research aspect of The Kangaroo Ace, particularly the idea that a female pilot could have secretly flown in the First World War.

The Witches of Witherwack was started in the Spring of 2022. He had started a personal memoir called the Chimney Sweeps Apprentice and had the third in his science fiction series well under way when the idea for this book evolved.

He was so engrossed that he dropped everything to focus on this story which he hopes you enjoyed. Tony already has an idea for a second story so look out for more adventures from the Witches in and around Sunderland and the beautiful Northeast of England.

As well as writing, he builds, host and maintain websites for businesses and private individuals.

During lockdown in 2020 I picked up my paint brushes again. You can see some of my work and links to my other books on www.tonybrassell.co.uk

I hope you enjoyed this book.

Tony Brassell
February 2023

**Other Novels by the Author**

Ten Days One Guernsey Summer
Journey Home
Battle for Guernsey

Project 75, Into the Dark
A New Future, A New Union

The Kangaroo Ace

**Future Titles:**

The Core Worlds
A Higher Order
The New Prince
What is Beyond?

The Chimney Sweeps Apprentice

Footsteps in the Sand – The Second Karen Dee Novel

Printed in Great Britain
by Amazon